Dead and Breakfast

Pennyfoot Hotel
Christmas Special Mysteries

Herald of Death
Mistletoe and Mayhem
Decked With Folly
Mulled Murder
The Clue Is in the Pudding
Ringing in Murder
Shrouds of Holly
Slay Bells
No Clue at the Inn

Manor House Mysteries:

An Unmentionable Murder
Wedding Rows
Fire When Ready
Berried Alive
Paint by Murder
Dig Deep for Murder
For Whom Death Tolls
Death Is in the Air
A Bicycle Built for Murder

For a complete list of titles,
visit doreenrobertshight.com.

Dead and Breakfast

A Merry Ghost Inn Mystery

Kate Kingsbury

CROOKED
LANE

NEW YORK

Published in the United States by Crooked Lane Books, an imprint of The Quick Brown Fox & Company LLC.

Crooked Lane Books and its logo are trademarks of The Quick Brown Fox & Company LLC.

Library of Congress Catalog-in-Publication data available upon request.

ISBN (hardcover): 978-1-68331-009-9
ISBN (ePub): 978-1-68331-010-5
ISBN (Kindle): 978-1-68331-011-2
ISBN (ePDF): 978-1-68331-012-9

Cover design by Louis Malcangi.
Cover illustration by Joe Burleson.
Book design by Jennifer Canzone.

Printed in the United States.

www.crookedlanebooks.com

Crooked Lane Books
34 West 27th St., 10th Floor
New York, NY 10001

First Edition: January 2017

10 9 8 7 6 5 4 3 2 1

To Bill, for listening, for understanding,
and for that strong shoulder when I need it

Acknowledgments

Many thanks to Laura Yokoyama, administrative assistant for the Cannon Beach Police Department. Your help with the research is much appreciated.

My thanks to my editor, Matthew Martz, for being so helpful and enthusiastic. It means a lot to me.

Thanks to my industrious agent, Paige Wheeler, for always finding time for me in her busy schedule, for working so hard on my behalf, and for being a good friend.

Chapter 1

The paper covering the bedroom walls was a dull beige, with green ferns and brown spots that could have been pinecones or hand grenades, depending on what frame of mind you were in. Melanie West's frame of mind was definitely leaning toward the grenades.

"This," she murmured, "should have been torn down years ago."

The woman at her side grunted in agreement. "Maybe we should hire someone to do it."

"We can't afford it." Waving the putty knife at the wall, Melanie added, "Besides, how hard can it be? Between the two of us, we should have this licked in no time." She tucked the edge of the knife into a small gap in the seam and peeled back a strip of paper. "See? It comes off easy enough."

Liza Harris leaned forward and poked at the gap. "The backing is still glued to the wall. It's going to take a while to get that off."

Melanie peered at the offending patch. "Shoot. I guess we'll have to soak it in something."

"Half fabric softener, half water. Very hot water."

"You've done this before."

"Many times, though it was a lot harder before fabric softener was invented."

Sighing, Melanie stepped back to survey the wall. "You might have warned me."

"I didn't want to put you off." Liza grinned. "You were so gung ho on doing it ourselves."

"I wanted to save us money." Melanie walked over to a white wicker chair and sank onto it. "I had no idea when we started on this renovation just how much it was going to cost."

Liza perched on the edge of the bed, wincing as she stretched out her legs.

Melanie felt a stab of sympathy. Her grandmother's hip was probably bothering her again.

"Look, Mel," Liza said, "I know it's been tough. When I asked you to partner me in this enterprise, I knew it was going to be a challenge. But that's what you needed. You were stuck in that miserable job in Portland, living all alone in that dingy apartment. You hated your life. You needed a change, and what better change can you get than becoming part owner of a bed-and-breakfast on our beautiful Oregon coast? You have to admit, it's a lot more fun than working for a stockbroker. Financial analyst even *sounds* stuffy."

"I was a good financial analyst," Melanie murmured.

"I know you were. You'll be an even better innkeeper."

Studying her, Melanie had to remind herself again of the wide difference in their ages. Despite the touch of arthritis and an occasional aching back, at times Liza had more energy and zip than her granddaughter.

Dressed in black slacks and a stylish blue sweater, with her short, golden-dyed hair fluffed around her face, Liza looked at least twenty years younger than her age. Comparing her own faded jeans and gray sweat shirt, Melanie felt positively tacky. The woman put her to shame. "You're right," she said, jumping up from the chair. "Let's do this. Hopefully it will get rid of the musty smell in here."

Liza pushed herself up from the bed. "Okay, we'll peel off as much of that vinyl as we can. Once we get it off, we can soak the backing and scrape it off. I have a couple of drywall knives that should do the trick."

Melanie shook her head. "Is there anything you don't have?"

"When you've lived as long as I have, you pretty much acquire everything you need." She trotted over to the wall. "The top layer shouldn't take long to peel off. It's coming apart at the seams in places." She ran her fingers over the paper. "It must have been on here for at least forty years. I wonder . . ." She broke off, staring at the wall, her fingers still resting on the wallpaper. "That's odd."

Something in her voice gave Melanie a chill. Ever since she'd moved down to Sully's Landing two weeks earlier, she'd been getting chills. The house she'd bought with her grandmother was over a hundred years old and had enough creaks and groans to wake the dead.

It didn't help that the locals were convinced the house was haunted by an invisible ghost, its presence known only by the objects it moved around. Not that Melanie believed that for one moment. Nor did she believe the rumors that the sound of laughter had been heard in some of the rooms. There were no such things as ghosts.

Liza, on the other hand, had been wildly enthusiastic about the possibility of a ghost—so much so that she'd insisted on calling their new investment the Merry Ghost Inn. It would bring in tourists, she'd assured her granddaughter, which they badly needed to survive.

The name didn't do much for Melanie, though she kept her opinions to herself. Once Liza made up her mind about something, it was set in stone. Right now her grandmother was staring at the wall, one finger slowly tracing downward.

Melanie moved closer. "What are you looking at?"

Liza tapped the wall with her polished fingernails. "This part has been taped up. The seam must have come loose . . ." Her words ended on a gasp as a portion of the wall clicked and swung inward a couple of inches. Her voice was hushed as she added, "It's a door! It must have a hidden trigger or something."

Already unnerved, Melanie's stomach lurched. "Where does it lead?"

"Let's find out." Liza pushed the door open wider and peered inside. "It looks like a large closet with a . . . *ohmygod!*"

Her shriek hurt Melanie's ears. "What is it? What did you see?"

Liza stared at her with wide green eyes. "It's a skeleton."

"No way! Are you sure?"

"I know a skeleton when I see one." Liza waved a shaking hand at the wall. "Take a look for yourself."

"No thanks." Melanie shot a glance at the gap in the wall. "Maybe it's a fake."

"It didn't look like a fake to me."

Melanie's stomach was beginning to perform some uncomfortable maneuvers. "Are you telling me there's a dead person behind that wall?"

"Very dead." Liza's face had turned pale, and she backed away from the wall.

"How in the world did it get there?"

"I don't know, but we have to get it out of there."

Melanie stared at her for a long moment. "Right." She fished her cell phone out of her pocket. "I'm calling nine-one-one."

"Wait!" Liza's hand still trembled as she laid it on her granddaughter's arm. "Think what the publicity will do to our grand opening."

"It will probably bring swarms of ghost-loving sensationalists down here to look at the thing."

Liza visibly brightened. "Really?"

Melanie pressed the phone to her ear, taking deep breaths until a crisp voice answered her call. When she explained about the skeleton, the officer asked to speak to her grandmother.

Liza's voice was high-pitched with excitement as she related what she'd seen. After a series of yeses and nos, she handed the phone back to Melanie. "He's sending someone over to take a look. He said not to touch anything."

"He's got no worries about that. I wouldn't go near that thing." Melanie shuddered. "Can't you shut that door?"

"There's no handle." Liza hooked a finger around the edge of the door and pulled it toward her. "That's as closed as it gets."

"Well, I guess we can forget about stripping the wallpaper in here today."

"Rats. I wanted to get it done today. I guess we could start on another room."

"I don't know about you, but I've had enough for one day." Melanie walked out of the room, followed by her grandmother. "We'd better wait for the police officer to come."

As she reached the top of the stairs, Liza announced, "It was wearing something."

"What?" Melanie stopped so sharply that her grandmother bumped into her.

"Ouch! I said it was wearing something."

Melanie didn't want to talk about the skeleton. Just the thought of it made her want to throw up. Still, for some reason, she wanted to know what it was wearing. "Okay. Man or woman?"

"Definitely woman."

"It's wearing a skirt?"

"It looks like a nightgown. She must have died in her sleep."

"More likely someone killed her while she was asleep. Why else would she be stuck behind the wall?"

"Maybe she was hiding from someone and couldn't get out. The door doesn't have a handle. No one would know she was there."

The conversation was doing bad things to Melanie's stomach again. "I'm going to make some coffee." She started down the stairs with Liza right behind her.

"Good idea. A shot of brandy in it might help."

Melanie rolled her eyes. "Any excuse."

"Hey!"

Minutes later, they sat in the kitchen, sipping the steaming-hot coffee. This was Melanie's favorite spot in the whole house.

The room was warm and inviting, with yellow walls that had probably replaced wallpaper when the previous owner had renovated the room. The cabinets had been painted white, and Liza had hung orange-checkered curtains at the leaded-pane windows. The island counter in the center of the room sat below a collection of her prized copper pots and pans.

The breakfast nook nestled in the corner with windows on two sides, where Melanie had a perfect view of the ocean. From where she sat, she could see the white flecks riding in on the waves. Foaming spray soaked the jagged rocks that soared out of the water like rockets ready for takeoff. The long stretch of sand and cliffs had disappeared in a gray mist, and dark clouds hovered over the water, promising a late-spring downpour.

"Who do you think she is?"

Liza's voice scattered Melanie's thoughts about the impending storm. "I have no idea."

"I think she was somebody's mistress." Liza cradled her mug and leaned forward. "I think the owner of the house hid her in that room when his wife came home unexpectedly."

Melanie nodded. "Okay. So why didn't he let her out later?"

"I don't know. Maybe he had a heart attack from all the shenanigans. Or maybe his wife never left the room for days, and the mistress starved to death. Maybe . . ." She paused as the doorbell chimed. "That must be the police."

Feeling only slightly relieved, Melanie stood up. "I just hope they get rid of that thing without us having to see it."

She walked down the hallway to the front door, conscious of her grandmother close on her heels. The walls on either side were also papered, but with a fairly innocuous pattern of pale-pink roses on a cream background. Not something she'd choose to live with but not terrible, either. It actually blended quite well with the navy-blue carpeting. The chandelier, however, with its ugly, tarnished metal framework, had to go.

Wondering why she was obsessing about the decor at such a nail-biting moment, Melanie pulled open the door.

The cop who stood on the doorstep had his back to her. He turned to face her when she muttered a "Good morning."

Towering over her five-foot-five frame, his steely-blue eyes probed her face as if trying to see into her mind. "Officer Ben Carter, SLPD. Mrs. Harris?"

"No, I'm her granddaughter, Melanie West." Melanie opened the door wider and shifted sideways to give Liza room. "This is Mrs. Elizabeth Harris."

Liza stepped up to the door, smiling up at the stern-faced cop. "Hi! I'm Liza. I'm the one who found the skeleton."

The man's sharp gaze raked her face. "Show me."

Liza's smile faltered a little. "It's upstairs." Her eyebrows were raised as she twisted around and gave Melanie a look that clearly said, *what the hell?*

Melanie would much rather have waited downstairs and let her grandmother take charge of the proceedings, but Liza's beckoning hand looked a little desperate. Wishing she were anywhere but in a purportedly haunted house with a resident skeleton, she trudged up the stairs behind her grandmother and the cop.

Reaching the bedroom, Liza paused at the door. "It's in there." She jerked her head at the door. "Behind the wall."

Officer Carter stepped into the room, paused, and then strode over to the gap in the wall. Seconds later, they heard him say something into his walkie-talkie and a spluttering of words answering him.

Liza leaned closer to Melanie. "Do you think he's going to take it away with him?"

"I hope so." Melanie shuddered. "It will probably fall to pieces when he picks it up."

"He doesn't have anything to carry it in." Liza turned toward the stairs. "I'll get a grocery bag."

"A body's not going to fit in a grocery bag."

"It's not a body. It's a bunch of bones."

"Mrs. Harris."

The deep voice behind them made them both jump.

"I'll have to put this room out-of-bounds for the time being." Officer Carter pulled a roll of wide yellow tape from his pocket and proceeded to stretch a strip of it across the doorway.

Melanie stared at the big black words written on the tape: *DO NOT CROSS*. "How long is that going to be there?"

"Until the investigation is completed." He moved to the head of the stairs. "No one is to enter that room."

"But we have to wallpaper it. We have a grand opening next month."

His expression suggested that he didn't consider that his problem. "I guess you'll have to postpone it. This is a crime scene now."

Liza's cry of dismay echoed her own. Melanie stared up at the cop's rigid features. "The whole house?"

"Possibly. It will depend on the detective and the medical examiner's report." His face softened a little. "You'll probably be allowed to stay here as long as you don't disturb anything in that room."

"But what about our guests? We have reservations."

He shrugged. "It's not up to me. You'll have to take that up with the chief. My guess is that he won't want people wandering all over the house while there's a possible murder investigation going on."

Liza exploded with a resounding "Bugger!"

The police officer raised his eyebrows.

"Sorry. English expression." Liza hunched her shoulders. "Not a very polite one."

"I got that." He glanced at Melanie.

"She's from England," Melanie assured him, "but she's been here since the sixties. She's an American citizen now." She had no idea why she'd felt compelled to explain all that, except for a nagging worry that her grandmother might be in some kind of trouble.

"What are we going to do now?" Liza sounded unusually fragile. "This is a disaster."

Officer Carter lifted his hand, and for a moment Melanie thought he was going to pat Liza's shoulder, but then he dropped his hand again. "I'm sorry. Maybe it won't take too long and you can have your grand opening." He looked down the carpeted hallway, where six more doors opened up into rooms. "Looks like a nice place."

"It will be, if we ever get a chance to finish redecorating." Liza gave him an accusing glare. "You tell that police chief of yours that we are depending on that grand opening to pay the bills. If we have to delay that, we might not be opening at all."

The cop gave her a brief nod. "We'll do our best to solve this quickly and get out of your hair. The crime team should be here before too long." He looked back at Melanie. "See you around." With that, he sped down the stairs and out the door.

Sick with dismay, Melanie stared after him. "Okay, so now what do we do?"

"I guess we have to wait and see what the police chief has to say." Liza started for the stairs and paused. "I wonder what he meant by that."

Still worrying about having to cancel the reservations, Melanie answered her with an automatic, "Huh?"

Liza turned to face her and, in a throaty growl, muttered, "See you around."

Her imitation of the cop's deep voice made Melanie laugh. "It's just an expression."

"I don't know. It seemed kind of personal." Liza started down the stairs. "I wonder if he's married."

Melanie rolled her eyes. "You can quit that right now. You know how I feel about your little matchmaking games. I'm not interested. Period."

Liza murmured something she couldn't catch.

"What did you say?"

Liza reached the bottom of the stairs and turned to face her. "Look, Mel, I know you've had a bad experience. A terrible experience. One that would crush most people for life. But you're not most people. You're my granddaughter. You're a survivor, like me. You're only thirty-two. You have your whole life ahead of you, and it's full of promise and possibilities. So don't shut yourself away from it. Embrace it." She threw her arms wide open, flinched, and dropped her hands. "Open that door to the glorious adventures awaiting you!"

Having heard various versions of that speech before, Melanie sighed. "I'm part owner of a haunted house involved in a possible murder investigation that is going to seriously disrupt our plans and probably wreck our credit scores for life. That's quite enough adventure for me. I just don't have the time or the energy for any more complications in my life right now."

Liza opened her mouth to answer, but just then, the harsh ringing of a telephone interrupted her.

For a moment, the two women stared at each other, then Liza twisted around and headed for the living room. "It's the landline," she called out over her shoulder. "We have to get used to having a regular phone again. Good thing, if you ask me. I never did like those cell phone things."

Melanie followed her into the vast room that looked out onto the street. An ancient piano sat in one corner, left there by the previous owner and included in the sale, as were the brown leather couch and two gold tweed armchairs that sat on either side of the wide marble fireplace. Bookcases, crammed with books, lined one entire wall, along with videos and knick-knacks that made Melanie cringe to look at them. All had been included in the sale.

Something else that had to be sorted through and disposed of, Melanie reminded herself. She'd been putting off the task, but now, with a possible murder investigation going on in the house, she'd probably have more than enough time to take care of it.

Liza was perched awkwardly on the arm of one of the chairs, the phone receiver pressed to her ear. "Yes, of course. That's great. Thank you so much." She hung up the phone. "That was the printer. The brochures are ready to pick up. I said we'd get them today, so we might as well go now. We can stop by the hardware store as well. We need a couple of things, and we can have lunch there."

Melanie raised her eyebrows. "Lunch in a hardware store?"

"I believe it's the only hardware store in Oregon where you can eat and have a beer or a glass of wine." Liza got up, rubbing her hip. "You'll love it. When we get back, we can paint the fence and the porch. That's outside the house, so it shouldn't bother the police."

"Speaking of which, shouldn't one of us wait here to let them in?"

"Oh, rats. I wonder how long they'll take to get here."

Melanie glanced at the bulky clock ticking away on the mantelpiece—another souvenir from the owner. "Why don't I go and get the brochures while you wait here for the detective? I'll probably be back before he gets here."

Liza looked disappointed. "Better take a rain jacket."

Melanie wasted no time in grabbing a jacket and heading for the front door. Ever since they'd discovered the grisly remains of that poor woman, she'd had an overwhelming urge to get out of the house and into the fresh air.

The wind greeted her as she ran down the porch steps, whipping her hair into her face. She brushed it back with one hand while she clicked the button on her key chain to unlock the door of her Suburban.

Although the garage was more than adequate to house her car as well as Liza's, right now it was stacked with boxes and pieces of furniture. Melanie's stomach churned when she thought of everything she and her grandmother had to do before the grand opening in four weeks. They barely had time to get it all done, and now this investigation was going to put them further behind in their schedule.

They had budgeted for the next four weeks, but after that, they were relying on accommodation fees to cover their costs. A delay would put a big dent in their bank account.

Lost in her troubling thoughts, she drove slowly onto the narrow main street of the little town. In spite of the unsettled weather, people strolled down the sidewalks, past antique stores and art displays, gift shops and restaurants. Some carried umbrellas, others braved the elements, and several dogs trotted along at the ends of their owners' leashes.

A line of customers spread out of the door of the nearby bakery, and as Melanie stepped out of her car, the delicious aroma of freshly baked bread reminded her that it was lunchtime.

The printer's shop was across the street, and she waited at the crosswalk for a small gray car to pass by. The driver must have seen her as he stopped, waving her across. As she started forward, the wind once more tossed her hair across her face. She slowed in front of the car to swipe it back and glanced at the driver. He started to wind down the window, and her heart seemed to stop.

She recognized that face. It was the face of the man who had shattered her life and almost destroyed her. The man she never wanted to see again. She thought she'd left him and the painful memories behind in Portland. But he was here, right in front of her, and she couldn't imagine what the hell he was doing in Sully's Landing.

Chapter 2

Minutes later, Melanie arrived back at the inn, her hand shaking so much she had trouble getting the key into the lock of the front door. Inside the hall, she yelled at the top of her voice, "Granny? *Granny!* Where are you?"

Liza's voice floated down the hall from the kitchen. "I thought we agreed you'd call me Liza from now on."

Melanie started forward as her grandmother appeared in the doorway. "Sorry. Old habits are hard to break."

Her distress must have shown in her face, as Liza's expression changed. "What's the matter? What's happened?"

Unable to form the words, Melanie gritted her teeth and shook her head.

"Get in here." Liza grabbed her arm and pulled her into the kitchen. "Sit." She pushed her down onto a chair. "Now, tell me what happened."

Melanie drew in a shaky breath. "Gary. He's here in Sully's Landing."

"What?" Liza eyes widened. "What's he doing here?"

"That's what I want to know."

"Are you sure it was Gary you saw?"

"Positive. He was driving the Honda. He stopped for me at the crosswalk and waved at me as I walked in front of him."

"Did you talk to him?"

She had to pause for another deep breath before answering. "No, of course not. I ran back to the car."

"He didn't try to follow you?"

"He didn't get the chance."

Liza walked over to fridge and took out a bottle of water. "How does he know where you are?" She poured water into a glass and handed it to her granddaughter.

"I don't know. Somebody must have told him." Melanie took a sip of the water, reassured to see her hand had stopped shaking. "There were people who knew I was moving to the beach. My landlord, for one."

"Well, just because he's here doesn't mean you have to talk to him." Liza sat down opposite her at the table. "I won't let him past the front door."

The sick feeling in Melanie's stomach intensified. "This is a small town. We're bound to bump into each other somewhere."

"This is ridiculous. It's been over a year since the divorce. What could he possibly want from you now? He knows how you feel about him."

"I don't know and I don't care." She fought back the threatening tears. "I just hope and pray I never have to see him again."

"You're not afraid of him, are you?"

"Afraid?" Melanie's laugh was bitter. "No, I'm not afraid of Gary. It's the memories that terrify me. It's taken me too long to put the past behind me, and I don't need him bringing it all up again."

Liza leaned forward and grasped her hand. "I'm sorry, Mel. I can't imagine how you must feel."

The sudden peal of the doorbell made them both jump. Melanie froze, staring at Liza, who seemed equally bereft of words.

The bell rang again.

"I'll get it." Liza rose to her feet. "You stay here. If it's him, I'll threaten to sue him for harassment if he doesn't go away."

She hurried out of the kitchen, leaving Melanie stuck to her chair, berating herself for being such a coward. She should face the bastard and find out what he wanted. Then tell him to go to hell.

She started to get up just as voices sounded in the hall. Deep, gruff voices that were nothing like Gary's soft tones. Liza appeared in the doorway. "It's the police. I'll show them upstairs."

Weak with relief, Melanie shot up. "I'm coming, too."

By the time she reached the hallway, Liza was already halfway up the stairs. Two men followed her, one wearing jeans and the other in khakis and carrying a black bag. Both wore jackets, their hair damp from the rain that had now started falling in earnest.

"It's in there," Liza said, gesturing at the door where the yellow tape displayed its warning.

The taller of the men took down the tape. "We'll let you know when we're done."

The second man smiled at Melanie. "It shouldn't take too long." He followed his partner into the room and closed the door behind him.

"The big one's a detective," Liza said, starting back down the stairs. "The other one is the medical examiner." She paused, her hand straying to her hip. "If I have to go up and down these stairs much more today, I'll be flat on my back. I'm not as young as I used to be."

Melanie grimaced in sympathy. "Sorry. Is it hurting much?"

"Nothing I can't handle. It must be the rain. Or I'm just getting old."

Melanie laughed at that. "You know you can outlast me any day." She followed her grandmother down the stairs. "I never picked up the brochures. We could go after they leave."

"Good idea. We'd better have lunch here, though. Who knows how long they'll be up there."

Melanie trailed after her grandmother into the kitchen, hoping that the men upstairs wouldn't take too long. She wasn't looking forward to going into town again, with the threat of seeing her ex-husband hanging over her.

If only she knew why he was in Sully's Landing. It could simply be coincidence, but she seriously doubted it. Gary was a prominent Portland lawyer and rarely did business out of the city. No, it was more likely he wanted to see her, to talk to her. Talk to her about what? They had hashed everything out over and over again during the divorce, and she'd made it very clear that there was absolutely no hope of reconciliation.

She swiftly shut down the memories and opened the fridge.

Liza was at the counter, spreading mayonnaise on slices of bread.

Melanie reached for a bowl of egg salad and carried it over to the counter.

"How's the research going?" Liza asked as she spread the salad on the slices.

It was a question she had asked every day for more than a year.

Melanie had been four years old when her father had died, leaving her mother, Liza's daughter, a widow and a single mother. Janice had fallen into a deep depression, and Liza had sent her to stay with relatives in England, hoping the change would help her. Janice had never arrived at her destination, and despite a prolonged search on both sides of the Atlantic, she remained a missing person.

Liza and her husband, Frank, had given Melanie a home. In spite of her losses, it had been a happy childhood. Knowing how hard it had been on her grandmother to lose her only child, Melanie had decided a year earlier to try to trace her mother's whereabouts using the Internet. So far she'd had no luck, but she was determined to find out what had happened to Janice, more for Liza's sake than her own.

The memories of her mother were no more than vague shadows in her mind, though she had to admit, curiosity had helped keep the project alive. That and Liza's never-abating hope that one day her daughter would return, alive and well.

Melanie knew that her grandmother had long given up on actually hearing any news, but hope kept her asking anyway. "Nothing new," she said, wishing she could have found something, no matter how trivial.

"You look a lot like her, you know." Liza sounded calm enough, but Melanie heard the catch in her voice. "You have the same heavy dark hair, but you have your father's beautiful hazel eyes. He was a nice-looking man. Such a shame he died so young."

Deciding it was time to change the subject, Melanie picked up her sandwich. "Let's eat. I'm starving."

It was over an hour later when heavy footsteps on the stairs signaled the completion of the police investigation. Melanie met them in the hallway, fingers crossed that they'd have good news.

The medical examiner carried a large black lawn bag, most likely containing the remains of the dead woman.

The younger man, who introduced himself as Detective Tom Dutton, looked sympathetic when he delivered the news. "I'm afraid we still have to cordon off the second floor." He nudged his head in the medical examiner's direction. "I'll be back after Colin here has completed the postmortem. We're hoping that will give us more to go on. Until then, the second floor is off-limits. I hope that won't be too much of an inconvenience."

Liza spoke from behind Melanie, frustration making her voice sharp. "How long is that going to take?"

Colin answered for him. "I'll be as quick as I can. A day or two at most, I should think."

Thanking them, Melanie showed them out and closed the door. "I guess there isn't much more we can do now, except wait," she said as she followed Liza down the hallway. "It's a good thing our bedrooms are on the first floor, or we'd be camping out in the living room."

Her grandmother muttered something under her breath. "I hate waiting. For anything. Such a waste of time."

"We can still paint outside," Melanie reminded her.

"If it stops raining. Rats. Just when things were going so well." She stopped short, tilting her head to one side like a curious bird. "Did you hear that?"

"Hear what?"

"Laughing. I heard someone laughing. Are those men still here?"

"I don't think so." Melanie walked into the living room and looked out the window. "No. The car's gone."

"I definitely heard someone laughing." Framed in the doorway, Liza looked worried.

"There's no one here but us." Uneasy now, Melanie walked over to her grandmother. "The back door is locked, and we would have seen anyone come through the front door."

"Then who did I hear?" Liza uttered a soft gasp. "You don't suppose it was our merry ghost?"

Melanie's laugh sounded abrupt. "That's ridiculous. Ghosts only exist in books and movies."

"Then who was it?"

Liza's face looked a little pale, and Melanie rushed to reassure her. "It was probably the rain on the roof or a bird outside. The ocean. Anything. We're in a strange house with a lot of strange noises. We're not used to them, that's all."

Her grandmother's lips tightened. "I know what I heard. It was laughter."

"What did it sound like?"

Liza thought for a moment. "Like a soft chuckling, as if he were enjoying a joke."

"It was a he?"

"Oh, yes. I'm sure of that."

"So where did the sound come from?"

"Down the hallway." Liza frowned. "I think on the stairs."

In an effort to bring some sense of normalcy to what was becoming a disturbing conversation, Melanie said firmly, "I thought ghosts only came out at night."

Liza raised her chin. "I thought you didn't believe in ghosts, period."

"I don't." Melanie sighed. "Okay, so if it was the ghost, what was he laughing at?"

"I don't know." Liza headed down the hallway. "But I'm going to find out."

Joining her at the foot of the stairs, Melanie peered up into the shadows. "You're not going up there again, are you?"

Liza stared upward for several seconds before shaking her head. "No. You heard the detective. It's off-limits. Let's go get those brochures."

Melanie wasn't sure which option was the least desirable. Somewhere in town, her ex-husband was prowling around. On the other hand, something else could be lurking at the top of the stairs.

In the next instant, she dismissed her ridiculous fancies. She was letting her grandmother's wild imagination get to her. Grabbing her rain jacket, she led the way out the front door.

The rain had tapered off by the time they reached the town. Rather than park on the street, as she had earlier that day, Melanie pulled in to the near-empty parking lot behind the post office. "It's a bit farther to walk," she said as she turned off the engine, "but we'll be less likely to be seen back here."

Liza gave her a look of sympathy. "You can't hide from Gary forever. Maybe you should just confront him and get it over with. Find out what he wants."

"I know you're right. I just don't know if I can talk to him without poking him in the eye." She climbed out of the car and closed the door with a little more force than was necessary.

The wind tossed the branches of the trees lining the parking lot, and heavy gray clouds still scudded across the sky. Liza joined her, looking as if she wanted to hug her. "Okay," she said, "let's forget about him for now. It's a great day for a walk, and the heavenly smell of that ocean is so salty fresh and clean, it's making me hungry again."

Melanie laughed. "You just had lunch."

"I know. And now I'm looking forward to dinner." She tucked her hand under Melanie's elbow. "I'm dying to see those brochures, aren't you?"

To Melanie's intense relief, they saw no sign of Gary as they strolled along Main Street, stopping every now and again to enthuse over the souvenirs and antiques displayed in the windows of the quaint little stores. Liza couldn't resist visiting the candy store and emerged carrying a bag of creamy fudge, insisting that Melanie sample a piece.

Munching on the chewy candy, they reached the printer's shop. The doorbell summoned the young man who had taken their order a week or so earlier.

"You will love these," he promised as he handed one of the brochures over to Melanie for inspection.

She studied the picture of the inn on the front while her grandmother peered over her shoulder.

"I wish we'd waited until we'd painted the porch," Liza murmured.

"We couldn't afford to wait," Melanie reminded her. "We need to get these brochures out to advertise the inn." She opened the slim leaflet and scanned the list of amenities and prices. "This looks good," she said, then opened her purse to find her credit card.

The assistant took it and swiped it. "Have you heard the ghost yet?" He handed over her card and the receipt. "Has it been laughing?"

Before Melanie could answer, Liza spoke up. "I think I did. I heard something that sounded like laughing."

The young man pinned his gaze on her. "Awesome! What did it sound like? Were you scared? Was it creepy?"

Liza shrugged. "Not really."

Melanie scribbled her signature on the receipt and held it out to him. "Thank you." After stuffing a few of the brochures into her purse, she picked up the box and headed for the door. Once outside, she waited for Liza to join her.

"You seem in a hurry," Liza remarked as they headed back down the street to the parking lot.

"I didn't want to answer a bunch of questions about our imaginary ghost." Melanie shifted the box to her other arm. "If you want to keep the legend alive, we need to be careful what we say about it."

"What if it's not a legend? What if it's real?"

"You know I don't believe in ghosts."

"But lots of people do, and like you said, it would be a great incentive to stay at the inn."

Melanie could hardly argue with that. Still, talking about the ghost made her uncomfortable, though she couldn't exactly explain why.

Walking into the hardware store a few minutes later, Melanie could smell beer fumes and the slightly musty odor of old wood. A few tables were scattered around the room, with a bar in the corner displaying a full array of beer and wine.

"It smells like an English pub," Liza said as she led the way into the other half of the building.

Here they were met with shelves filled with all kinds of gadgets and tools, packets of seeds, spray cans of paint, and a large display of bathroom fixtures.

"We need new switch plates for the bathrooms and a towel rack," Liza said, plucking a couple of packets off the hook that held them.

Melanie wandered down the narrow aisles, fascinated by the array of fixtures and fittings.

Liza, meanwhile, had found her towel rack. "I'm going to pay for these," she said.

"Where do you pay for them?" Melanie looked around. "I can't see a counter anywhere."

"You pay for them in the pub." She headed for the bar, and Melanie followed her, intrigued by the whole setup.

The big man behind the bar greeted them with a gruff voice and a wide grin. There were deep laughter lines at the corners of his dark eyes, and with his white hair and trim beard, he reminded Melanie of Santa Claus.

They gave him the switch plates and towel rack and waited for him to bag them before Liza handed him her credit card. He examined it closely, reading her name aloud. "Elizabeth

Harris. You must be the new owner of the Morellis' house. I hear you found one of them still in residence."

Liza stared at him. "How'd you know all that?"

The man winked. "Small town. News travels fast."

"Yes, but—"

The man leaned forward and lowered his voice. "My brother's a reserve police officer. I get to know just about everything that happens in this town. If you want to know anything, just ask me." He straightened and raised his voice again. "I'm Doug Griffith, the owner of this place." He looked at Melanie. "And you're the partner?"

She nodded. "Melanie West. Pleased to meet you."

"Same here. Seen the ghost yet?"

"No," Melanie said sharply, while Liza added, "But I did hear him."

Doug's eyes widened. "No kidding. Maybe it's that skeleton's ghost, looking for revenge."

Liza snorted. "I seriously doubt it. The skeleton was female, and the laughter I heard was definitely male."

"The victim was a woman? Know who she was?"

"Not yet. You'll probably find out from your brother before we do."

"I might at that." Doug handed her the card. "Anything else we can do for you?"

"No, thanks." Liza leaned over the counter, her voice softening. "Tell me, Mr. Griffith, did your brother have any idea how long the investigation will take?"

"Sorry, he didn't tell me that." He handed her the receipt. "And it's Doug. Nobody calls me Mr. Griffith unless they're arresting me. Nice accent, by the way. Australian?"

Melanie winced, knowing how her grandmother hated to be mistaken for an Australian.

Liza straightened her back. "I'm English, and proud of it."

He gave her an approving nod. "Good for you. Okay, English, hope we see you back again soon. Stop for a couple of beers next time. You'll feel right at home in here."

Melanie almost laughed out loud at her grandmother's affronted expression.

"Do I look like a beer guzzler?" Liza muttered as they walked to the door.

"I think he just meant it would remind you of England." Melanie pushed the door open and stepped out into the street. Once more, the wind whipped her hair across her face, making her wish she'd tied it back. "You said yourself it smelled like an English pub."

Liza seemed unconvinced as they trudged back to the car. She brightened, however, as they passed a shop with mannequins in the window wearing stylish dresses and pantsuits. "I really like these outfits. We have to come back here soon so I can take a look inside."

Melanie didn't answer. She'd caught sight of a man walking briskly along in front of them, and his back looked uncomfortably familiar. Heart thudding, she poked Liza with her shoulder. "Does that look like Gary to you?"

"What! Where?" Liza peered ahead. "Good heavens, no. You know Gary wouldn't be caught dead in those sloppy jeans and jacket." She patted Melanie's arm. "You're letting your worry get to you. If it was Gary you saw earlier this morning, he's probably on his way back to Portland by now. You know how he hates to be away from his office."

Feeling only slightly reassured, Melanie reached the car and unlocked the doors. All she wanted to do now was get home and off the street. She just hoped Gary wouldn't come knocking at the door. At least she had the option of not opening it.

Arriving back at the inn, she began to feel a little more relaxed. Maybe Liza was right, she thought as she followed her grandmother into the house. Maybe it was simply a coincidence that Gary was in town and he'd gone back to Portland already.

Wishing she could convince herself of that, she hung up her jacket and joined Liza in the living room.

"I think we should paint this room," Liza said when Melanie walked in. "The walls are much too busy. I guess we could paint over the paper. What kind of fascination did these people have with wallpaper anyway?"

Melanie studied the wall. "Wasn't there a time when it was really popular and everyone was putting it on their walls?"

"Yeah, about forty or fifty years ago." Liza squinted at the wall. "Come to think of it, this stuff could have been on there that long." She sighed. "I suppose if we're going to paint, we really should strip it first."

Melanie sank into an armchair and stretched out her feet. "Do we have time to do all that?"

"Not really." Liza grunted as she lowered herself onto the couch. "I just wish we had the money to hire someone. I get tired just thinking about all the things that need to be done."

"Well, I think the walls in here are okay." Melanie scanned the room. "What if we buy light-colored drapes for the windows, maybe lavender or rose, and matching cushions for the couch and chairs? We could even manage a nice creamy rug to put in front of the fireplace." She nodded at the mantel-piece. "We can get rid of all that stuff and put something more elegant up there, like a delicate vase or a sculpture. That clock is downright ugly."

Liza pursed her lips. "All that stuff could be worth money. I do believe those figurines are French antiques."

"Really?" Melanie looked at the peasant boy and girl fig-urines with renewed interest. "I didn't know you knew that much about antiques. How much do you think they're worth?"

"I don't know that much about them. I just remember my mother having something similar. I used to play with them when I was little. Have you tried picking them up? Those mar-ble bases weigh a ton."

Melanie got up and walked over to the fireplace to study the pair. "They're pretty and really old-world. I'm surprised Tony Morelli let them go along with the house."

"I'm surprised they are still here, considering how long the house sat empty. Mr. Morelli probably didn't know what they were worth. He didn't strike me as being too smart. Besides, he lives all the way over there in New Jersey. He told me his father had refused to sell the house while he was alive. He probably didn't want to be bothered getting rid of everything, which is why we ended up with this." Liza got up and pounded the couch. "I don't think there's any springs left in this thing."

"He was here for the sale of the house." Melanie ran a fin-ger down the smooth back of the peasant girl figurine. "He could have taken care of it all then."

Liza uttered a short laugh. "He couldn't wait to get back to the East Coast. He seemed a bit shifty to me. He seemed relieved when I agreed to take care of the contents, and he did give us a good price on the house, which is why we could afford it."

"And thanks to Grandpa's life insurance and my divorce settlement."

Liza's sad face made Melanie feel bad she'd mentioned her late grandfather. Her grandparents had been the happiest couple she'd ever known, until Frank Harris's heart attack had taken him. They had raised her since she was four years old, and she never once saw them have a serious fight.

They argued now and then, but more often than not, the argument ended in a joke and a hug. Too often, Melanie had compared their marriage to her own, wishing she could have had the close companionship and love that Liza had found with her husband.

Reminded once more of Gary and his disquieting appearance in town, she tried to shake off the depressing memories.

The sudden chime of the doorbell froze her thoughts. She looked at her grandmother, worried that she had conjured up the man she was trying so desperately to avoid.

"I'll get it," Liza said, then left the room.

Melanie stood where she was, trying to breathe normally. Her grandmother was right. Now was the time to face Gary and find out what he wanted. Dreading the confrontation, she waited with mounting anxiety for Liza to open the door.

Chapter 3

The murmur of voices down the hall did nothing to ease Melanie's tension. The visitor was a man, she could tell that much, but the voice was too quiet to recognize. Moments later, Liza appeared in the doorway, followed by a young man wearing a jacket emblazoned with the New York Yankees logo. His dark hair stuck up in spikes, and a light stubble covered his jaw.

"This is Mr. Phillips," Liza announced, waving a hand at the smiling stranger. "He's a reporter and wants to interview us for the local newspaper."

Melanie waited a moment to regain her breath. "About the inn?"

"About the skeleton, and it's Josh." He held out his hand. "Pleased to meet you."

Melanie grasped the strong fingers. "Nice to meet you, too." She moved back to let him walk into the living room.

He stood for a moment, scanning the room as if searching for something, then nodded. "Nice place. Mind if I sit down?"

"Go ahead." Liza beckoned to an armchair. "That one's pretty comfortable. Better than the couch."

Josh grinned at her. "I'll take your word for it." He sat down and pulled a phone from his pocket. "Mind if I record our conversation?"

"I think we're all right with that." Liza looked at Melanie for confirmation.

It took a moment for Melanie to answer. She wasn't sure she wanted her connection to the inn published in a newspaper. On the other hand, the publicity would be invaluable.

"It's okay if you'd rather not," Liza said, nodding emphatically while her face expressed otherwise.

Melanie smiled at the reporter. "That's fine." After all, she told herself, Gary would never waste his time reading a small-town newspaper.

Liza beamed. "Good." She sat on the couch and turned to Josh. "So what do you want to know?"

"Well, first, tell me about the skeleton. How did you find it?"

Seated on the other armchair, Melanie listened as her grandmother explained about the wallpaper project. Josh seemed fascinated by the account, occasionally interrupting to get a better understanding of her words.

Meanwhile, a vision of the skeleton filled Melanie's mind. Who was that woman? How had she died? Had she become trapped in the secret room behind the wall? If so, how come nobody heard her yelling and pounding for help?

She envisioned herself in that dark, suffocating place, frantically screaming for someone to hear her until all hope died. She lay on the floor, her life gradually ebbing away, and no one could help her. Cold fingers closed around her heart, and she shuddered.

"Melanie? Are you all right?"

"What?" Melanie blinked, realizing that her grandmother and the reporter were both staring at her as if she'd grown horns. "Oh, sorry. I was thinking about that poor woman up there."

"Oh, do you know who she is?" Josh leaned forward, his intensity making his features seem harsh.

Melanie shook her head. "No, no, I don't." She looked at Liza for help.

"The police are still investigating," Liza said, then launched into a lengthy account of her partnership with her granddaughter, their plans for the inn, and how the investigation was holding things up. "You can be sure," she told Josh, "we will do our utmost to open next month as planned."

"Well, good for you." Josh looked back at Melanie. "So what are you calling this place when you open?"

"We're calling it the Merry Ghost Inn." She waited for the inevitable question.

Josh nodded. "I take it you've heard about the ghost."

"Not only heard about it," Liza said. "I've actually heard it myself."

"No kidding!" He looked impressed. "What did it sound like?"

"Like a man laughing." Liza glanced at Melanie. "My granddaughter thinks it's something in the house making that noise, but I think it really is a ghost."

"That's wild." He turned back to Melanie. "So tell me more about the skeleton. Did you get a good look at it?"

"No, I didn't see it. I didn't want to."

He nodded. "I can believe it. It's not something you want hanging around your bedroom."

"I can think of something I'd rather have hanging around," Liza murmured.

"The police took it away," Melanie said hurriedly as Josh gave her grandmother a lecherous smirk. "They can probably tell you more than we can about it."

"They can." Josh turned off his recorder and stood up. "Whether they will or not is another question. I usually have to second-guess what they mean when they say anything, but it's worth a shot." He held out his hand to Liza, who got up from her chair. "Thanks for your time. I'll drop a copy of the *Gazette* off for you, okay?"

"We'd love it. Thanks."

He turned to Melanie. "It was real nice talking to you, Melanie. I hope we bump into each other sometime."

He held on a little too long to her hand, and she pulled it back. "Thank you. We'll look forward to seeing the story." She watched him leave with a vague feeling of uneasiness. It was too late now, but she couldn't help wondering if she'd made a mistake by advertising where she lived.

"He seems nice," Liza said as she closed the front door. "I wonder if he's married."

"Why?" Melanie said sweetly. "Are you thinking of dating him?"

Liza huffed out her breath. "Don't put it past me. I may be ancient on the outside, but inside, I'm still a vibrant, thirsting woman, ready for anything."

"Thirsting?" Melanie grinned. "You're incorrigible. You may be a lot of things, Granny, but ancient isn't one of them."

"Well, calling me Granny makes me feel ancient, so cut it out, okay? It's Liza from now on. You promised."

"Okay, Liza. I'll try to remember."

"Good. It's too late to start anything ambitious today." Liza nodded at a bookcase. "Why don't we sort through that lot and see if we have anything worth keeping?"

Melanie joined her at the shelves, wondering just how long it would be before they could tackle the wallpaper in the upstairs bedroom again.

By the time she finally crawled into bed that night, all she could think about was falling asleep and hopefully waking up to sunshine. Her last thoughts before drifting off were pleasant ones, reflecting on how much more interesting and enjoyable her life had become since accepting her grandmother's offer of a partnership. Now if she could just get Gary off her back once and for all, life would be perfect.

She awoke a few hours later, starting up from her pillow without knowing what had disturbed her sleep. Raised on one elbow, she peered around the darkened room, where only the vague shapes of the dresser and chest of drawers hovered in the shadows.

All was deathly quiet. Reassured, she settled down, only to be brought up again by a sound that chilled her bones. Somewhere in the darkness, she'd heard a soft chuckle.

Her first thought was that Gary had somehow found his way into her bedroom. She lunged for the lamp on the nightstand, only to smack her hand against it so hard it skidded off and crashed to the floor.

She scrambled out of bed, frantically scrabbling for the lamp, and at last, her fingers closed around the base. To her relief, when she turned the switch, the light almost blinded her. Holding the lamp as a weapon, she scrambled to her feet.

There was no one in the room. She stared at the closed door of the closet. Was her ex-husband hiding in there? There was only one way to find out. "Gary? If you're in there, come out here, right now."

The door of her bedroom flew open, and she almost dropped the lamp.

Liza appeared in the doorway, her ruffled hair standing on end. "What the blazes is going on in here?"

"I thought I heard someone." Melanie stared at the closet. "You don't think . . . ?"

Liza muttered something under her breath, marched across the room, and flung open the closet door. "There. No one's hiding in there. You must have been dreaming."

Still not convinced, Melanie looked around the room. There was nowhere else to hide except under the bed, and she wasn't about to make a fool of herself by looking. "Sorry, I didn't mean to wake you up."

"This whole skeleton business is playing games with our heads." Liza closed the closet door and tightened the belt of her robe around her waist. "Try to forget it, Mel. Get some sleep. We need our energy to get this house in order." She walked over to her granddaughter and gave her a hug. "See you in the morning."

She was almost out the door before Melanie said quietly, "I thought I heard someone laughing."

Liza paused for a moment before turning back. "A man?"

"I think so."

Liza beamed. "Our merry ghost."

"You know that's ridiculous." Melanie looked up at the ceiling. "Something must be making that noise. It's probably the pipes or something. It just sounds like laughing."

"Well, if it is something like that, we'll keep our mouths shut about it. We want our visitors to believe there really is a ghost haunting the inn."

"Isn't that false advertising?"

"Not at all. It's providing entertainment for our guests. Besides," she added as she turned back to the door, "we still don't know that it isn't a ghost, do we?" She closed the door behind her before Melanie could answer.

Left alone, Melanie glanced at her bedside clock. Two AM. She needed to get back to sleep. For a moment she hesitated, then quickly bent down and aimed the lamp under the bed. There was nothing but a couple of dust balls and what appeared to be a crumpled tissue.

Shrugging, she got to her feet and crawled into bed.

Half an hour went by, and still she felt wide awake. Reaching for the lamp, she switched it on and stared at the ceiling. She must have been nuts to think Gary could have broken into the house. The solid front and back doors had dead bolts, and all the downstairs windows were locked. Somehow she couldn't see her uptight, nit-picking ex crawling up the drainpipe to get in through an upstairs window.

Thinking about Gary stirred her memories, and she switched her thoughts to something else. A vision of the cop crept into her mind. What was his name? Carter. Ben Carter. She could still feel the impact of his sharp blue eyes probing her face. Thinking of him reminded her of the skeleton. With a muffled groan, she threw off the comforter and climbed out of bed.

Her laptop lay on her bedside table. Taking care to move quietly, she pulled her chair over and sat down.

The file where she kept her research on her mother's disappearance contained a list of towns and villages that her mother might have visited. There was also a photo of her mother, taken thirty years ago, that showed a pretty, dark-haired woman with Liza's green eyes and a chin that attested to the family tenacity.

Melanie had sent the pic of her mother to various people she might have had contact with in the UK, but so far no one had recognized the woman in the photo. She had, however, made several e-mail friends and discovered distant relatives through her efforts, which had helped ease the pain of losing the so-called friends who had deserted her after her divorce.

Opening her in-box, she found an e-mail from England, which came from Vivian Adams, a woman who had been so intrigued by Melanie's story, she'd offered to help in the search for Janice. Vivian wrote that she had found a man who thought he recognized the missing woman in the photo. After contacting him, however, Vivian had been disappointed to learn he was mistaken.

Another dead end. After writing to thank her friend, Melanie closed the lid of her laptop. It seemed an impossible task. The authorities on both sides of the ocean hadn't been able to find a trace of her mother. What chance did she have?

She climbed into bed and pulled the comforter up to her chin. Maybe there wasn't much hope to cling to, but as long as there was the faintest chance that her mother could be found alive, until she actually had proof of her death, she would not give up the search.

Turning onto her side, she closed her eyes and tried not to think about the sound of soft laughter in the shadows.

She woke up a few hours later to see bright sunlight filtering through the drapes at the window. Aware that she'd overslept, she peered at her clock. The digital display showed eight forty-five. She lay still for a moment until the fog in her mind cleared, then swung her legs out of bed.

Padding across the room to the closet, she wondered if the reporter would bring the newspaper by as he'd promised. She tried to remember his name as she opened the closet door and reached for her robe. Much to her surprise, the hanger was empty.

Frowning, she stared at it, trying to remember where she could have left her robe. She could have sworn she'd hung it up in its usual place the day before. Normally, she was a creature of habit, methodically following a routine without even thinking about it. Then again, not much about her life had been normal lately.

Slowly, she went down the row of shirts, pants, and sweaters until she reached the few dresses she owned. Her robe was not among them. *Where on earth?* She must have left it in the bathroom. That would be the last place she'd worn it.

She was about to close the door when a bundle of pale-blue terry cloth at the very end of the closet caught her eye. Catching her breath, she bent down and reached for it. The soft folds of her robe fell open in her hands.

No, it wasn't possible. She would never have thrown it into the opposite end of the closet like that. Just to be certain, she checked the end of the rod. There were no empty hangers from which the robe could have fallen.

Feeling decidedly uneasy, she thrust her arms into the sleeves of the robe and tied the belt around her waist. Maybe she *had* thrown the darn thing in there. Her mind had been so messed up lately, what with the upheaval of giving up her life in Portland, buying an inn, finding a skeleton, and coming face-to-face with her worthless ex—it was no wonder she couldn't remember what she'd done the day before.

The enticing smell of coffee drifted along the hallway as she walked to the kitchen. Liza sat at the table in her rose-patterned robe, a mug steaming in front of her. "There's nothing like the smell of coffee in the morning to get you out of bed," she said as she got to her feet.

Melanie sat down at the table, smothering a yawn. "How long have you been up?"

"Not long." Liza poured coffee into a mug and brought it over to her. "I slept late."

"Thanks." Melanie took a sip of coffee and set it down. "Sorry I woke you up last night. I must have been dreaming."

Liza narrowed her eyes. "You look frazzled. Are you okay?"

Trying not to think of her misplaced robe, Melanie nodded. "I'm fine. Just sleepy. The coffee helps." She took another sip.

"I do enjoy coffee in the morning, but I must admit I sometimes miss my cup of tea." Liza lifted her mug. "We all used to drink tea first thing in the morning, remember? It took your grandfather a while to get used to it at first, but he knew it was important to me, and he ended up enjoying it as much as I did."

"Of course I remember." Melanie felt a stab of sympathy. "We have tea in the cabinet. You could still have your cup of tea in the mornings."

Liza shook her head. "I'm used to coffee now, and I love the smell of it. It gives me the jolt I need to get going in the mornings. My old bones need all the help they can get."

Melanie laughed. "Your old bones are doing just fine."

"Speaking of old bones," Liza said, smothering a yawn, "I wonder how the investigation is going. Maybe we should stop by the police station and ask."

"Or we could just call."

"There's no fun in that." Liza took another sip of coffee. "I've always wanted to visit a police station. This would be a good excuse. Besides, I was sort of hoping we'd bump into that nice policeman again. What was his name?"

"Ben Carter."

"Aha!" Liza's voice rang with triumph. "So you've been thinking about him."

Mel sighed. "It's a little hard not to think about finding a skeleton hidden behind a wall in your home."

"But you remembered the officer's name." Liza leaned forward. "You never remember names."

Mel glanced at the time displayed on the microwave. "We'd better have breakfast before we shower or we'll be combining it with lunch."

To her relief, Liza accepted the change of subject and drained her coffee. "You're right. Let's get going or this day will be over before we get anything done. I'd like to get started on painting the porch while the weather is good."

An hour or so later, Mel was perched on a ladder on the porch, paintbrush in hand, when a gray car drew up in the driveway. Liza was on her knees, smoothing cream paint on the railing, and got slowly to her feet as the lithe figure of the newspaper reporter climbed out of the car.

He headed for the steps, waving a folded newspaper at them. "Brought you a copy of the article," he said, pausing at the foot of the steps. "The police identified your skeleton." He looked up at the porch. "Wow! You two are ambitious."

Liza put down her paintbrush. "I may look it, but that doesn't mean I feel it." She gestured at Melanie. "At least I don't have to climb up a ladder."

Melanie peered down at the reporter. *Josh!* That was his name. She waved her paintbrush at him.

"I'd offer to help," Josh said, grinning up at her, "but I'm afraid of heights."

"The steps need painting, too," Liza said hopefully.

"Sorry, I have an appointment." He walked up the steps and handed the newspaper to Liza. "Maybe another time?"

"I'll hold you to that." Liza took the newspaper. "Thanks so much for this."

Feeling compelled to say something, Melanie called out, "Yes, thanks for bringing it by, Josh."

He looked up at her. "No problem. The police think they've identified your skeleton, by the way. She was Angela Morelli. Vince Morelli's wife. The people who owned the house before you bought it."

Melanie realized she'd been listening to the shocking news with her mouth open and quickly shut it.

Liza seemed equally shocked. "Oh my! Do they know who killed her?"

"Not yet. It's all in the article." He looked back at Melanie. "Hope you like it."

Melanie swallowed. "I'm sure we will." She was suddenly eager to see it and wished he would leave so she could take a look at it.

As if reading her mind, he gave her a quick wave and ran down the steps to his car.

Melanie waited until he was out of sight before climbing down the ladder.

Liza already had the newspaper open and was scanning the pages. "Here it is. Not a big story but a nice picture of the inn. He must have taken it when he left yesterday. I wish he'd waited until we'd painted the porch."

She handed the paper to Melanie. "Here. Read it to me. My reading glasses are in the kitchen."

Melanie sat down on the wrought-iron bench and waited for Liza to get comfortable at her side before starting to read out loud. *"The gruesome discovery of a skeleton behind a bedroom wall of the Merry Ghost Inn has handed the Sully's Landing Police Department a mysterious cold case to solve. The police suspect the remains are that of Angela Morelli, wife of the previous owner of the house, Vincent Morelli. It will take a few days, however, for a positive identification."*

"Goodness! Tony Morelli's stepmother! Didn't he say his father lived here with his second wife?"

"I guess so. If it is his wife." Melanie went back to the article. *"Angela Morelli had supposedly left her husband and moved back to her home in New Jersey seven years ago. Attempts to locate her, however, have been unsuccessful, leaving the authorities to assume she is the victim. Police found a packed suitcase next to the remains. According to the autopsy, the victim had been killed by a blow to the head. It was also determined that she had been pregnant at the time of her death."*

Melanie's cry of dismay was echoed by Liza's.

"Poor thing," Liza muttered. "Life can be so cruel. Does it say how she got behind the wall or who killed her?"

Melanie went on reading. *"So far, the police have no clues as to who might have been responsible for the alleged murder and are looking into the case."*

"I'm betting it was her husband. He found out she was leaving him, and he killed her in a fit of rage. I wonder if he knew she was pregnant."

Melanie squinted at her grandmother. "You've been reading too many mystery novels."

"Enough to make me a pretty decent detective."

"Detectives don't guess. They find evidence and solve clues."

"Well, it seems pretty obvious to me. Go on, what else does the article say?"

Melanie turned back to the newspaper. *"Meanwhile, the renovations of the Merry Ghost Inn are on hold while the investigation is ongoing, and the new owners, Mrs. Elizabeth Harris and her granddaughter, Ms. Melanie West, will have to wait for the grand opening of what will eventually be a charming and intriguing bed-and-breakfast."*

Liza beamed. "What a sweet man. We'll have to invite him over for dinner sometime."

"He mentions the ghost." Melanie continued to read out loud. *"The Merry Ghost Inn is a century-old house, named for the rumored ghost that haunts the ancient halls. Mrs. Harris confessed she has heard his eerie laughter and is convinced the ghost is real."*

"Oh, that's wonderful!" Liza's eyes were bright with excitement. "I hope this article is picked up by the *Oregonian.*"

Thinking of Gary, Melanie wasn't sure how she felt about that. Folding up the newspaper, she stood up. "Time to get back to the painting. I'd like to get this side of the porch finished before lunch."

By the time they'd finished supper and cleaned up the kitchen that night, Melanie was more than ready to crawl into bed. "I don't know how you do it," she told Liza as they walked down the hallway toward the bedrooms. "Every muscle in my body is screaming in pain."

"Believe me, so are mine." Liza paused at her door. "Then again, I'm used to being in pain. That's part of getting old."

Melanie smiled. "You, my dear Granny, will never be old."

"Tell that to my creaking joints." Liza opened her door. "Go ahead and use the bathroom. I can wait."

Still smiling, Melanie wished her grandmother a good night's sleep, then headed for the lone bathroom on the first floor. It was small, as bathrooms go, but quaint, with its pedestal basin and claw-foot tub. The shower had obviously been added later, with a convoluted arrangement of pipes and faucets that nevertheless delivered a satisfying spray of water.

The large mirror on the wall had an impressive white frame carved with tiny rosebuds and sprays of lily of the valley. Melanie thought it was the bathroom's best feature. Glancing at it now, she caught sight of her reflection in the mirror and shuddered. She looked a mess, with her hair tangled by the wind, her old yellow T-shirt stained with paint, and . . . she paused and leaned forward.

There was something else on the mirror. Something that hadn't been there that morning. Lipstick. Smeared in the shape of a bow.

Chapter 4

"I called the police station this morning," Liza announced when Melanie walked into the kitchen the next morning. Seated at the table with the pages of the *Oregonian* spread out before her, she added, "Apparently Detective Dutton, the cop who's in charge of the case, has been called out of town, so our case is on hold right now."

"What?" Melanie headed for the coffeepot. "They only have one detective?"

"I guess so. Ben said the detective works with the Clatsop County major crimes team, and they take care of several towns, not just ours."

Melanie poured coffee into a mug and carried it over to the table. "You talked to Ben Carter?"

"I asked to talk to him." Liza took off her glasses and laid them down on the table. "He's such a nice young man. So helpful and sweet."

"Not that helpful, apparently." Melanie sat down, her gaze going immediately to the window. Just a few white clouds drifted across a pale-blue sky. The ocean was calm, and already people strolled along the beach while a couple of dogs romped around, chasing each other into the water and out again. She watched them for a moment or two, smiling at their antics.

She could see all the way down the coastline, until the line of cliffs and rocks faded into the distance. For a moment, she felt a deep sense of peace, until Liza said, "Josh's article is in the *Oregonian.*" She tapped the paper. "It's the same one that was in the *Sully's Landing Gazette.*"

Dragging her attention back to her grandmother, Melanie sipped her coffee before answering. "There's nothing new in there about the case?"

"Nothing." Liza shook her head. "And we need to do something about it. If we don't get this resolved soon, we'll have to cancel all our reservations."

"I don't see what we can do. Obviously the police don't think our case is a priority."

"Well, they should. Angela Morelli's killer is still at large. Unless it was her husband, in which case he's where he belongs."

"Exactly. If Vincent killed his wife, then he's not going to harm anyone else. If it was someone else, the murder was seven years ago. The killer is probably a thousand miles away from here."

"Maybe, but that doesn't solve our problem. We still have to face the probability of having to cancel the reservations, which will put a serious dent in our finances. Without that money, we won't be able to get the new roof, or the heating system overhauled, or any of the major renovations we need . . ." Her voice trailed off and her eyes misted over.

It was so rare to see her grandmother look that defeated, and Melanie felt a stab of alarm. She reached out for Liza's hand, which felt icy cold. "We'll think of something, Granny. Don't worry."

Liza gave her a weak smile. "I'm trying not to worry. Which is why I want to do something about it."

"Like what?"

"Like doing a little investigating ourselves."

Melanie let go of her hand and sat up. "Investigating?"

"Yes." Liza already looked brighter. "We can talk to the locals. Find out what we can about Vincent and Angela and see if we can come up with something that will move this case along."

"But what about the redecorating? We don't have time to run around town talking to everyone."

"There's no point in redecorating if we can't open the inn. Please, Melanie. I really want to do this, and I don't want to do it alone."

For a long moment, Melanie studied her grandmother. In some ways, she was right. There was no point in spending time and money on the inn if they couldn't open it up to their guests.

She seriously doubted that they could solve a murder case, but she knew how much her grandmother loved mystery novels. If doing some snooping around town made Liza happy while they waited for the police to solve the case, then who was she to deny her?

Reaching for Liza's hand again, she clasped it in her own. "Okay, Nancy Drew, let's give it a shot."

"Great!" Liza's smile melted away Melanie's doubts. "I'll make breakfast now."

"I'll help." Melanie got up from the table. "By the way, what's the point behind the lipstick bow on the bathroom mirror?"

Liza frowned. "Lipstick?"

"Yes." Melanie opened a cabinet door and took down a couple of plates. "You drew a bow on the mirror. I was wondering if it was some kind of message."

"I didn't draw anything on the mirror." Liza paused in the act of slicing an English muffin. "I didn't see anything on there this morning."

Melanie was beginning to get an uncomfortable feeling in her stomach. "I wiped it off last night. Are you telling me you didn't put it there?"

Liza's gaze was intent on her face. "Positive. Are you quite sure you saw it? You didn't dream it?"

Melanie felt sick. She wasn't sure of anything anymore. "Maybe I did." She opened the fridge door. Either she was hallucinating, or Liza was doing things without remembering she'd done them.

Neither scenario seemed feasible. Liza's mind and memory were sharper than most people Melanie knew, and as for her own sanity, she was fairly certain she was solid in that department.

All the stress was getting to them. Maybe Liza was right, after all. Maybe they needed to do something positive to try to solve their problem before they both lost their minds.

Just to reassure herself, when she went into the bathroom to take her shower, she looked in the wastebin. The tissue she'd used to wipe the mirror the night before lay inside, still smeared with red lipstick.

Quickly, she snatched it up and flushed it down the toilet. She did not believe in phantoms, she told herself as she turned on the faucet for the shower. Liza was having fun with her, trying to make her believe in the merry ghost. Well, she would just go along with it and let her grandmother enjoy the game. It would take her mind off their money troubles.

Only half-convinced, she climbed into the shower and did her best to banish the niggling disquiet that would plague her for the rest of the morning.

It was after lunch when the two of them set off for town. Liza suggested they stop in the clothing store, killing two birds with one stone, as she explained to Melanie. She was eager to take a look at what the store had to offer, and they could talk to whoever was in there.

Entering the store a few minutes later, Liza headed at once for the racks, while Melanie wandered over to a display of glittering scarves. She'd never been that interested in sequins and sparkles, but the scarves were so appealing, she couldn't resist a closer look.

"They're pretty, aren't they?"

Melanie turned to face the middle-aged woman who'd spoken behind her. "They are. I don't wear scarves, but I'm almost tempted to buy one."

The woman laughed, one hand straying up to brush back blonde bangs from her eyes. "Maybe I can persuade you." She plucked a purple-and-green scarf from the stand. "I like this one. It will bring out the green in your eyes."

"Oh, do buy it, Mel." Liza appeared at Melanie's side. "It's beautiful."

Feeling pressured, Melanie hesitated. "I'm not really a scarf person."

"Oh, rubbish. Here, I'll buy it for you. An early birthday gift." Before Melanie could protest, Liza had carried the scarf over to the counter and was digging into her purse for her wallet.

The blonde woman followed her over to the counter and walked behind it. "Good choice. Let me wrap it for you."

Melanie joined her grandmother at the counter. "You can't afford to buy me a birthday gift."

"Of course I can. That's what credit cards are for."

Melanie sighed. "Thank you. That's very sweet of you, and I do love the scarf."

"I know. I could see it in your eyes."

The woman finished wrapping the scarf in pink tissue and slipped it into a small, cream-colored paper bag with black drawstrings. Handing it over to Liza, she said brightly, "Thank you for shopping at Felicity's Fashions."

Liza smiled back. "Are you Felicity?"

The woman laughed. "No, I'm Sharon Sutton, the owner of this store. I just liked the way the name Felicity sounded."

"It's certainly one you'd remember." Liza put a hand on Melanie's arm. "This is my granddaughter, Melanie West. I'm Liza Harris, and we're the new owners of the Morelli house. Soon to be the Merry Ghost Inn."

Melanie was intrigued to see Sharon Sutton's expression change at the mention of the inn. For a second or two, she actually looked scared, but then she recovered almost at once, and the smile was back in place. "Well, welcome to the neighborhood. Though I'd guess finding a skeleton in your house isn't exactly the welcome you'd expected."

Liza nodded. "It was a bit of a shock, I can tell you. Did you know the Morellis?"

Sharon hesitated. "I didn't have much to do with them. I saw Angela around town now and then, but her husband, Vincent, was in a wheelchair and never left the house. I heard that he was in a car wreck about two years before Angela left . . ." She paused, then corrected herself. "Before Angela died." She leaned forward and lowered her voice. "If you ask me, *he* killed her. Found out she was leaving him and lost his temper."

"That's certainly possible." Liza handed the bag to Melanie. "Though if he was in a wheelchair, it might have been difficult for him to kill her and stuff her body behind the wall."

"They say anything's possible when you're in a rage. The adrenaline gives you added strength." Warming to her subject, Sharon launched into a long, meandering description of an elderly, crippled woman who saved a dog from drowning in the ocean.

Her attention wandering, Melanie glanced around the store. Although small, Sharon had managed to stock a wide variety of dresses, pantsuits, blouses, and sweaters. They were a little mature for her taste but stylish all the same.

She was contemplating taking a closer look at a short black dress with a low scoop neckline when Liza announced, "Well, we must get back to it. We have a lot of renovating to do before we can open the inn."

Sharon nodded. "I hear you're being held up by the investigation. That must be annoying."

"A little. We hope to be open soon, though." Liza gave Melanie a look that she interpreted as, *let's get out of here.*

She was about to follow her grandmother when Sharon called out, "He had a nurse, you know."

Liza turned back. "Pardon?"

"Vincent. He had a nurse." Sharon frowned. "Noriko, that was it. Chinese or Japanese, I think. Anyway, I believe her last name was Chen. Yes, that was it, Noriko Chen. She could probably tell you more about the Morellis, if you're interested. She was Vincent's nurse for a couple of years."

Liza walked back to the counter. "Do you know where I can find her?"

"Sorry. I haven't seen her since Vincent left. She may still be in town, or she may have moved on." Sharon sighed. "People come and go in Sully's Landing. Hardly anyone sticks around anymore. There's not a lot of work in a seaside town this size."

Leaving the store, Melanie opened the bag to take another peek at the scarf. "It's really gorgeous. Thank you."

"You're welcome." Liza smiled. "That would look lovely with the little black dress you were ogling back there."

Melanie stared at her. "How did you know?"

"I saw you gazing at it with lust in your eyes."

"I don't waste my lust on clothes."

"Good to know. I was beginning to think you'd given up on men entirely."

Melanie quickened her pace to keep up with her grandmother. "Maybe I have. Right now I don't feel in the least interested."

Liza gave her a sly look. "Not even in Officer Ben Carter or Josh Phillips?"

A vision of the cop flashed through her mind. "Not Josh Phillips," Melanie said firmly. "And definitely not Ben Carter."

"What's wrong with him?"

"Nothing, as far as I know. He's just not my type."

Liza looked disappointed but chose not to answer, much to Melanie's relief. Maybe now her grandmother would quit trying to match her up with the cop.

Back at the house, the two of them tackled the painting once more and kept at it until the cream-colored porch, steps, and railings all glowed a faint orange in the rays of the setting sun.

Well-satisfied with their work, the two women cleared away the empty paint pots, brushes, and ladder and stowed them in the garage.

"We have to sort out this mess soon," Liza said as Melanie edged the ladder between two piles of boxes. "And we have a ton of stuff to go through in the basement."

"We'll start on it tomorrow." Melanie glanced around at the stack of cartons, chairs, tables, and shelves. In the weeks they had waited for the sale to go through, they had scoured thrift stores and used furniture outlets for the extra pieces they would need for the inn.

"It's going to take a few days to go through it." Liza gazed mournfully at the mountain of goods. "We can't move most of it until we redecorate the upstairs rooms."

"We can unpack the boxes and figure out where everything goes." Melanie pulled a carton toward her and peered at the words scribbled on it. "This one says kitchen. We can start there. Maybe by the time we get these unpacked, the Clatsop

County crime team will have finished with our detective and he can go back on the case."

"I sure hope so." Liza slapped a hand down on one of the cartons. "Anyway, I'm done for the night. Let's go get something to eat. My stomach has been complaining for the last hour."

Watching her grandmother limp into the house, Melanie felt a deep surge of guilt. If only they could afford to have someone do the redecorating for them, Liza would be spared the pain. Several times, Melanie had insisted that she could manage the work on her own, but her grandmother wouldn't hear of it.

"We do it together," she'd said when Melanie had suggested she paint the porch herself, "or we don't do it at all." Sometimes the Harris women were too stubborn for their own good.

"We need to talk to the nurse," Liza announced when they were seated in the kitchen nook later, enjoying a plate of chicken Alfredo.

Alarmed, Melanie studied her grandmother. Liza's face looked drawn and tired and just a little too pale. Visions of her lying still and silent in a hospital bed sent a wave of panic throughout Melanie's body. "Where does it hurt? Do we need to go to the hospital? Is it your heart?"

Liza looked at her as if she'd lost her mind. "What on earth are you talking about?"

"You said . . . oh!" Feeling foolish, Melanie picked up the fork she'd dropped on her plate. "You're talking about Vincent Morelli's nurse."

"Of course I am." Liza shook her head. "You've got to stop worrying about me. I may be getting old, but I'm far from decrepit. I'm as healthy as a horse."

Liza smiled. "And I hope you stay that way. You do look tired, though."

"Tired I'll admit to, reluctantly. It's been a long day. But about this nurse. How do we find her? Do you think Ben could help with that?"

Melanie raised her eyebrows. "How does Officer Carter feel about you using his first name?"

"He didn't say I couldn't." Liza dug into her pasta. "Actually, I think he rather likes it."

Melanie felt it wiser not to probe too far into that statement. "Well, I might be able to track the nurse down online. If I can remember her name."

"It's Noriko Chen."

Melanie sighed. "You never cease to amaze me. How did you remember that?"

"I made a mental note of it in Sharon's store. I knew we would have to talk to her."

"Are you sure you want to do that?"

"What do you mean? Of course I want to do that. I want to find out more about the Morellis and maybe pick up a clue as to who might have killed Angela. Don't you?"

"Well, yes." Melanie put down her fork and reached for her glass of chardonnay. "But not if it means stepping on the toes of the Sully's Landing Police Department. How does your friend Officer Carter feel about us butting our noses into one of their cases?"

"I didn't ask him." Liza leaned back in her chair. "The police aren't doing anything about the case right now, and anyway, all we are doing is asking a couple of people about the Morellis. Since they once owned this house, surely we're entitled to know more about them."

"Put that way, I guess it can't do any harm."

Liza grinned. "I knew you'd see it my way."

"That's what scares me." Melanie took a sip of wine. "I'm beginning to think like you."

"Well, it's about time." Liza yawned and stretched. "Ouch. Speaking of time, I think I need to get some beauty sleep."

"Good idea." Melanie got up and reached for the plates. "You go ahead. I'll take care of these. I'm going to watch the news and spend a little time on the computer before I go to bed."

Liza's face clouded. "More research on your mother?"

"Maybe. But first I'm going to look for Norika Chen."

"It's Noriko." Liza spelled it out. "I used to know a woman with that name. That's how I remembered it. Nice lady. I hated her dog, though. Nasty little yappy thing."

"I thought you loved all dogs. You're always talking about getting one."

Liza yawned again. "I do. Just not that one." She climbed slowly to her feet, wincing as she pushed back her chair. "Thanks for doing the dishes. I'll take my turn at them tomorrow."

Melanie walked over to her and gave her a hug. "Have a good night's sleep. I'll see you in the morning."

She watched her grandmother walk stiffly to the door, cursing the lack of funds that would have saved Liza from all that work. Maybe she could find a part-time job while they were waiting for the police to close the case. Although Karen—or Sharon, whatever her name was—had said there was little work in town. She could maybe commute to another town close by, but then that would leave Liza alone. Knowing her grandmother, Liza would then tackle the renovations on her own, and heaven only knew what trouble she'd cause for herself.

Melanie made short work of the dishes, then switched on the TV in the living room, keeping the volume low so as not to disturb her grandmother. She was at the point of dozing off when the news anchor's words snapped her to attention.

"The discovery of remains behind a bedroom wall in a local inn has police wondering who could have chosen such a bizarre hiding place. The victim, who was pregnant at the time of her death, was identified as the wife of the previous owner of what is now called the Merry Ghost Inn, situated on the cliffs in Sully's Landing. The new owners, Elizabeth Harris and her granddaughter, Melanie West, received the gruesome surprise while renovating the house in order to turn it into a bed-and-breakfast. Let's hope the merry ghost doesn't chase the customers away. In other news . . ."

Melanie reached for the remote and switched off the TV. Well, now the news was all over town, and Gary would know exactly where she could be found. There wasn't much she could do about that, except pray he would stay out of her life.

Minutes later, she sat down at her bedroom desk and opened her computer. It didn't take her long to find a news story about a nursing home in Tillamook and a picture of the staff. Noriko Chen was listed as one of the nurses. She appeared to be in her forties, with short jet-black hair and beautiful dark eyes. Her kind smile warmed her face as she looked down at a frail man in a wheelchair.

Melanie had to wonder what the nurse could tell them that would help track down a murderer. Still, she scribbled the address on her sticky notepad and pulled the sheet off. If Liza wanted to go visit Noriko Chen, that was fine with her. It would give her grandmother a rest from the redecorating.

She clicked out of the web page and was about to close her laptop when an idea occurred to her. She had often wondered if the reason her mother couldn't be traced was because she'd been involved in an accident and lost her memory. After all, there had been no reports of her death.

She'd checked with every hospital she could find in the UK, but none of them could find any record or recognize the photo of the woman who seemingly had vanished off the face of the earth. She hadn't checked nursing homes, however. With a renewed sense of hope, she opened her laptop.

She awoke the following morning to the sound of someone singing. The memory of ghostly laughter brought her wide awake, but in the next instant, she realized it was the voice of Engelbert Humperdinck crooning one of his ballads. Liza must have the radio going full blast.

Joining her grandmother in the kitchen, she had to smile at the sight of Liza waltzing around with her arms wound about an imaginary partner, her pink-and-white robe floating around her ankles.

Melanie had to raise her voice to be heard above the music. "Mind if I cut in?"

Liza dropped her arms with a guilty grin. "Be my guest. Though I must warn you, he's a little heavy with the footwork." She danced over to the radio on the counter and switched it off.

"From what I've seen of him," Melanie said as she headed for the coffeepot, "he has some pretty racy moves."

Liza laughed. "He does indeed, but I wasn't dancing with Engy. I was dancing with your grandfather."

Immediately contrite, Melanie said quickly, "Of course you were. I should have known that."

Liza walked over to the table, where a mug of coffee sat waiting. "It keeps him close in my mind. Though I have to admit, the thought of boogieing with Engelbert can put a spring in my step, too. Not that I could keep up with him."

"You could keep up with Justin Bieber." Melanie brought her coffee over to the table. "How long have you been up?"

"Not long." Liza glanced at the clock. "I was hoping we could visit that nurse today. Did you have any luck finding her?"

"I did. She's still working, in a nursing home in Tillamook."

Liza's eyes sparkled with excitement. "Really? I knew you could do it. Let's go this morning."

"I hope you won't be too disappointed if she can't tell us anything helpful."

"Of course not." Liza waved a hand at the window. "It's a lovely day out there. Perfect for a drive down the coast."

Looking out the window, Melanie had to agree with her. A calm ocean, a blue sky empty of clouds, and a soft breeze swaying the branches of the pines—what more could they need? "I'll call the nursing home," she said, "and see if Nurse Noriko can join us for lunch. By the way, we were on the news last night."

"Really?" Liza's eyes flashed with excitement. "Did they mention the inn?"

"Yes, they did." Melanie repeated what she could remember of the piece. She decided to leave out the bit about chasing the customers away. Liza was so certain the ghost rumors would bring in the visitors, not frighten them off. The last thing she wanted to do was take that light out of her grandmother's eyes. "I checked online as well but didn't find anything."

"Oh, well, at least we're getting some publicity out of it. I wonder—" She broke off with a start as the shrill ring of the telephone echoed around the room. "Goodness. I'd forgotten how loud a landline can be."

Melanie jumped up and hurried over to the counter. "Maybe it's your friend at the police station to tell us the investigation is over."

"Oh, I hope so."

Picking up the receiver, Melanie could tell her grandmother was practically holding her breath. She was disappointed when the voice on the other end of the line asked about making a reservation. After a brief exchange with the woman, she hung up.

"The publicity's working," Liza said as Melanie sat down again. "I guess that's one silver lining in a very dark cloud."

"I wrote her name down while she was talking to me." Melanie reached for her coffee. "She gave me her e-mail address so I can let her know when we're taking reservations again."

Liza beamed. "Thank heaven for the Internet."

"She also said she couldn't find a website for the inn."

Liza gasped. "Why didn't we think of that?"

"There's so much to think about, it's not surprising we'd forget something. I'll get to work on one tonight." Melanie put down her mug. "Meanwhile, I'll make that phone call to the nurse. Let's hope she can tell us something that will help end this investigation."

Liza raised her mug. "Amen to that."

Chapter 5

The drive to Tillamook was every bit as pleasant as Melanie had anticipated. Although she had visited the town a few times, she had never driven the coast road herself. It was quite a different experience. The views were spectacular, with wide sweeps of rocky cliffs, long stretches of gray sand, fir-covered mountains, and quaint little towns that she had barely noticed before.

"Did Noriko seem okay with us wanting to talk about the Morellis?" Liza asked as they rounded a curve to be greeted by yet another picturesque bay.

"I think so." Melanie slowed down behind a truck pulling a trailer. "I didn't actually say we wanted to ask her about the murder. I just said we'd bought the house and were turning it into an inn, and since she'd lived in it for a couple of years, we hoped she could tell us more about it."

"She probably knows we want to ask about the murder."

"Maybe. I just hope she's willing to talk about it."

"So do I. By the way, have you ever visited the Tillamook cheese factory?"

"No, I haven't. Have you?"

"Your grandfather and I visited it a few years ago. It's really fascinating. They have a museum room with pictures of how it all got started and a fantastic gift shop with all kinds of souvenirs and products that they make there. You can see where the cheese is made, and taste samples of it, and get a scrumptious ice cream cone at the creamery." Liza looked at her watch. "They make the best fudge in the world. I can taste it now. Why don't we stop in on the way back?"

"Sounds good to me. Where is it?"

"Just a couple of miles before we get to the town. We should pass by it soon."

Minutes later, she pointed out the long white building as they drove past, where a group of visitors wandered between the parking lot and the impressive entrance.

Melanie was still thinking about the fudge as she drove into town and headed for the nursing home.

Reaching the crowded parking lot, she pulled into a space between a small gray car and a large black SUV that barely gave her room to make the turn. She had to squeeze through her partially open door to get out and then waited for Liza to climb out and edge between the cars.

"Why don't they make parking spaces big enough to fit those tanks?" Liza complained, giving the SUV a murderous glare.

"We've got a tank ourselves, and that one is parked too close to the line." Melanie took her arm and began leading her toward the door. "It will probably be gone by the time we leave."

As she expected, most of the chairs in the reception room were taken. She found a seat for Liza and stood by her side until a tired-looking woman on the other side of the room got up and left.

Melanie sat, fidgeting with impatience until a petite nurse finally rushed in and announced, "Ms. West?"

Recognizing Noriko Chen, Melanie stood up. "I'm Melanie West."

"I hope I didn't keep you waiting too long. Things are so unpredictable here; I never know exactly when I can get away." The nurse glanced at the gold watch on her wrist. "I can manage at least half an hour, but I should get back soon."

Liza rose to her feet. "I'm Melanie's grandmother, Elizabeth Harris. Can you suggest somewhere to have lunch in half an hour?"

Noriko smiled. "I'm afraid it will have to be the cafeteria. Anywhere else would take too long."

Liza looked a little crestfallen, but Melanie was quick to answer. "The cafeteria's fine."

Still smiling, Noriko led them through a long hallway and around a corner, stopping every now and then to speak to one of the ailing residents they passed on the way.

The nurse seemed to really care about her patients, and Melanie had to admire the woman for dedicating her life to helping people in need. One day, she told herself, she could end up in a place like this. She hoped if that happened, there'd be nurses like Noriko to take care of her.

The thought depressed her, and she was relieved when they reached the cafeteria, where a few people, some of them dressed in white coats, sat at tables by large windows that overlooked a pleasant garden.

After choosing a turkey sandwich and a soda from the long counter, Melanie followed her grandmother and the nurse to a table in the corner.

After exchanging pleasantries as they all sat down, the conversation soon turned to the Morellis, and Noriko appeared willing to talk about them. She disclosed that Vincent and Angela Morelli had left the East Coast soon after they had married and had bought the house from the Sullivan family.

"The Sullivans built the house in 1905," she said. "Paul Sullivan was the last of the family to own it. He and his wife, Brooke, lived there for a few years before selling it to the Morellis. You must have heard of them. They own most of the land in the area. The Sullivan family settled on that part of the coast during the late 1800s and built the town. Sully's Landing is named after them."

Liza uttered a soft gasp. "I didn't know that."

Fascinated now, Melanie joined in the conversation. "There must be a lot of Sullivans in the area."

"I don't think so." Noriko took a bite of her sandwich and swallowed it down. "I believe most of them have moved away."

"Have you met any of them?"

"Paul Sullivan used to visit the house a lot. He had . . . business dealings . . . with Mr. Morelli."

She'd spoken as if the business dealings were in the same category as horse droppings.

"So how did you come to work there?" Liza asked, exchanging a meaningful glance with Melanie.

"I was working at the hospital in Seaside when I heard that Mr. Morelli had been in a car accident and needed a live-in nurse. I applied for the job and was hired that day."

Liza leaned forward, her gaze intent on Noriko's face. "What was Mr. Morelli like? Did you like him? Was he difficult to look after?"

The nurse didn't respond right away. She took a bite of her sandwich and seemed to be thinking over her answer before she spoke again. "He was a good man. He was in a lot of pain and could be irritable at times, but he always apologized for his bad mood later and made up for it in some way. He was a very generous man."

Melanie wondered if he paid the nurse extra cash or gave her expensive gifts so that she would forgive him for being a grouch. "What about Angela Morelli?"

Noriko shrugged. "Mrs. Morelli was okay. One should never speak ill of the dead."

"You didn't like her," Liza said.

Melanie could tell from Noriko's expression that they'd hit a nerve. She lowered her voice. "I know you must have heard about Angela Morelli's remains being found. That must have been a terrible shock for you."

"It was." A dark shadow crossed the nurse's face, but then she seemed to shake it off. "We all thought she'd left to go back to New Jersey." She paused. "I must have been the last one to see her alive." She gulped and added quickly, "Except for whoever killed her, of course."

"Have the police talked to you yet?" Liza asked.

Noriko dropped her sandwich on her plate. "No. Anyway, I don't have anything to tell them. I talked to them after Mrs. Morelli left and told them everything I knew."

Caught up in the story now, Melanie had to hear the rest of it. "Can you tell us anything about the last time you saw Angela Morelli? Did she seem upset or afraid?"

She thought at first that Noriko wasn't going to answer, but then she started speaking in a low, fast voice that Melanie had to strain to hear.

"I had settled Mr. Morelli for the night and stopped by Mrs. Morelli's room as I always did, to see if she needed anything. She was standing by the bed, packing a suitcase. She said she was leaving her husband. She was wearing a coat, and I thought she was going to leave right away, but she said she was leaving the next morning." Noriko shook her head, her face creased with pain. "I pleaded with her to talk it over with him, but she said she couldn't stand to be with him anymore. I went back to warn him, but he was fast asleep. I decided it would be better to wait until the next morning and be there for him when his wife broke the news."

Melanie waited throughout the long silence that followed, until she was compelled to ask, "So what happened when she told him?"

Noriko started as if woken from a bad dream. "She never did tell him. I was asleep that night when something woke me up. I thought I'd heard the doorbell ring, but I was so sleepy, I didn't get up right away. I lay there, listening, but I heard nothing after that, and I fell asleep again. When I got up the next morning, Mrs. Morelli was gone, and poor Vincent . . ." She cleared her throat. "He was heartbroken. I didn't think he was going to survive the shock. Two days later, he ordered me to pack up his clothes and a few belongings. I took him to the airport and got him on a plane. I assumed he'd followed his wife back to the East Coast. I never saw him again."

Feeling sorry for the nurse, Melanie said gently, "And you were out of a job. That must have made things difficult for you."

Noriko's eyes were misty when she met Melanie's gaze. "It did, but it was so much worse for Mr. Morelli. I wonder now if he would have taken it better if he'd known his wife was dead. It destroyed him to think she'd abandoned him when he needed her the most."

"You didn't hear anything that night after you heard the doorbell?" Liza asked.

Noriko shook her head. "I thought at the time that the ringing of the doorbell was a cab driver arriving to take Mrs. Morelli to the airport, since both cars were still in the garage." She paused and uttered a heavy sigh. "I think now that whoever rang the doorbell must have killed her. She was wearing her nightgown when she died, so someone must have come to the house after she'd gone to bed."

Liza leaned forward again. "Do you think Vincent Morelli could have murdered his wife?"

Melanie thought the nurse was going to choke on her sandwich. She carefully put it down on her plate and took a deep breath. Her face still looked calm and serene, but there was a fire in her dark eyes, and her hands had clenched into fists.

"Mr. Morelli couldn't possibly have killed his wife," she said with just a slight quiver in her voice. "He was confined to his wheelchair and was far too weak to kill her and drag her body behind that wall."

Liza nodded. "So we heard. Besides, I doubt that even a man in anger would kill the woman carrying his child."

Noriko's voice rose a notch. "I can't believe that was Mr. Morelli's baby. He and Mrs. Morelli barely talked to each other. They slept in separate rooms all the years I was with them. I even heard Mrs. Morelli tell someone on the phone one night that she only stayed with her husband because of his money."

Melanie couldn't stop herself from saying, "Then Angela Morelli must have had a boyfriend."

"Of course she did." Liza smiled at Noriko. "I don't suppose you know who he was?"

As if aware she'd said too much, the nurse looked at her watch. "I'm sorry. I should be getting back . . ."

"No, wait." Liza held out her hand. "If you have any idea who Mrs. Morelli was involved with, you really need to tell us."

Noriko rose, her face flushed. "I'm sorry, I can't help you. Now I must go."

She gathered up her purse and started to leave, but Liza obviously wasn't ready to let it go. "What kind of business did Paul Sullivan have with Mr. Morelli?"

"I have no idea. Good-bye, Mrs. Harris, Ms. West." Noriko's voice was firm as she stepped out into the aisle. "Thank you for my lunch. Have a pleasant trip home."

Melanie got to her feet. "Thank you, Noriko, for taking the time to talk to us. We're very eager to find out who killed Angela Morelli, and we appreciate your help."

The nurse paused and slowly turned her head. "Be careful. It doesn't pay to pry. Some people will go to great lengths to keep their secrets." She hurried off, leaving Melanie staring after her.

"She knows more than she's telling us," Liza said as Melanie sat down again. "She was warning us about someone. I just wish she'd told us who."

"Probably the mysterious boyfriend. Or Paul Sullivan." Melanie picked up her soda. "He's obviously an important person in the community. He probably wouldn't be too happy if he found out we were poking into his business."

"Well, that's a chance we'll have to take. Did you get the feeling that Noriko doesn't like him?"

"I don't think she liked anyone connected to that house."

"Except maybe Vincent Morelli." Liza reached for her purse, which she'd stashed under her chair. "We'd better get going. Tomorrow I want to stop off at the hardware store again. Maybe this time we can have lunch there."

Melanie smiled. "So you can guzzle beer?"

Liza wrinkled her nose. "So we can ask that cheeky Mr. Griffith if his brother told him anything new about the case. Now let's go and buy some of that fudge at the cheese factory."

As she followed her grandmother out of the nursing home, Melanie had to admit the conversation with Noriko had been intriguing. Her analytical mind relished the challenge of unraveling the mystery behind Angela Morelli's death.

If Noriko was right and the baby didn't belong to Vincent Morelli, then who was the mysterious father of the child? Was he the killer? Or had Vincent found the strength to kill his wife in a jealous rage?

Fascinating stuff. Then again, Noriko's warning still hovered in her mind. After all, they had a business to consider. It might not be such a good idea to make waves with people as prominent as the family who founded Sully's Landing.

"Well," Liza said as they drove out of town, "if Angela was planning on leaving town with her boyfriend the next morning, she wasn't expecting whoever it was who rang the doorbell that night. She was wearing her nightgown, so she was probably asleep in bed."

"If it was the doorbell that disturbed Noriko." Melanie slowed down as they rounded yet another curve. "She said she *thought* it was the doorbell. She wasn't sure, so it could have been something else that woke her up."

"Such as?"

Melanie shrugged. "I doubt if someone could have killed Angela and stuffed her body behind the wall without making some noise. When you're woken up out of a deep sleep like that, it's easy to be confused about what you heard."

"True." Liza was quiet for a moment, then added, "Did you believe her story? About Angela, I mean. She made her sound pretty narcissistic."

"I think Noriko had personal feelings for Vincent. As for her story . . . I don't know." Melanie frowned. "It's been seven years. People remember things differently over time."

Liza pointed at the windshield. "There's the factory ahead. By the way, I was impressed at how you questioned her. I should have known that with your logical mind, you'd make a great detective."

Melanie gave her a sideways glance. "I have to admit, I enjoyed talking to her and trying to figure out the meaning behind what she was telling us."

"I'd give anything to know who the father of that baby was."

"I'm sure the police would, too." Melanie slowed down to pull into the factory's parking lot.

"Maybe Paul Sullivan knows who he was. We need to talk to him."

Melanie parked the car and applied the brake. "Liza, I know how eager you are to solve this murder. I am, too, but I've been thinking about it, and as much as I'd love to keep looking into it, I really think we should leave it up to the authorities. Let them take it from here, before we get into trouble. It wouldn't be good for business to get on the wrong side of influential people like the Sullivans."

Liza sounded disappointed when she answered. "I suppose you're right. Anyway, the police have better resources than we do to conduct an investigation. And we do need this thing resolved as soon as possible. Still, it would have been nice to have solved a murder."

"Well, let's hope the police can do it for us, and soon."

"Amen to that," Liza said as they walked over to the entrance to the factory. "Though I was hoping for an excuse to go see that nice Officer Carter again."

Rolling her eyes, Melanie followed her grandmother through the door.

They spent a pleasant hour roaming around the factory eating fudge, watching the cheese being made, and tasting samples of it. Melanie enjoyed the historical photos of the factory, and they were both munching on ice cream cones when they returned to the car.

"That was a very satisfying day," Liza remarked as they drove back along the coast road.

Melanie had to agree with her.

That evening, after her grandmother had gone to bed, Melanie spent over an hour working on a website for the inn. When her eyelids started drooping, she gave up and climbed into bed.

Before long, she was dreaming she was being chased across the beach by a hooded man carrying a rifle. The sand slowed her down, and he was gaining on her. Her chest hurt with the effort to breathe. She woke up with a start, heart pounding, to find her face buried in her pillow.

She lay awake for some time, going over in her mind their conversation with Noriko. She still couldn't shake the feeling that the nurse was holding something back. She pictured her arguing with Angela and running to Vincent to warn him, only to find him sleeping. She must have been torn between the urgency of the situation and the reluctance to wake him up. Had she blamed herself the next morning when Angela was gone, leaving a devastated husband behind? Noriko had lost a job and a home that day. That must have been so hard for her.

Turning over, Melanie finally fell asleep and woke up the next morning feeling desperately in need of her morning coffee.

Minutes later, as she was pouring the freshly brewed liquid into her mug, Liza waltzed through the door, humming something that sounded vaguely familiar.

She held a newspaper in her hand and dropped it onto the kitchen table. "I challenge anyone to stay in bed with that heavenly smell permeating the house," she said as she walked over to the counter and reached for a mug from the cabinet.

Melanie took the mug from her and filled it with coffee. "You sound perky this morning. Sleep well?"

"I did. I hope you did, too?"

Shutting her mind against the memory of her nightmare, Melanie handed her the coffee. "Like a baby."

"Good." Liza carried her mug over to the table and sat down. Peering at the window, she added, "Looks like it's going to be a nice day. Mel, I've been thinking about this, and I really think we should go to the police station today. We need to tell them about our conversation with Noriko. Just in case there's something there she didn't tell them."

Melanie sat down opposite her and cradled her coffee in her hands. "He could be married, you know."

Liza gave her an innocent stare. "Who?"

"You know who I'm talking about. Officer Carter. He's probably married."

Liza shook her head. "He doesn't look married."

Melanie gulped down a mouthful of coffee. "What does that mean?"

"Exactly what I said. Besides, he's not wearing a ring. I looked."

Still wondering what being married was supposed to look like, Melanie shook her head. "Don't you ever give up?"

"Never!" Liza's eyes misted over. "You deserve to be happy. You deserve a lovely man to take care of you."

Melanie gripped the handle of her coffee mug. "Granny, I know you mean well, but I'm just not ready to go down that road again. I don't know if I ever will, so please, let it go. Okay?"

Liza looked contrite. "I'm sorry, Mel. It just pains me to see you alone when you have so much to give."

"I'm not alone. I have you." Melanie drained her mug and reached for the newspaper. "Do you want to read this now, or shall we wait until after breakfast?"

Accepting the change of subject, Liza popped on her glasses and held out her hand. "Let's read it now. I want another cup of coffee before I get dressed."

Melanie took out the Living section and handed her the rest of the paper. After skimming through the comics, she checked her horoscope. The caution about obstacles to her goals and a warning about pitfalls ahead prompted a cynical smirk. The story of her life.

"What are you sneering at?" Liza asked as she turned a page. "The news can't be that bad."

"It's not exactly heartwarming. I—" She broke off as a headline caught her eye. "Oh, here's something—a charity dinner at the Windshore Inn tomorrow night. It's for the Humane Society. One of your favorite causes."

Liza looked up. "Really?"

Melanie scanned the article. "Guess who's going to be there."

"The president of the United States?"

Melanie laughed. "Seriously? In Sully's Landing?"

"One can always live in hope."

"Well, it's nobody that illustrious. Just the Sullivans, that's all. Paul Sullivan is giving a speech."

Liza sat up straighter. "All right! We should go!"

"I thought we were going to let the police handle the investigation."

"Oh, not to question them or anything." Liza's eyes gleamed with excitement. "Aren't you just a little bit curious? They must have fascinating stories to tell. After all, their family built this town."

"And what makes you think they'd tell us their stories?"

"We bought the house they lived in. That gives us something in common."

Melanie sighed. "You know the discovery of the skeleton is bound to come up. They can hardly ignore that. It's all over the news."

"So it would be natural to casually include it in a conversation. It's not going to hurt if we manage to learn something, is it?" Liza tapped the newspaper. "After all, the police don't seem too eager to pursue it. There's no mention in the paper about it. Come on, Mel. It will be fun. How long has it been since you went dining and dancing?"

"Who said anything about dancing?"

Liza shrugged. "They always have dancing at these things."

Melanie leaned forward. "No dancing. And no questioning."

"All right. Does that mean you'll go?"

Melanie stared at the article again. "Okay. I guess I would like to know more about the Sullivans."

Liza waved her coffee mug in triumph. "Yes! I knew you couldn't resist. Now you have to buy that little black dress we saw in Felicity's Fashions."

"I can't afford a new dress."

"Of course you can. I told you, that's what credit cards are for." She glanced up at the clock. "We'd better get dressed and have breakfast or it will be lunchtime before we get to the police station. But first, I'm going to call and order tickets for that dinner."

A few hours later, Melanie parked the car in the public parking lot in front of City Hall. Like most of the structures in Sully's Landing, cedar shingles covered the walls, and a wide overhang shadowed the small windows, lending it a rustic charm that reminded her more of a farmhouse than a municipal building.

The police station was tucked away in the back, where a treelined side street led to a narrow parking lot. The door opened onto a small foyer, with another door across the room and a glassed-in counter on the right. On the other side of the glass, two women in plain clothes sat at desks, staring at computers.

One of them sprang to her feet as Melanie walked in, followed closely by her grandmother.

Now that she was actually in the police station, Melanie began to have second thoughts about talking to Officer Carter. What if he was angry with them for butting into police business? What if—? She jumped when the woman interrupted her thoughts with a pleasant, "Can I help you?"

Suddenly tongue-tied, Melanie hesitated.

Before she could say anything, Liza said firmly, "We'd like to speak with Officer Carter, please."

The woman seemed surprised. "I'm not sure he's back yet. Let me check." She went over to her desk and picked up her phone. Seconds later, she spoke into the receiver. "Ben, there are two ladies here to speak with you. Can you give them a minute?" She paused and added, "They didn't say."

"Tell him we're the owners of the Merry Ghost Inn," Liza said.

The woman repeated Liza's words, then replaced the receiver. "He'll be out in a minute."

Melanie could feel her heart beginning to thud. They should have just called him on the phone. They were wasting his time. He was going to be annoyed with them for interfering in police business.

The interior door opened, and Melanie's mind went blank. She'd forgotten how tall he was. He seemed to fill half the space in the tiny foyer that had suddenly become stifling.

He was frowning. Not a good sign. She tried to smile, but her lips felt stiff.

Liza seemed to have no such trouble. She bounced forward and held out her hand. "So good to see you again, Officer Carter. Thank you for giving us some of your precious time."

Ben Carter's eyebrow twitched. "What can I do for you ladies?"

Melanie glanced at the two assistants who were blissfully watching the encounter, curiosity stitched all over their faces. "Is there somewhere we can talk in private?" she asked, hoping that didn't sound too provocative.

The officer's gaze rested briefly on her face, then he waved a hand at the door. "We can talk outside if you prefer."

"We prefer," Liza murmured, then hurried out the door.

Melanie followed her, wishing she was back home in the kitchen nook with a cup of coffee.

Once outside, she let Liza do all the talking, interrupting now and then to clarify a point.

Ben Carter listened to their account of their visit with Nor-iko, giving nothing away by the stern expression on his face. By the time Liza was done with her story, Melanie's stomach was in knots.

A long moment of silence followed, broken only by the harsh squawking of a sea gull overhead. The sun warmed Melanie's back, and she wished she'd worn a lighter sweater than the heavy white fleece she'd thrown on with her jeans that morning.

Finally, Officer Carter fished a pair of sunglasses out of his shirt pocket and slipped them on. For some reason, that unnerved Melanie even more. "Was there a special reason you went down to Tillamook to talk to Ms. Chen?"

He'd spoken calmly enough, but Melanie sensed he wasn't too happy with them. "We wanted to find out more about—"

She had meant to say the house, hoping that would avoid a confrontation, but Liza jumped in and finished the sentence for her. "About the Morellis. We were hoping that would shed light on the murder, since your investigation seems to have stalled."

The cop seemed unfazed by the accusation. "Detective Dutton is out of town right now, but we're expecting him back in a couple of days. I'll pass along what you've told me, but you should know that most of what Ms. Chen told you is already on file. She gave us the information when Mrs. Morelli was reported missing."

"What about the baby Angela Morelli was expecting?" Liza peered up at him, determination making her frown. "You didn't know about that until the autopsy. Noriko was certain it wasn't Vincent's baby. There had to be another man in the picture."

"We'll look into all that when Detective Dutton gets back. Until then, the investigation is on hold. It'll stay that way until the detective is free to work on it."

"Oh."

Liza's disappointment was visible on her face, and Melanie said quickly, "Thank you for your time. We'll get out of your way now."

She couldn't see his eyes behind the dark shades, but she could feel his gaze on her face. "No problem. Have a good day." He turned to leave, then stopped, looking back over his shoulder. "And you're right. We didn't know about the pregnancy back then. What Ms. Chen said about that might be of some help."

Liza brightened. "Oh, good. Then our trip wasn't for nothing."

Officer Carter hesitated, then walked back toward them. "Look, I know things aren't moving as fast as you'd like, and I'm sorry about that. Detective Dutton is aware of your situation, and I'm sure he'll get on the case just as soon as he can. Meanwhile, I have to warn you both against going around asking people questions about the murder. That's a good way to get yourselves in all kinds of trouble. Let us do the investigating. Just try to be patient, okay?"

Before either of them could answer, he twisted on his heel and marched back inside the station.

Melanie puffed out her breath. "Did he sound mad?"

"No, he didn't. He sounded concerned." Liza took hold of Melanie's arm. "It's nice that he's worried about us. That's a good sign. Now let's go and get lunch. I'm hungry."

"You're always hungry." Melanie eyed her grandmother's slender figure. "I don't know how you keep the weight off."

"Sheer determination." She let go of Melanie's arm. "Oh, shoot. I forgot to ask him something. Wait here. I'll be right back."

Before Melanie could protest, Liza had disappeared inside the police station.

Melanie waited a moment or two, then started for the door, only to halt as her grandmother emerged again, wearing a satisfied smirk.

"Okay," she said, "now we can go to lunch. I need to sit. My back is killing me."

Half afraid of the answer, Melanie asked cautiously, "What did you ask him?"

"I asked him if he was taking his wife to the charity dinner at the Windshore."

Her suspicions having been confirmed, Melanie rolled her eyes. "So what did he say?"

"He said he didn't have a wife." Liza punched her arm. "Told you so! So then I asked him if he was going."

"And?"

"He said he didn't think so, but I liked the look on his face when he said it."

"You really are incorrigible."

"I know." Liza beamed as she slipped her hand under Melanie's elbow. "Aren't you glad you went into partnership with me?"

"Ecstatic." She headed out of the parking lot, trying not to think about a rugged, good-looking cop gliding around the dance floor.

Chapter 6

The hardware store was just a short walk from the police station. After stopping by City Hall to pick up the tickets for the charity dinner, they crossed the parking lot to the store.

Seated at a table by the window, Melanie studied the menu. "The prawns and chips look good," she said as Liza stuffed her purse under her chair, "but if I eat that now, I won't have an appetite for dinner."

"Try the chicken sandwich." Liza smiled at the young server approaching them. "It's light but satisfying."

"Sounds good." Melanie gave the woman her order and leaned back to take a longer look around the pub. Colorful posters and signs clung to the walls, and what appeared to be a large patterned rug was pinned to the ceiling. On one end of a table sat a bust of a female mannequin wearing a hard hat.

She was still staring at it when a gruff voice spoke from behind her. "Well, hi there, English! Come to enjoy a beer with us?"

Liza sat up on her chair. "I don't drink before five o'clock."

"You don't know what you're missing." Doug Griffith moved around to face them both. "Hope you both enjoy your lunch."

Liza smiled up at him. "Do you have a minute? We were wondering if you'd heard anything new on the case."

Doug hesitated a moment, then reached for a chair and pulled it up to the table. Sitting down, he folded his arms and leaned on them. "I might have."

Liza pursed her lips. "So you want us to pay for the information?"

Melanie flinched, but Doug merely laughed. "Not unless you think it's worth something. What are you offering?"

"Nothing you'd be interested in."

"Oh, I wouldn't say that."

Liza looked at him, one hand straying to her hair.

Intrigued, Melanie recognized the familiar gesture. Something was unsettling her grandmother. Obviously, she wasn't the only one who realized Doug Griffith was flirting.

Liza seemed to have recovered her composure when she asked, "So do you have anything you can tell us?"

Doug leaned back in his chair. "I heard there's a case going on up north, and it looks like it might be a while before Dutton gets back to town." He shrugged. "I know it's not what you want to hear, but I guess a murder investigation is going to take priority over a cold case in our little town."

"Bugger it. Officer Carter said it would only be a couple of days." Liza flicked a sheepish glance at Doug. "Sorry."

He shook his head. "Am I missing something?"

"She's apologizing for swearing," Melanie said helpfully, earning a dark look from her grandmother.

"I'll have to remember that one." He looked around the store, then leaned forward and lowered his voice. "As a matter of fact, I do have one little snippet that might interest you."

Liza's face brightened, and Melanie felt a quick stab of hope.

"I heard that there were no prints or DNA on the corpse," Doug said, "which means the killer probably wore gloves." He straightened up. "Nothing's cast in stone, of course, so don't quote me on that."

"We won't breathe a word to anyone," Liza promised. "I—" She broke off as the server arrived with their order.

Doug got up from his chair. "Well, ladies, I'll leave you to enjoy your lunch. Don't be a stranger, English. Come in after five, and I'll buy you a beer."

Liza gave him a look from under her lashes. "I prefer a nice glass of wine."

He grinned at her. "Done. See you soon."

He strolled off, and Liza picked up her sandwich. "Saucy devil."

Melanie laughed. "You enjoyed every moment of that."

"I was buttering him up so he'd tell us what he knows." Liza took a bite of her sandwich. "Not that he knew anything useful. Mmm, this is good."

"You were flirting with him."

Liza chewed for a few seconds and swallowed. "Well, maybe I was. I might be old, but I'm not dead. You might want to try it sometime. It's very rejuvenating."

"No, thanks." Melanie reached for her sandwich. "Been there, done that."

Liza gave her a long look. "You'll change your mind one day."

"Until then, I'll get my kicks watching you and Big Doug."

Liza's eyes gleamed. "He is rather bulky, isn't he? I like bulky men."

"Like Grandpa?"

Liza was silent for a moment or two. "I loved your grandfather," she said finally, her voice so soft Melanie could barely make out her words. "I miss him every day. Every minute. I've mourned him for almost two years, and I'll always love him, until the day I die. But I know he wouldn't want me to be miserable without him. That would make him miserable, too. So I'm moving on, and that doesn't mean I'll forget him. Ever. It just means I'm living the rest of my life the way he would want me to."

Melanie put down her sandwich. "I'm sorry, I didn't mean—"

"I know you didn't." Liza reached out and patted her hand. "I just want you to realize you can't wallow in misery the rest of your life. At some point, you have to move on."

Melanie struggled to suppress the stab of resentment. "I will. When the time is right."

Liza nodded. "I just worry about you, that's all."

Her irritation fading, Melanie managed a smile. "Don't worry about me, Granny. I'm doing just fine."

Liza flicked a quick glance at the bar, where Doug stood talking to a customer. "You won't be doing fine if you keep calling me Granny."

Melanie held up her hands. "Sorry, Liza."

Her grandmother shook her head. "So what do you think about the piece of information Doug gave us?"

"About the gloves? I'm not sure." Melanie frowned. "Do you think Vincent Morelli hired someone to kill his wife?"

"It's a possibility." Liza stared at her iced tea for a moment. "Though I doubt very much that a hired killer would simply ring the doorbell in the dead of night and wake everyone up to carry out a hit, or whatever you call it. Don't they usually hide on roofs and shoot from afar?"

"In the movies they do. I don't know what they do in real life."

"We need to find out who rang the doorbell that night. If Noriko didn't hear anything after the doorbell woke her up, then Angela must have let the killer into the house. Which meant she knew him."

Melanie thought for a moment. "The article in the newspaper didn't mention finding a murder weapon."

"The killer probably took it with him when he left and got rid of it somewhere."

"Buried it?"

"Perhaps." Liza frowned. "Or threw it in the ocean, in which case we'll never find it."

Melanie finished her sandwich and picked up her soda. "What happened to the agreement that we let the police handle this from now on?"

"You heard Doug." Liza waved a hand toward the bar, where the owner was talking to a young man at his side. "They have an important murder case in another town. It could take them weeks to solve it. We can't afford to wait that long. Noriko said Paul Sullivan visited the house a lot. Let's talk to him at the charity dinner and find out if he knows who else Angela Morelli knew well enough to invite into the house in the middle of the night. The more information we can give the police, the better."

Melanie wasn't entirely comfortable with that scenario, but knowing her grandmother, no amount of protests would deter her from her chosen path. Liza was going to talk to Paul Sullivan, no matter what she said or how she felt, so she might as well go along with it and worry about it later.

As they drove out of the parking lot, Liza kept insisting that they go back to Felicity's Fashions to buy the black dress. "You should have a new dress for such a significant event," she said. "We need to make a good impression if we're going to meet the Sullivans."

Melanie snorted. "That's so archaic. I have a couple of really decent dresses that will do just fine. It's not like they're royalty."

"If they were, *I'd* be buying a new dress." Liza nudged her arm. "Come on, Mel. How long has it been since you dolled yourself up to go boogieing?"

"I told you, no dancing."

"How are you going to have an intimate conversation with Paul Sullivan if you don't dance with him?"

"Who said I was going to have an intimate conversation with him?" Melanie slowed down at the crosswalk to allow a couple walking a dog to cross in front of her. "Why don't you talk to him? You're the one with all the charm."

"I get the feeling he'll be a lot more receptive to you than he will to me. I'll tackle Mrs. Sullivan. I probably have a lot more in common with her. Maybe she'll know something that could help."

Melanie sighed. "You're not going to let this go, are you?"

"Nope. Turn right here. We can park behind the post office again."

Giving in, Melanie turned the corner and drove up the block to the parking lot. It had been a while since she'd bought a new dress, she told herself as she parked the car. It wouldn't hurt to at least try it on.

A few minutes later, she stood in front of a long mirror in Felicity's Fashions, reluctantly acknowledging that the dress did look good on her. In fact, she'd forgotten how it felt to wear a dress and heels instead of her usual jeans and sneakers.

"Gorgeous!" Liza announced, her eyes sparkling. "You'll knock 'em dead at the charity dinner."

Sharon Sutton appeared in the mirror behind Melanie. "Oh, is that where you're going? This dress will be perfect. I heard it's going to be quite a fancy affair."

Melanie smoothed down the skirt. "It doesn't look too tight on me?"

"It was made for you." Sharon looked at Liza. "Don't you think so?"

"Totally." Liza nodded at Melanie's image in the mirror. "You have to buy it. It's your dress."

"I'll take it." Melanie felt a little surge of satisfaction. This had been more enjoyable than she'd anticipated.

Liza was talking to Sharon at the counter when Melanie emerged from the dressing room with the dress draped over her arm.

"We were just talking about the Sullivans," Liza said as Melanie laid the dress on the counter. "Sharon says they do a lot of work for charity."

"That's nice." Melanie dug in her purse for her credit card.

"We heard that they owned our house before the Morellis bought it," Liza said, smiling at Sharon. "Apparently Paul Sullivan visited them a lot after he sold it to them."

Sharon had her back turned to them, fiddling at her computer. She seemed to take a long time before she turned around to face them. "That must have been nice for Mr. Morelli. I don't suppose he saw many people, being stuck in a wheelchair like that."

"I would imagine his wife would have taken him out for a change of scenery now and then," Liza murmured, poking around a tray of colorful buttons on the counter.

Sharon handed the card and receipt to Melanie. "Maybe. I really didn't know them that well. They never came in here." Her laugh sounded strained. "I think Mrs. Morelli must have gone to Portland to shop for clothes."

"More than likely." Liza picked up a brochure advertising the local theater. "We talked to Noriko Chen, by the way. She said that Paul Sullivan had a business relationship with Vincent Morelli. That must have helped relieve the boredom."

Sharon's hand shook as she took the signed receipt from Melanie. "Really? I wouldn't know about that." She tucked the receipt in the drawer. "Well, it was nice seeing you again, Mrs. Harris." She nodded at Melanie. "I hope you enjoy the charity event. I know you'll look beautiful in that dress."

Thanking her, Melanie picked up the bag containing her dress and followed her grandmother out of the store.

Liza waited until they were out of earshot before saying, "Did you see how jittery she got? I think she knows something she doesn't want us to know."

"She did seem nervous about something." Melanie shifted the bag to the other hand as a woman pushing a stroller approached them. "She hardly knew the Morellis, though, so she can't know too much about them."

"She could know someone who did know them well."

"True. Though from what we've heard so far, I got the impression that the Morellis didn't socialize all that much."

"Me too."

"Maybe Sharon is friends with the Sullivans. They seem to be the only people who had close contact with the Morellis."

"That's what I'm thinking." Liza turned the corner to head for the parking lot. "Now I can't wait to meet them."

*   *   *

The following evening, Melanie studied her reflection in the bathroom mirror, happy to note that her stomach didn't stick out too much in the close-fitting dress. She'd toyed with the idea of draping the scarf Liza had given her around her neck but ultimately decided that it would look too business casual for such a formal occasion.

Instead, she'd added a multichain gold necklace to fill in the low scoop neckline. Her grandfather had given it to her when she'd turned twenty-one, and Liza had added the matching earrings the following Christmas. A gold clasp pinned her hair in a sophisticated swirl at the back of her head, and she'd used just a touch of light makeup.

She only owned two pair of heels. Black pumps and gold sandals. After a lot of deliberation, she went with the sandals.

Liza's nod of approval went a long way to bolster her confidence, and she was actually looking forward to the evening when she climbed into the car and turned on the engine.

Her grandmother, looking energetic and glowing in a pale-mauve dress with long, filmy sleeves and a flowing skirt, settled herself on the seat next to her and pulled her black wrap closer around her shoulders. "It's still chilly at night," she murmured. "I'll be glad when summer gets here."

"We're used to wearing jeans and sweaters." Melanie pulled away from the curb. "I feel naked in this dress."

"You look fabulous. Too bad Officer Ben Carter won't be there to see you."

Melanie pinched her lips together. "One more word about Officer Carter and I'm going back to Portland."

"No you won't. You're having too much fun."

It was true, Melanie thought as she drove slowly along the winding coast road. She was having fun. In spite of the money worries and the bad memories that still lingered in the back of her mind, she liked her new life.

Tonight, she told herself, she'd put all the bad vibes behind her and just enjoy the evening. It had been so long since she'd been anywhere exciting, and this promised to be a fun night. Nothing was going to spoil it for her.

Minutes later, they pulled up in the parking lot of the Windshore Inn. Lights blazed from the windows and the decorative lamps lining the curb. Women in long gowns and men in tuxes strolled through the doors of the foyer, and Melanie was glad she'd listened to Liza and bought the dress. Her grandmother could be annoying at times, but she knew how to make the best of a situation.

"I've been dying to see what this hotel looks like inside," Liza said as she took hold of Melanie's arm. "I've seen pictures, but it's not the same as seeing the real thing."

They stepped over the threshold into a vision of luxury. A thick, dark-blue carpet patterned with gold-and-silver swirls cushioned their feet as they walked toward the wide double doors of the ballroom. Glistening chandeliers hung overhead, and in one corner of the vast lobby, Melanie was impressed to see huge gold-and-silver wreaths painted on the elevators.

A burst of lively music greeted them as they entered the ballroom. Round tables filled with chattering partygoers were clustered on three sides of the room, and a small orchestra played on the stage at the rear. Flickering candles glowed on every table, and enormous bouquets of roses, ferns, and baby's breath blossomed in baskets clinging to the walls.

A smiling young woman in a black dress greeted them, took their tickets, and led them to a table close by the doors. Several people already seated there nodded or murmured a greeting, then went back to their conversations.

A young server with red hair and freckles carried a large tray of glasses filled with wine over to their table. He seemed a bit nervous as he asked, "Would you like some wine?"

"I'd love some." Liza beamed up at him.

"Red or white?"

"Oh, white, please. Is it chardonnay?"

"Yes, ma'am." He placed a brimming glass in front of her and turned to Melanie. "And you, ma'am?"

"I'll have the chardonnay, too."

His hand shook as he set the glass down in front of her. She thanked him, and with a timid nod, he took off for the next table.

"I bet this is his first job as a waiter," Liza observed, watching him hover over an elderly couple.

"He could be a volunteer, since this is for charity." Melanie took a cautious sip of her wine. "This is good."

Liza lifted her glass. "To an exciting evening. Did you notice the TV cameras? We could end up on the news."

"I don't think a TV reporter would find us exactly newsworthy."

"Are you kidding? The opening of a haunted inn? That's what makes a TV story."

"I'm sure the reporter is a lot more interested in the Sullivans." Melanie touched glasses with her grandmother. "Do you know what they look like?"

"No, but if Paul Sullivan is giving a speech, we'll soon find out." She peered at the stage. "They're probably sitting down there in the front. We'll have to find a way to get to them after dinner."

Melanie tried not to think about that as she enjoyed the surprisingly delicious chicken cacciatore that arrived a few minutes later.

Several people at their table, after learning they were the new owners of the Morellis' house, seemed interested in their plans to turn it into an inn. No one, however, seemed to have known the Morellis very well, and only one couple remembered seeing Vincent after the crash that had put him in a wheelchair.

Before that, according to the young woman sitting at Melanie's side, he had been a frequent visitor to the bank where she worked. "He was not very friendly," she told Melanie. "He was a big man, tall with a heavy build, kind of forbidding. I don't think I ever saw him smile, and he barely answered me when I spoke to him. I gave up trying to be nice to him after a while.

Mrs. Morelli was much nicer. I saw her a lot after the accident. She seemed so lonely, though. I guess she didn't have many friends. Not surprising, being married to a grouch like that."

But Angela did have a friend, Melanie thought as a server placed a lemon meringue tart in front of her. The father of her baby. That's if Noriko was right about Vincent not being the father.

Minutes later, Liza put her fork down on her plate with a satisfied sigh. "That was excellent. Now I don't feel like doing anything more strenuous than sitting here and watching everyone else on the dance floor."

They were still drinking coffee when an attractive, middle-aged woman with immaculate bleached-blonde hair took the stage and introduced herself as Eleanor Knight, the mayor. She gave a short but inspiring speech on the importance of the Humane Society and the great work that the organization was doing in saving animals from being euthanized.

She then announced that Paul Sullivan, one of their most generous benefactors, would address the audience.

Melanie's nerves twitched as a tall, lanky man stepped up onto the stage. His light-brown hair stuck up in little tufts in the latest style, and his jaw had just enough stubble to be fashionable. He looked the epitome of sophistication in his designer tux, and the thought of talking to him, much less dancing with the man, gave her hives.

She barely heard a word he said as she frantically rehearsed in her mind what she would say to him. She would much have preferred tackling Brooke Sullivan, whom Paul had introduced at the beginning of his speech, although the woman was almost as intimidating in a sleek, dark-blue gown studded with sequins and crystals.

Deciding she needed a little help, she grabbed her wine glass, which was still half-full, and downed the contents. Across the room, she saw the redheaded server carrying a loaded tray. She managed to catch his eye, and he headed toward her. Seconds later, she was sipping her second glass of chardonnay.

A burst of applause signaled the end of Paul Sullivan's speech, and with a casual wave of his hand, he stepped off the stage and sat down at one of the tables.

Liza jumped up, announcing, "Let's go. The sooner we get their attention, the better."

Melanie got up from her chair, mentally scolding herself for being such a wimp. The Sullivans were just people, and if talking to them helped get closer to finding out the truth about the murder, then she was definitely going to give it a shot. One way or another, they were going to find out who killed Angela Morelli and get their inn back.

Chapter 7

Liza was winding her way between the tables, and Melanie hurried after her, eager now to get it all over with so she could start enjoying the evening. The ballroom was festive, the music made her feet itch to get out on the floor, and the wine was beginning to melt away all her inhibitions.

By the time they reached the Sullivans' table, Melanie had convinced herself that she could take on the president of the United States if necessary.

Paul Sullivan sat talking to a silver-haired man next to him while Brooke Sullivan leaned back in her chair, a cocktail in her hand and a look of pure boredom on her face. She appeared to be ignoring the rest of the people at her table, all of whom were chatting to each other.

Liza edged behind Paul's chair and leaned down to make herself heard against the blaring music from the stage.

Melanie couldn't hear what she was saying, but she assumed her grandmother was introducing herself as the women shook hands. Just then, the orchestra came to the end of the number, and Brooke looked up at her.

"My partner, Melanie West," Liza said.

Brooke gave a languid wave of her hand. "Pleased to meet you."

Paul Sullivan ended his conversation to stare up at Liza. "You said you bought the Morellis' house?"

"Yes." Liza smiled down at him. "We're turning it into a bed-and-breakfast. The Merry Ghost Inn."

"Ah. So you must have heard our ghost." Paul Sullivan unfolded himself from his chair and laid a hand on the back of it. "Would you like to sit?"

Liza's face lit up. "I'd love to! Thank you." She sat down next to Brooke. "I just love your dress." She peered at the bodice. "Those crystals are gorgeous. It takes a great body to show off a gown like that, and you do it so beautifully."

Brooke smoothed an imaginary stray blonde hair from her forehead. "Well, thank you. What did you say your name was?"

"Liza Harris." She leaned closer. "I would love some advice on interior decorating. Since you lived in the house, you are the perfect person to advise us. You have such excellent taste."

Melanie had a tough time trying not to roll her eyes. Surely the woman would see through the inflated snow job.

Brooke, however, seemed to be eating up all the phony praise. "I would love to. There was so much I wanted to do to the house." She sent her husband a reproachful glance. "Paul would never let me change anything. Now if I'd had my way, I would have had all that ancient wallpaper torn off and . . ."

Paul Sullivan shook his head and looked at Melanie. "Excuse me. I'm being rude. I didn't catch your name."

"Melanie West." She held out her hand. "Part owner of the future Merry Ghost Inn."

His handshake was firm. Up close, he looked older than she'd first thought. Probably late forties or maybe early fifties. He was still an attractive man, if one went for the finely chiseled Italian-type look. Personally, she preferred the husky, outdoors type. A mental vision of a certain cop hovered in her mind for a second before she clamped down on it.

The music started up again, this time mercifully quieter as the orchestra played a slow-tempo song.

Paul was still holding onto her hand. "Well, Melanie West," he murmured, "since there are no seats available at this table, would you like to dance?"

It had been so long since she'd been on a dance floor. Before she met Gary, she'd boogied, as Liza called it, every chance that came along. Her ex-husband, however, had never shown any interest in dancing, and she'd almost forgotten how good it felt to be moving in time to the music, feeling her whole body relax.

Paul was an excellent partner, with no fancy steps to trip her and not too slow to make things uncomfortable. "So what do you think of the house?" he asked as he sidestepped her out of the way of another couple. "Obviously you like it, since you bought it, but what gave you the idea to turn it into an inn?"

"It was my grandmother's idea. She offered me a partnership in it, and I liked the sound of it, so here I am."

Paul's eyebrows rose. "That woman is your grandmother? She must have been an infant when she had your mother."

"I'll tell her you said that. She'll be bragging about it for weeks."

Paul's pale-blue eyes glinted with amusement. "Well, I'm glad you're turning the house into an inn. It's been in my family for over a hundred years. I like the idea that people from all over the country will get to enjoy it."

She looked up at him. "Even if we do some renovating?"

He laughed. "Don't listen to my wife. She wanted to turn the dining room into a gym and put a casino in the basement. I'm sure your ideas are not nearly so radical."

"We did think about taking down the wallpaper and remodeling the bathrooms."

He nodded. "That I can live with. Besides, it's not my house anymore. It hasn't been since I sold it to the Morellis fifteen years ago."

It was the opening she'd been waiting for, and she pounced on it. "It must have been a huge shock for you to hear about the skeleton we found in the bedroom."

"Totally." He shook his head. "I still can't believe it. All this time, I've imagined Angela happily living out her life on the East Coast. We all thought she'd left Vincent to go back home."

"Wouldn't she have kept in touch with her friends, though? Surely they must have wondered why she hadn't contacted them."

"I don't think Angela had many friends. I never saw anyone else at the house." A shadow crossed his face. "I could never understand why she married that man. Even before the accident, he was a miserable, bad-tempered grouch. Completely the opposite of Angela."

"There must have been something she saw in him," Melanie murmured, remembering Noriko's comment about hearing Angela say she only stayed with Vincent for the money.

"Beats me. The last time I saw her was about a week before she went missing. I was over at the house taking care of some business with Vincent and ran into her on my way out. She looked like she was about to totally fall apart. I left for a conference in New York right after that, and when I got back, I heard that they'd both left town." His jaw hardened. "If I'd only known . . ." He broke off with a light laugh. "But enough of this dismal stuff. Tell me about you. What did you do before you became an innkeeper?"

Melanie would have given her right hand to know what he was going to say before he stopped himself. If he'd only known Angela was pregnant? Or that she was planning on leaving Vincent? Would he have stepped in somehow and perhaps saved her life?

She debated asking him, but it would seem like prying, and Noriko's warning still echoed in her mind. In any case, he was out of town when Angela Morelli was murdered, so he wasn't going to be of much help.

Realizing she'd kept him waiting for her answer, she said quickly, "I worked for a stockbroker in Portland. Financial analyst."

"Impressive. Yet you gave up that busy, glamorous city life to come and live in our little town. I smell a story behind that."

The stab of pain under her ribs took her by surprise. She dropped her chin. "I just felt like a change. And my grandmother needed me." The music came to an abrupt end, much to her relief. She pulled away from him. "Thank you. That was nice."

He dropped her hand. "Entirely my pleasure. I wish you the best of luck with your new venture. I have a feeling it will be a roaring success."

"I hope you're right." She started to walk back to the table where Liza still sat talking to Brooke Sullivan.

"You must have heard the ghost to have given your inn that name," Paul said as they reached the table.

"That was Liza's idea." Melanie glanced at her grandmother, who was getting up from her chair. "She thought it would attract customers."

Liza bounced over to them. "You're talking about the ghost?" She looked up at Paul. "You lived there for so long. You must have heard it."

"Many times." He looked amused. "We never could figure out what he was laughing at."

Remembering the lipstick on the mirror and the robe at the wrong end of the closet, Melanie was tempted to ask him if he'd seen any physical signs of the ghost. Wary of sounding weird, she decided to keep her thoughts to herself.

"I have enjoyed talking to your wife," Liza said. "She has given me some great ideas for the house."

Paul flicked a glance at Brooke. "I hope it didn't include a casino."

Liza looked confused. "What?"

Melanie took hold of her grandmother's arm. She was eager now to know if Liza had learned anything from Brooke. "We should get back to our table."

"Of course." Liza turned to wave at Brooke, who nodded at her, then reached for her glass.

"It was a pleasure meeting you both," Paul said, smiling at Melanie.

"Nice to meet you, too." She could feel his eyes on her back as they walked away. For some reason, it gave her chills.

They had almost reached their table when a man in a tux and wearing dark-rimmed glasses stepped out in front of them.

Melanie froze, her heart bumping against her ribs. She heard Liza's gasp, and for a moment the urge to run was almost impossible to resist. Then the anger exploded, sweeping away all her qualms. She stared up at her ex-husband, hardly recognizing her own voice when she demanded, "What the hell are you doing here?"

Gary West flinched as if she'd hit him. "I was invited here by a client," he said, giving Liza a curt nod. "I had no idea you'd be here."

"You don't have to talk to him," Liza said, taking hold of Melanie's arm.

"I just need a moment, and then I'll get out of your way." He looked back at Melanie. "There's something I need to tell you."

She hesitated, then decided she might as well find out what he wanted and get it over with. "It's okay," she told Liza. "Why don't you go ahead to the table? I'll be there in a minute."

Liza looked like she'd like to argue, but she took the hint and, after giving Gary a withering look, sauntered off.

"I'm not here to stalk you," Gary said, apparently reading her mind. "I'm here on business. One of my clients has a summer home here. I've been staying here at the hotel while we work on a case." His mouth twitched in the vestige of a smile. "Plus, I'm getting in a little R and R. I just saw you from across the room and knew I had to speak to you. You look gorgeous, by the way."

Ignoring the compliment, Melanie pulled in a deep breath. "I think we've said all there is to say to each other."

His features hardened, reminding her of his quick temper. "I know what you said, but that doesn't change the fact that I still love you and I won't give up on you." His eyes softened behind his glasses. "We belong together. You know that. The divorce was a mistake. We should have stayed together and worked things out. It's been three years since the accident, Mel. It's time to let it go and move on."

Her anger almost cut off her breath. "*Let it go*? Forget that you destroyed any chance I had of having children?" She was trembling so hard she could barely get the words out. "I'll never be a mother because of you, and you never once said you were sorry. You never even seemed to grieve. You couldn't understand why I was grieving for so long. Instead of trying to comfort me, you were nagging me to get over it."

"Of course I was grieving. I was devastated, and at first the guilt almost destroyed me. But you can still be a mother. We can adopt children."

"It wouldn't be the same. You just don't understand, do you? Because of you, I will never know what it's like to give birth to a child. You will never understand how much that hurts."

"But it wasn't my fault. It was an accident. I didn't crash the car on purpose."

The pain sliced through her like a knife. "You were distracted by a phone call. You admitted that. Your work has always come first. Your damn phone meant more to you than the safety of your wife."

"For a split second, that's all. I told you. I didn't answer the phone."

"But it took your attention away from the road." She shook her head. "We've been all over this so many times, and this isn't the place to have this conversation. Maybe one day in the distant future I can forgive you. Maybe. But I will never forget. Never. You and I are finished, Gary. I don't know how many times I have to tell you that before you'll believe it."

He took hold of her arm, pinching her so hard she cried out. "You and I will never be finished. We belong together. One day you'll realize that."

He flung her arm away from him and stalked off, leaving her shaking at the edge of the dance floor.

"Are you okay? Did that man hurt you?"

Melanie blinked as she looked into the eyes of the woman she'd sat next to at her table. "I'm fine, thank you."

The woman still looked worried, and Melanie forced a smile. "Just an old acquaintance. There's no problem, really." Catching sight of Liza hurrying toward her, she added, "I'm coming back to finish my wine."

"Good idea." Looking a little less concerned, the woman led the way back to their table.

Liza got there just as Melanie sat down. "What happened?" she muttered as she eased down onto her chair. "I saw Gary belting out of here like the Hound of the Baskervilles was after him."

"I told him to get lost," Melanie murmured as she reached for her wine.

"I'm assuming he didn't take it very well."

Melanie's hand shook as she lifted her glass and tipped wine down her throat. "He's not giving up easily."

"Sorry, Mel." Liza laid a hand on her arm. "Want to get out of here?"

Melanie was only too happy to agree. Grabbing her purse, she murmured her good-byes and followed Liza to the lobby. Her anxiety that she might run into Gary again faded away when she saw no sign of him.

She took hold of Liza's arm as they crossed the soft carpeting to the door. "Are you okay? You look tired."

"I am, a little." Liza smiled at her. "What about you? Are you okay?"

Melanie puffed out her breath on a sigh. "More than okay. I've been worried about seeing Gary again ever since I saw him in town. Now that I've faced him and survived, I can quit obsessing about it."

"I'd say you did more than survive. You sent him off with his tail between his legs. His face was as red as a tomato."

Melanie felt a twinge of apprehension. "I just wish he would take no for an answer. He can be so stubborn about things that are important to him."

"His pride will probably keep him out of your way. Gary's not the type to grovel."

Outside in the cool night air, Melanie felt that she could breathe normally again. The swish of waves brushing the sand soothed her nerves as they crossed the parking lot to the car. Lifting her chin, she closed her eyes for a moment and concentrated on the salty smell of the ocean. It never failed to bring her peace.

She opened her eyes again to find Liza staring at her. "Are you sure you're okay?"

Melanie smiled. "I'm good. Let's go home."

"I had an interesting conversation with Brooke Sullivan," Liza said as Melanie drove out of the parking lot onto the coast road. "She told me that Angela Morelli did have one good friend. You'll never guess who it is."

Melanie had almost forgotten why they had gone to the charity dinner. Her curiosity aroused now, she eagerly grabbed at the chance to concentrate on something else other than her ex-husband. "Is it someone we know?"

"Someone we just met."

"At our table tonight?"

"No, before tonight."

Melanie frowned. "Well, if it's not Noriko, the only other person I can think of is Sharon Sutton."

"Right! According to Brooke, Angela Morelli and Sharon Sutton were close friends."

"But Sharon said she didn't know Angela very well. She said she never came into the shop."

"Yes, she did." Liza's voice was tight with excitement. "So why did she lie to us?"

Melanie slowed down for the turn that would take them back to the house. In front of her, she could see the ocean, shimmering in bright moonlight, with the dark silhouettes of the jagged rocks rising above it. "If it was such a secret, I wonder how Brooke knew about it."

"Exactly. She knew a lot more about Angela Morelli than we thought. I can tell you one thing—it was pretty obvious to me that Brooke hated Angela."

"She told you that?"

"No, but I could tell by the way she talked about her."

"I wonder why Noriko didn't tell us that. She said Paul visited the house a lot. She never said anything about Brooke being there."

"Maybe she was worried we'd want to question Brooke. Remember she warned us about prying?"

"Why would she worry about it?"

"I don't know, unless she's afraid that it will make trouble for her, seeing as she's the one who told us about the Sullivans in the first place."

Melanie pulled into the driveway and switched off the engine. "If so, I wonder what reason she'd have to be afraid of the Sullivans."

Liza shrugged. "They're powerful people, and people with that kind of influence can make all kinds of trouble for someone."

"But why would they care what Noriko said about them, unless they had something to hide?"

Liza smiled. "And there you have it."

Melanie stared at her. "Are you saying that the Sullivans had something to do with Angela's death?"

"I'm saying that they are at the top of the list of our suspects."

"Well, you can cut Paul Sullivan off that list. He told me he was in New York when Angela was killed."

Liza's voice chilled her when she said quietly, "That's interesting. Brooke told me they were both in Hawaii when Angela died."

They stared at each other for a long moment, until Melanie found her voice. "I wonder if the police know about that."

"I guess we'll have to pay another visit to the police station." Liza opened her door. "And we need to talk to Sharon Sutton again. All these lies have to add up to something. We just have to find out what it is everyone is hiding."

Melanie climbed out of the car, her nerves tingling again—this time with excitement. When Liza had first suggested they conduct their own investigation, she'd seriously doubted they'd achieve anything more than annoying people with their questions.

Now, however, it seemed they might actually be getting somewhere, and the thought that they might be able to solve the mystery of Angela's death was exhilarating. She could just imagine the look on Officer Ben Carter's face when they presented him with the solution.

"What are you grinning at?"

Liza's question jerked her thoughts back to the present. "I'm just thinking how great it would be if we could solve this murder and get back to working on the house."

Walking up the path to the front door, Liza said over her shoulder, "I know. We can't open unless the murder is solved, and we can't work on the house if we're running around looking for clues. The way things are going, we'll have to open the inn without redecorating."

"We can't do that." Melanie paused at the doorstep, waiting for her grandmother to open the door. "There's so much work left to do, and if we don't do it before we open, we'll never have the time."

"I know." Liza turned the key in the lock and pushed open the door. "But we're going to run out of money real soon, unless we can get another loan. Maybe if we go to the bank again and offer our souls—"

She broke off her words as the soft sound of laughter echoed down the hallway.

Melanie's breath froze in her throat while Liza stepped inside and yelled, "That wasn't funny!"

The silence that followed was almost as creepy.

Switching on the lights, Liza murmured, "You're not going to tell me that was birds on the roof again, are you?"

Shaken, Melanie stepped inside and closed the door behind her. "I don't believe in ghosts."

"Then we have an intruder in here with a warped sense of humor."

"There has to be some explanation for that sound."

"There is. We have a ghost who sees the comical side of everything."

"I mean a realistic explanation." Melanie cast a nervous glance down the hallway. "Maybe we should have someone come and check it out. Find out what's causing it."

"Like ghostbusters?"

Melanie gave her a scathing glance. "Like a housing inspector."

"We had an inspection done when we bought the house. There was nothing unusual in the report." Liza led the way to the kitchen. "I'm going to make a cup of tea. We should be able to catch the local news. Want to join me?"

Reluctantly, Melanie let go of the subject. Nothing would convince her there was an actual ghost haunting the house. Liza, however, seemed just as convinced the ghost was real, and once her grandmother got an idea in her head, it would take an army to shift it. "No tea," she said, "but I'll watch the news with you."

"Good." Liza poured water into the kettle and set it on the stove. "Why don't you go and warm up the TV. I'll be there in a minute."

Melanie wasn't too sure she wanted to go back down the hallway on her own. Annoyed with herself and her ridiculous qualms, she marched to the living room and turned on the TV.

The news had already started, and she sat down to watch the weather report. The weatherman had just assured his audience that the showers expected in the morning would be short-lived when Liza walked into the room, carrying a mug in one hand and a cookie in the other.

"Would you like one?" she asked, waving the cookie at Melanie. "I'll fetch you one if you do."

Melanie pulled a face. "No thanks. I'm still stuffed from dinner." She shook her head. "I don't know how you can eat so much and stay so slim. I only have to look at a cookie for it to go to my hips."

Liza lowered herself onto her chair and placed her mug on the side table next to her. "Nervous energy. And for the record, it wouldn't hurt for you to put on a pound or two. You've been looking a bit frail lately."

Melanie studied her face. "Are you telling me I'm looking haggard?"

"Haggard? No, of course not." She munched on her cookie. "A bit malnourished, maybe. That meal tonight was the most I've seen you eat since you moved down here."

Melanie was about to answer when the news anchor's words caught her attention.

"The fundraiser being held tonight at the Windshore Inn in Sully's Landing had some unusual guests when a pair of raccoons appeared in the ballroom, apparently searching for food."

"I didn't see any raccoons. Did you?" Liza slipped her glasses on. "Look, there you are, dancing with Paul Sullivan."

Melanie stared at the screen, mesmerized by the sight of herself gliding around the floor while Paul appeared to be talking earnestly in her ear.

"You two look really cozy," Liza said.

"We were talking about Angela's murder." Melanie leaned forward. "Look, I can see you over there in the corner, talking to Brooke."

Liza squinted at the screen. "Where?"

"It's gone. It was only a glimpse."

The view of the ballroom disappeared to be replaced by the anchor at his desk, droning, "In other news . . ."

Liza finished her cookie. "Well, that was a brief moment of fame. Too bad we didn't get the chance to talk to the news reporter. We might have managed to get a blurb in about the inn." She yawned. "I think I'll go to bed. All this excitement is tiring me out." She took off her glasses and laid them on the table, then got up slowly from her chair and reached for her cup and saucer. "It was fun, though, wasn't it? I'm so glad we went."

Melanie smiled at her grandmother. "Me too. Sleep well."

"Oh, I will." Liza blew her a kiss. "You too."

Left alone, Melanie watched the rest of the news, then switched off the TV. She was still feeling too edgy to sleep and decided to do some more research into her mother's disappearance.

Opening her laptop in her bedroom, her hopes leapt when she saw an e-mail with an attachment from one of the nursing homes she'd queried. Quickly, she scanned the words on her screen:

I'm sorry to inform you that no record of the woman you describe can be found in our files. During my search, however, I found this copy of a newspaper that contains the story of your mother's disappearance and subsequent search for her whereabouts. I'm sending it to you with the hope it might be useful.

After writing back and thanking the woman and promising to let her know if she discovered anything new, Melanie downloaded the attachment and printed up a copy of the newspaper article. Her excitement mounted as she realized it was one she hadn't seen before. Could there be something in the article that would help her find out what happened to her mother? Was she finally going to find a way to solve a thirty-year-old mystery?

Turning to the article, her hands shook. What if she found out her mother had died? Did she really want to know that? To shatter all hope of seeing her again? More importantly, how in the world would she be able to tell Liza the bad news?

Wondering why she hadn't thought of that before, she began to read.

Chapter 8

Minutes later, frustration crushed Melanie when she realized the article held nothing that she didn't already know. Yet another dead end. How many more promising leads were going to end in a letdown?

The intensity of her disappointment surprised her. Maybe the search for her lost mother was becoming more important to her than she realized.

She was still dwelling on that when she crawled into bed and pulled the comforter up to her chin. In an effort to think about something else, she channeled her thoughts back to earlier that evening.

Gary's infuriated face popped into her mind, but she blocked that out, concentrating instead on her conversation with Paul Sullivan.

We never could figure out what he was laughing at.

Paul had said that with a perfectly straight face and a note of conviction. Did he really believe there was a ghost, or was he just perpetuating a myth? She'd have given anything to know for sure.

As if to mock her, she thought she heard a whisper of laughter somewhere in the room. She sat up, nerves stretched tight as she strained her ears. After several moments of silence, she settled down again and pulled the comforter over her ears. She was tired, and if the ghost wanted to laugh, he could just go ahead. She was going to sleep.

The next morning, Melanie had showered, dressed, and eaten a couple of slices of French toast by the time Liza appeared in the kitchen doorway.

"I overslept," she said, brushing stray bangs out of her eyes. "How long have you been up?"

"Not long." Melanie watched her grandmother walk over to the counter. "Are you okay? You're limping again."

"I limp every morning until my body gets used to moving again. It comes with growing old."

"I'm sorry. I just can't think of you as being old."

Liza picked out a mug from the cabinet and poured coffee into it. "In my head and my heart, I'm as young as you are. It's my body that's wearing out. That's something young people don't understand. No matter how old we get—for most of us, anyway—in our minds, we never get older than thirty-nine."

Melanie grinned. "I like that."

"Me too." Liza sat down at the table. "I just wish my body could keep up with my mind. It's raining, by the way. I was hoping we could get some of that furniture in the garage sorted out today."

"We could go through the stuff in the basement."

Liza sighed. "I think we're going to need some help getting everything where it's supposed to be. Those steps to the basement are so narrow. I didn't think about that when I had the delivery guys take all those boxes down there. I was just thinking about where to store it all until we got the redecorating done. Like the furniture in the garage. It all has to be carried into the house."

"We'll manage somehow." Melanie got up and carried her plate over to the sink. "What would you like for breakfast?"

"Oh, just cereal. I'm not very hungry this morning. I ate too much last night."

Melanie poured the cereal into a bowl and set it down in front of her grandmother. Liza was worrying her. She sounded so crushed. That was so out of character, it made Melanie uneasy. "You sound tired. Didn't you sleep well?"

"I slept like a baby." Liza sighed as she picked up her spoon. "I'm just beginning to wonder if we haven't taken on too much with this house. It would be different if we had the money to hire people to help us. Right now, we've barely got enough to pay the bills."

"Well, why don't we talk to the bank manager today and see if we can get another loan?"

"I was hoping it wouldn't come to that, but I guess you're right. We could call in at Felicity's Fashions while we're out."

"Good idea." Melanie picked up her coffee mug. "And if we can't get another loan, we'll just go ahead and open without redecorating. After all, the wallpaper isn't that bad. It's . . . vintage, like the house."

"Isn't that just another word for antiquated?"

"Well, what I mean is, the decor is part of the house's charm. People love antiques, and the wallpaper is . . . er . . . well, it's . . ."

They looked at each other in silence for a long moment, then Liza giggled.

Melanie felt a laugh bubbling up, and then the two of them were laughing helplessly, with tears spilling down Liza's cheeks.

"Let's face it," Liza said between gasps for breath, "that wallpaper is atrocious. But if we can sell it as genuine antique, then let's go for it."

"Agreed." Melanie wiped her eyes with the back of her hand. "And who knows, maybe it won't come to that. Maybe we'll get another loan and can hire a decorator."

"Or maybe we'll solve this murder and get the police out of our house so we can do the work ourselves."

Melanie's amusement faded. "We need to decide soon about the reservations. We can't wait until the last minute to cancel them if we can't open on time."

Liza nodded. "I know. I've been worrying about that, too. It's been hard enough having to turn down new bookings, but I don't think we have any choice. Who knows when this investigation will be over? I just hope everyone will understand."

"I'm sure they will if we explain what happened."

"All right. So when shall we make the calls? Today?"

"Let's wait until the end of the week. We might have a better idea by then of how long it's going to take to open up."

"Sounds good." Liza finished her cereal and picked up her bowl. "I'm going to shower and get dressed, then we'll pay a visit to the bank and Sharon Sutton. I can't wait to hear her explanation of why she lied about being friends with Angela Morelli."

Melanie took the bowl from her. "I'll do the dishes. You go and get dressed."

Half an hour later, the two of them were on their way to the bank. The showers that the weatherman had predicted were tapering off, leaving a sky studded with white-and-gray clouds. The air smelled salty fresh when Melanie climbed out of the car. She could hear birds chirping in the branches of the spruce trees behind the bank, and someone was playing music too loud on a car radio. Out on Main Street, visitors crowded the sidewalks and wandered across the road, heedless of cars waiting impatiently to proceed.

The summer season was fast approaching, and the thought brought a knot to Melanie's stomach. They badly needed bookings for the inn to survive. Already they'd had to turn down several prospective guests, and by the end of the week, they would have to cancel the rest of the reservations. The summer was their peak period. People were making plans, and if they didn't open soon, they would lose their most valuable customers.

Warren Pierce, the friendly bank manager who had granted their current loan, was sympathetic when Liza explained their predicament. He seemed genuinely sorry when he turned them down. "Once you have opened the inn and can show me a balanced profit and loss statement," he said, "I might be able to arrange something. Until then, I'm afraid I can't manage a new loan."

"Oh, well, it was worth a try," Liza said, getting up stiffly from her chair. "Thank you for listening, anyway."

Melanie also stood up, wishing there was something she could say to change his mind. "We'll make a success of the inn," she said, "once we can open it up."

Warren smiled, peering up at her over the rims of his glasses. "I'm sure you will, and I wish you both the best of luck. I think the house will make a wonderful inn. Just what our town needs—a charming, picturesque establishment with an old-world look. So much nicer than those modern eyesores farther down the coast, thanks to our dedicated city planner. Jim Farmer works really hard to preserve the authentic coastal look in town. You won't find any ugly box stores here in Sully's Landing."

"Well," Liza said crisply, "I just hope we can survive long enough to open the inn. If not, we might have to sell to an out-of-towner who might very well turn it into a bunch of ghastly avant-garde condos." She turned and marched a little lopsidedly to the door.

Melanie hurriedly thanked the manager and chased after her grandmother.

Once outside, Liza let out a groan. "Idiot. Can't he see a viable investment when it's handed to him?"

"Don't worry. We'll work it out." Melanie took hold of her grandmother's arm. "Just look at this place." She nodded at the crowded sidewalks. "It's so popular. We won't have any trouble filling the rooms once we open."

"A lot of these people are day-trippers." A gust of wind snatched the ends of her scarf, and she tucked them inside the neck of her sweater. "We're close enough to Portland to make a comfortable trip there and back in a day."

"I read somewhere that people from all over the country come to stay on the Oregon coast."

"That they do." Liza smiled. "You're right. We'll get this investigation going far enough to get the police out of our house, then we'll fill up our rooms with happy visitors. Let's go and see what Sharon Sutton has to say for herself."

Felicity's Fashions was just a couple of blocks down Main Street. Except for a couple of women browsing among the embroidered T-shirts, the shop seemed deserted. Sharon was nowhere to be seen, but Liza wasted no time in ringing the bell that sat on the counter.

Seconds later, Sharon appeared through a pair of curtains, looking a little anxious when she saw them. "You're back again! How was the charity dinner?"

"It was very nice." Liza looked over her shoulder at the two customers browsing the racks. Apparently deciding that they were out of earshot, she added, "We met the Sullivans there. Very interesting people."

"Yes, I know." Sharon fidgeted with a display of decorative combs. "I saw you both on TV last night on the news." She looked at Melanie. "I saw you dancing with Paul."

It was almost an accusation, making Melanie feel uncomfortable.

Before she could answer, however, Liza said abruptly, "Brooke Sullivan told me you were good friends with Angela Morelli. She said you were frequently at the house. We were wondering why you didn't want us to know that."

Sharon's face seemed to shrink, and Melanie began to feel sorry for her. "We're just trying to find out what happened the night she was murdered," she said, giving the woman a smile. "It's important to us. This investigation is holding up all our plans for our opening. If you can help us at all, we'd be extremely grateful."

For a long moment, Sharon appeared to be struggling with her conscience, her face a mask of conflicting emotions. Finally, she let out a long sigh. "I'm sorry. I hate lying to anyone. I'm not good at it at all. Brooke was right. I was close friends with Angela. I believe I was her only friend here in Oregon. It hurt me terribly when I thought she'd left to go back to the East Coast without even telling me she was going."

"I'm sorry."

"So sorry."

Liza and Melanie had spoken in unison, and Sharon shook her head. "I knew that Angela was miserable here, but I never thought she'd leave Vincent, with him being in a wheelchair and everything. When I found out she'd been killed, I kept wondering if she'd planned on telling me she was leaving and died before she had the chance."

"What we don't understand," Melanie said, "is why you didn't want us to know you were close friends with Angela."

Sharon shrugged. "I may not be much of a liar, but I know how to keep a promise. Angela told me something she didn't want anyone else to know and made me promise not to tell a living soul. I swore on her Bible I wouldn't tell anyone. If the police know I knew her that well, they'd question me." She held up her hands. "How am I going to lie to the police?"

Melanie leaned toward her. "Sharon, your friend was brutally murdered and shoved behind a wall, hidden from anyone who would have given her a decent burial and mourned her passing. She deserves retribution for that. If you know anything that can help find out who did this to her, I know she would want you to tell us."

"If she were standing here now," Liza put in, "what do you think she'd be saying to you?"

Sharon chewed on her bottom lip for a moment or two, then leaned forward. Lowering her voice, she muttered, "God forgive me. I know who got Angela pregnant." She sent a worried glance over at the browsing customers.

Liza exchanged a meaningful look with Melanie. "Angela told you?"

"Yes, she did." Sharon glanced over at the customers again. "When I first found out that she was having a baby, I thought that Josh Phillips might be the father."

Liza gasped. "The newspaper reporter?"

Sharon nodded. "He was always hanging around her, making excuses about interviewing her, but I could tell he had a big crush on her. What's more, she seemed to enjoy the attention. She didn't get much from her husband. But then one night, she called me in a terrible state. She sounded so desperate, I rushed right over there."

She paused as one of the customers approached the counter, holding a couple of T-shirts.

Still intrigued by the idea of Josh Phillips idolizing Angela Morelli, Melanie waited in a fever of impatience while Sharon took the money, wrapped the shirts in tissue paper, and placed them in a bag.

The customer chatted for a moment or two, then left. She was barely out of earshot when Liza pounced on Sharon. "So what happened when you went to see Angela?"

For a moment, Melanie thought the woman wasn't going to answer. Her lips were pressed together, and she had a look of fear in her eyes. "I shouldn't be telling you this," she muttered.

"You know Angela would want us to know." Melanie gave her an encouraging smile.

Sharon sighed. "When I got there that night, Angela was crying. Worse, she was drinking. A lot. I told her it was bad for the baby, and she said she hoped the booze would get rid of it." Sharon's face crumpled. "I wanted to help her, but I didn't know what to do. Then Angela told me who had gotten her pregnant." She looked over at the door as an elderly couple walked into the store. Lowering her voice again, she whispered, "It was Paul Sullivan."

Melanie caught her breath. Liza's eyebrows rose, but she said nothing as Sharon glanced at the customers again. "Angela had told him earlier that night, and he'd sworn up and down it wasn't his. He said he couldn't be the father because his army didn't have any weapons."

Liza blinked. "What?"

Sharon waved a hand. "You know, he said he was infantile, or whatever that is when you can't make babies."

"Infertile," Liza said helpfully.

"That's the word." Sharon looked relieved. "He could do the deed, but there couldn't be any results."

"I think we've got the picture," Melanie said, shutting her mind to the vision.

"Well," Sharon said, "Angela swore he was lying. He was the only one she'd been with except for Vincent, and she hadn't slept with him in years. He couldn't perform at all, you know, after he ended up in that wheelchair. That must have been hard to live with."

"I'm sure it was," Liza murmured.

"I'm going to hell," Sharon said, choking on the words. "I swore on the Bible."

Liza reached out and grasped her hand. "I'm quite sure God will forgive you. So will Angela when whoever murdered her is rotting in prison. The sooner this investigation is over, the sooner she can have a proper burial. Then she can rest in peace forever."

Tears spurted from Sharon's eyes. "That was beautiful. Thank you."

"Just no more lies, okay?" Liza let go of her hand. "If the police come to question you, tell them the truth."

"Okay, I will." Sharon nodded so hard a hank of blonde hair fell across her eyes. She brushed it back with an impatient hand. "It will be such a relief not to have to lie anymore."

"Thank you for being honest with us," Melanie said, holding out her hand. "We appreciate it very much."

Sharon shook her hand, then backed off as a customer approached the counter. "Good luck with the investigation," she muttered, then pasted a bright smile on her face as she turned to the customer. "Good morning. Did you find something you like?"

Melanie followed her grandmother out of the shop, turning over in her mind what they had just heard. So Paul Sullivan was Angela's secret boyfriend after all. That part didn't surprise her. She'd tagged Paul as a ladies' man the moment she'd set eyes on him.

Outside on the sidewalk, Liza waited for an elderly couple walking an inquisitive dachshund to pass by before turning eagerly to say, "What do you make of all that?"

"I'd say it doesn't look good for Paul Sullivan." Melanie took her arm and began walking back to the parking lot. "He had a strong motive to get rid of Angela if she threatened to tell everyone he was the father of her baby."

"Just like a man to deny everything. He must have been lying about being infertile, though it wouldn't have taken much to prove he was the father if Angela had tests done."

"Exactly. Which is why he had to kill her. It was the only way he could be sure no one would find out."

"I don't know." Liza frowned. "When you put it all together, it doesn't make sense. According to Noriko, Angela was all set to go back to the East Coast. That doesn't sound like she was going to make trouble for Paul. It sounds more like she was giving up on the whole thing and going back home to start a new life."

"Maybe Paul didn't know that. Maybe he killed her before she had a chance to tell him she was leaving."

"Or maybe he didn't kill her at all. What if Brooke found out about the baby and killed Angela in a jealous rage?"

Melanie caught her breath. "I didn't think of that. It's possible, I guess."

"What do you think about Josh Phillips having a thing for Angela? He never said a word about that. He didn't seem all that broken up about her being murdered."

"No, he didn't." Melanie frowned. "Then again, neither did Paul Sullivan. He and Angela had obviously been having a hot-and-heavy affair. You'd think he'd feel some regret at the way she died."

"Unless he was responsible for it. Both he and Brooke would have known about the hidden room in the bedroom. They both had motive and opportunity. Now if only we could find the murder weapon, that might help to find the means."

"The what?"

"The means." Liza waved her free hand. "You know, the mantra of mystery—means, motive, and opportunity. A suspect has to have all three to be viable, and both the Sullivans had at least two, and probably the third. After all, it doesn't take much to clobber someone over the head."

The familiar sharp ache of grief took Melanie by surprise. This time it was for someone else. "It's so sad," she said as they walked toward the car. "There were two lives lost that night. That little baby never had a chance to see the world." She almost choked on the last word and pinched her lips together.

"I'm sorry, Mel." Liza squeezed her hand with her arm. "This must be hard on you. Try not to think about that part of it. Just keep your mind on finding out who did this to Angela."

Melanie nodded, let go of her grandmother's arm, and opened the passenger door for her. "I do think we have more than enough to take to the police now."

Liza settled herself on the car seat and beamed up at her. "Yes, let's go there now. I can't wait to see that gorgeous Officer Ben again."

Melanie pulled a face at her before shutting the door. Walking around to the driver's side, she let out a sigh. This whole business was unsettling. It seemed the more they learned, the more complicated things became. It would be a relief to put it in the hands of the police and let them handle it. Yet after everything they'd learned that morning, she felt personally invested in the hunt for Angela's killer.

She wasn't sure why it was so important to her, but she did know that she wanted to keep digging into the events of that night. With or without the help of the police.

Minutes later, she parked in front of City Hall, and the two of them walked around the corner and down the street to the police station. The same two women were sitting in the front office, and the one who had spoken to them before smiled as she got up from her chair. "Can I help you?"

"We'd like to speak to Officer Carter," Liza said while Melanie tried to ignore the fluttering in her stomach.

"I'm sorry, Officer Carter is out on patrol. Is there someone else who can help you?"

Liza exchanged a quick glance with Melanie and shook her head. "Thanks, but we'll come back later. Do you know when he'll be back?"

"Probably not until tomorrow." The woman looked over her shoulder at her coworker. "Is Ben in the office tomorrow?"

The other woman looked up from her computer. "No, he'll be in Seaside for training sessions. He should be here the following day."

"Well, thanks." Liza nodded at the two of them and headed for the door with Melanie close on her heels.

"I always feel like I'm intruding in there," Melanie said as they walked back to the car. "Those two women must wonder why we keep asking for Officer Carter."

"He's handling our case, so it's perfectly understandable why we'd want to talk to him."

"I thought Detective Dutton was handling our case."

"Well, technically, I suppose." Liza halted at the car. "But he's not here, and Ben Carter is, and he's the one who came to the house when we first found Angela's bones, so we're talking to him." She peered into Melanie's face. "I thought you liked him."

"I do. I mean . . . he's okay. I just don't want to seem like I . . . er . . ."

"Fancy him?"

"If that means what I think it means, then yes, I don't want him to think it's personal."

"Even if it were."

"Which it definitely is not."

Liza grinned. "Too bad. You could be missing a great opportunity."

Melanie opened the car door. "Get in. We're going home. I want to sort through that mess in the basement this afternoon."

"Yes, ma'am." Still grinning, Liza climbed slowly into the car and collapsed onto the seat.

Back at the house, Liza made sandwiches for lunch. Melanie suggested they eat them on the back deck overlooking the ocean, and Liza eagerly agreed.

Warmed by the sun and sheltered from the wind by a thick stand of western hemlock, the deck provided a perfect lookout spot to view the long stretch of sandy beach stretching down the coastline.

The sea was calm, with gentle waves creeping in over the sand. People strolled along the water's edge while children pulled kites or chased after bounding dogs, occasionally braving the chilly ocean.

"We need to put more chairs and tables out here for our guests," Liza said when she'd finished her roast beef sandwich.

"We could even serve breakfast out here when it's warm enough. Some people love to eat outside."

"Good idea." Melanie sipped at her soda and put the glass down. "We'd have to buy the extra furniture, though. We barely have enough for the dining room."

"More expense." Liza gazed out at the ocean, where a thin line of gray hovered above the horizon. "We need to buy lottery tickets."

"Or find a wealthy benefactor."

"Maybe we can blackmail Paul Sullivan. We can tell him we know he was the father of Angela's baby, and we'll tell Brooke if he doesn't own up."

Melanie rolled her eyes. "Good way to get ourselves killed, if he is the killer. One of them had to be lying about where they were when Angela died. Paul said he was in New York, while Brooke said he was with her in Hawaii. He can't be in two places at once."

"I've been thinking about that." Liza leaned back on her chair and gazed up at the sky. "I'm wondering if Brooke knows he killed Angela and is covering for him."

"Don't they talk to each other? I'd think if he needs an alibi, they'd at least get their story straight."

Liza sat up again. "That is weird, isn't it? I wonder if we can find an excuse to talk to them again."

"Once we tell the police what we know, I'm sure they will question both Paul and Brooke Sullivan."

"I guess you're right." Liza got up from her chair. "But I wish we'd been able to solve the murder ourselves. That would've been very satisfying."

"Very." Melanie got up and collected up the plates and glasses. "Though I'm not sure where we would have gone from here. It's very unlikely that the Sullivans would tell us the truth, and they would probably have us tossed out of the house if we started throwing accusations at them."

"Maybe. We would have to find a good excuse to visit them again." Liza sighed. "I guess we'll have to leave it for now. If you want to sort out that chaos in the basement, we'd better get started."

"Right." Melanie carried the plates into the kitchen and put them in the sink. "I'll get the flashlight. The light down there isn't very good."

"Good idea." Liza opened the door to the basement. "I don't fancy crawling around that place in the dark. I just hope our jolly ghost doesn't decide to join us down there."

"I was hoping you wouldn't mention that." Melanie pulled a flashlight from a drawer and tested it to make sure the batteries were still working. "I don't need to be worrying about weird noises while we're working."

Liza grinned. "Ghosts can't hurt you, my dear."

Melanie walked over to the door. "I don't believe in ghosts."

"So you've said."

"I'll go first." She stepped through the door, onto the stairs, and flipped on the light. "Be careful going down here. These steps are really narrow." She edged down them one by one, trying not to think about a ghostly figure lurking in the shadows.

Reaching the bottom, she shone the flashlight onto the last few steps for her grandmother. Holding the railing, Liza crept down to the floor. "I wouldn't want to have to come down here in a hurry," she muttered as she let go of the railing. "Maybe we should think about putting wider stairs—"

She broke off when something interrupted her—a sound that sent cold chills down Melanie's back. From out of the dark corners of the basement came the distinct echo of throaty laughter.

Chapter 9

Melanie felt as if her entire body had turned into an iceberg. Her fingers hurt from gripping the flashlight as she focused the beam of light into the far corner.

Liza had given a squeak of surprise when she'd first heard the sound, and now her voice sounded a little shaky as she whispered, "He must have heard me upstairs."

Melanie was annoyed to see the beam of light wobbling as she pointed it at the other corner. "We have to find out what's making that noise and put an end to this."

"No way." Liza's voice sounded stronger. "That sound is going to keep visitors coming to hear our laughing ghost. He will be our biggest attraction. We'd be crazy to get rid of him. Besides, the inn is named after him, so he has to stay."

Melanie turned the flashlight on her. "So you do admit something is making that noise."

"Of course something is making that noise."

"I meant something real, not a ghost."

"I didn't say that." Liza raised her chin. "Point that thing in another direction before you blind me."

"Sorry." Melanie switched the beam to where furniture and boxes were stacked along the wall. The back of her neck tingled when she thought about what might be hovering in the corners behind her.

"I brought the box cutters," Liza said, handing her one. "Let's tackle these boxes and get out of here. It's so cold down here. This place gives me the creeps."

Melanie couldn't agree more. Reaching for the closest box, she tried to ignore the feeling that someone, *something*, was lurking in the shadows, watching them.

Several of the boxes contained dishes, cups, saucers, and glasses, and Melanie stacked them near the bottom of the stairs to be carried up later. Liza found sheets and pillowcases, towels and shower curtains.

"Good," Melanie said when her grandmother held the curtains up for inspection. "We'll only need those for the three bedrooms that have showers in the bathrooms. The other three will just need towels for the tubs."

"We'll have to charge a lot less for the bedroom that doesn't have a bathroom." Liza piled the towels back into their box. "I hope that won't turn out to be a problem. Most people insist on having a private bathroom."

"It's right next door to the main bathroom." Melanie picked up the box. "It should work out okay."

"Right now there's not a lot that's working out okay. I just wish we had the money to add showers to the rooms that don't have them."

Realizing her grandmother was getting tired, Melanie dumped the box of towels onto the growing stack. "We've been working for three hours. Time for a break. Let's go watch the news."

"Good idea." Liza pocketed the box cutter and headed for the stairs. "I'll make some tea."

"It's almost dinnertime. How about a glass of wine?"

"Even better."

Liza's smile went a long way to reassuring Melanie as she followed her grandmother's leisurely climb up the steps. Even so, her nerves tingled as she imagined ghostly eyes probing her back.

Just as she closed the door, she could swear she heard the laughter again. Silently cursing Liza's wild imagination, she closed the door and turned the key in the lock for good measure.

Liza headed straight for the living room, and Melanie paused in the kitchen just long enough to pour two glasses of wine, then followed her grandmother.

The TV blared out a commercial as Liza settled herself on her chair.

Melanie set the glass of wine down next to her.

"Thank you." Liza stared at the table. "That's weird."

"What is?"

"I left my glasses here last night. Now they're gone."

"They are probably in the kitchen. I'll get them."

"But I didn't wear my glasses this morning. We didn't have a newspaper."

"I'm sure I'll find them in the kitchen." Melanie put down her glass and hurried out of the room. A thorough search in the kitchen failed to turn up the glasses, and she went back to the living room to find Liza watching the news, her glasses perched on her nose.

"Oh, you found them!" Melanie crossed the room to her chair. "Where were they? On your chair?"

Liza's face wore a strange expression when she turned to look at her. "No. I found them on the mantelpiece. Did you put them there?"

Melanie felt a pang of uneasiness. "On the mantel? No, of course not. Why would I put them there?"

"Exactly." Liza straightened the glasses on her nose. "And since I am positive I didn't put them there, how in the world did they get there?"

"Are you sure? Maybe you were looking at something on there and took your glasses off for a closer look."

Liza shook her head. "I haven't been near that mantelpiece since you moved in. I would never put my glasses up there." She took them off and looked at them. "I think our merry ghost is playing games."

Melanie sat down and reached for her wine. Her grandmother was getting old, she reminded herself. Older people sometimes get forgetful. Liza most likely left her glasses on the shelf and forgot they were there. There was no point in arguing about it. If Liza wanted to believe in a ghost, then she'd just go along with it. "Well," she murmured, "as long as he leaves my wine alone, he can play all he wants."

"Aha." Liza raised her glass in the air. "You're beginning to believe he exists."

It would take a lot more than misplaced glasses to convince her they had a real ghost haunting the house, Melanie thought as she turned her attention back to the TV, where an earnest young meteorologist was explaining how the latest El Niño was ravaging the world.

Liza thankfully dropped the subject, and they spent a pleasant evening playing Scrabble, until Liza declared she was tired and was going to bed.

Melanie soon followed her, but her mind refused to quit working on the puzzle of Angela Morelli's murder, and it was more than an hour before she fell asleep.

*   *   *

After spending the next day catching up on the housework, Melanie managed another good night's sleep. The following morning, she arrived in the kitchen to find Liza had once more woken up before her. Her grandmother sat at the table with the newspaper spread out in front of her and the usual mug of coffee at her elbow.

Her expression, however, was anything but cheerful when she murmured, "Good morning."

Heart sinking, Melanie walked over to the counter and filled a mug with coffee. Something was wrong. She prayed it wasn't something to do with her grandmother's health.

"There's been another murder," Liza said as Melanie sat down opposite her. "Right here in our neighborhood." She handed the newspaper over. "We didn't watch the news last night or we might have seen it on TV."

The familiar chill had already taken hold of Melanie. "Where did it happen?"

"Just two blocks from here. A woman was walking her dog two nights ago, and someone stabbed her." Liza shivered. "Makes you wonder if this is a safe neighborhood to live."

Melanie found the story and quickly scanned the lines. "Poor woman. It does say here, though, that this is only the second murder to happen in Sully's Landing in more than fifty years. I don't think we have to worry too much about the neighborhood."

"Except there's another killer roaming around. That's not all." Liza tapped the newspaper with her finger. "Look at the photo of the victim."

Melanie studied the grainy picture. "I don't recognize her." She inspected the photo again. It had been taken on the beach. The young woman stood with her back to the ocean, holding a dog on a leash. She was smiling as the wind blew her hair across her face while the dog stared eagerly into the distance. "It says her name is Ellen Croswell. Do we know her?"

"You don't think she looks like you?"

Melanie looked at it again. "Not really. Same hair, I guess."

"And about the same height, same age. She even has the same heart-shaped face as you."

"Other than that, she doesn't look like me."

"She might in the dark."

The chill spread deeper into Melanie's bones. "What are you trying to tell me?"

Liza looked at her for a long moment, then shook her head. "Nothing. Just my imagination at work, that's all. As you say, I've read too many mystery novels."

Still uneasy, Melanie started to read the rest of the story. "It says here the dog was taken to a shelter. Poor thing. I wonder if he tried to protect her. He must be so miserable. He's lost his best friend, and now he's shut up in a cage." She looked back at the picture of the victim. "Look at them. They both look so happy. How sad this happened to them."

For some reason, she felt tears forming and quickly got up from her chair. "I'll be back in a minute." She fled from the kitchen and made it back to her bedroom before the tears began to fall.

She hadn't cried in months, and she didn't know why she was crying now. After a few moments, she managed to control the flow of tears and mopped her eyes with a tissue. It was the dog that upset her, she told herself. It was the thought of him being all alone in a cage, unable to understand what had happened to his happy life.

She knew how that felt. She knew the terrible agony of loss. The thought of that poor dog locked up and possibly facing death was unbearable.

Making up her mind, she marched purposefully back to the kitchen. "I think we should adopt him," she announced as Liza gave her a look of concern.

"Are you all right?" Liza peered up at her. "You've been crying."

"I'm fine." Melanie sat down. "So what do you think?"

Liza studied her for a moment. "Are you actually considering taking in that poor woman's dog?"

She nodded.

"Melanie—"

"I know what you're going to say. You're going to tell me that we have enough problems right now without adding to them. That taking on a shelter dog is a lot of work. I know all that, but if we don't rescue that dog, he could be put down. I know it's crazy, but I feel responsible for him. As if I'm meant to save him. If I don't do this, he will haunt me forever."

Liza stared at her for several seconds, her face creased in concern. Finally, she said quietly, "All right. Maybe it's what you need—something to take care of and love."

"Exactly." At last, Melanie could smile again. "I'd like to go to the shelter today, before something bad happens to him."

"Okay." Liza tapped the paper again. "Did you read the whole story?"

"I think so. Why?"

"It says the major crimes team is putting everything on hold until they solve this case. Which means our cold case will go to the bottom of the list."

Melanie sighed. "Well, I guess it will give us more time to work on the house."

"It also means it's up to us to solve our case." Liza folded up the newspaper. "I don't know about you, but I can't just sit here waiting for the police to find time to work on it. We need to get this over with and out of our hair."

"You're right. The question is, where do we go from here?"

"I think the big question here is why the Sullivans lied about where Paul was when Angela was killed. Someone has something to hide. We have to come up with an excuse to talk to them again."

"That won't be easy."

"I know." Liza frowned at the newspaper. "I wonder if we should talk to Josh Phillips. If he was hanging around Angela as much as Sharon said he was, he might know something that could help us."

"If he's willing to talk about it." Melanie drained her mug and got up. "He wasn't very forthcoming about it when he interviewed us."

"I guess there was no reason for him to talk about it. After all, he doesn't know us that well." Liza gave her a sly look. "Although I got the impression he'd like to know you better."

Melanie chose to ignore that. "Okay, let's get going. I want to get that dog out of the slammer."

Liza grinned. "Spoken like a true detective."

"In books, maybe. I've never heard a cop actually talk like that."

"Too bad. It might make them more sociable." Liza pushed herself up from her chair. "All right, let's go and free Fido."

*　*　*

The ride north took them along the coast road, with more spectacular views to enjoy. At times, a sea mist shrouded the beaches and hid the peaks of the coastal range, but now and then, they'd have a clear view of the ocean, reminding Melanie once more how lucky she was to be living in such a gorgeous area of the country.

"We have everything here in Oregon," she remarked as they turned off the main road and swept around a long curve sheltered by towering firs. "We have the beach and mountains, the desert and forests, beautiful cities and quaint little towns. We have it all."

"We do indeed." Liza gazed out the window. "Your grandfather and I visited more than half the states in the country, and there isn't anywhere else I'd rather live."

Melanie felt a pang of envy. "You were so happy with Grandpa. It must be wonderful to have a truly happy marriage. I don't think too many people have that."

"More than you think." Liza turned to her. "You'll have that one day, Mel. I know it."

"I wish I knew it."

"Trust me. It's when you're not looking for love that it finds you."

"Oh, look! This must be Warrenton." Thankful for the change of subject, Melanie slowed down as houses and buildings started popping up on either side of her.

"I've never seen this place," Liza said as they drove into the town. "I've stayed across the bay in Astoria. Have you been there?"

"I've passed through it, but I haven't really visited it."

"We'll have to spend a day there. It's a lovely little town. I—"

The GPS interrupted her with instructions to turn right, into a business park. The shelter stood at one end of the park, and Melanie pulled up outside. She was excited and at the same time anxious, worried that the dog would be traumatized and difficult to handle.

Once inside, she was surprised at how many people were sitting around the main reception room, wandering in and out of the doors and lining up at the counter.

Liza chose to sit while Melanie waited in line, getting more and more impatient as time dragged on. Finally, she reached the counter, where a tired-looking woman with silver hair sat with a sheaf of forms in front of her.

Melanie started to explain why she was there, and as she talked, the woman's frown grew deeper.

"Have you seen the dog?" she asked when Melanie came to the end of her speech.

"Just a picture in the newspaper," Melanie admitted. "But I know it's the dog I want."

The woman studied her for a long moment. "Max hasn't been screened yet. We don't release a dog until it's been checked out for any health or behavioral problems."

"Oh." Melanie tried out the name Max in her mind and liked it. "How long does that take?"

"Three or four days, depending on how busy we are."

Cursing herself for not calling first, Melanie fought down her disappointment. "I'll have to come back later then. Can I at least see him? I've come up from Sully's Landing to get him."

The woman looked about ready to refuse but, after a moment or two, nodded. "It's down the hallway on the right. You'll find his name on the cage. Call us later this week, and we'll let you know if he's ready to adopt."

"I will. Thanks."

Melanie thought about going back for Liza, but when she looked across the room, her grandmother was deep in conversation with another woman. Deciding to leave her to enjoy her chat, Melanie headed down the hallway marked "Dogs."

Emerging into a long room filled with cages on either side, she saw dogs of all shapes and sizes, some cowering behind the bars, some leaping up, some sleeping on blankets. Her heart ached to think of so many animals abandoned or lost, and she felt compelled to stop at a cage or two to pet the eager-looking animals.

She found Max at the very end of the row. He was bigger than she'd realized, with shaggy brown-and-white hair, a square head and jaw. Mostly sheepdog, she guessed, with a few other mixes thrown in. He sat with his back to the bars, his head hanging down. She wanted to cry for him and blinked back tears as she softly called out his name.

His ears pricked for a second or two, then drooped again.

"Max? Here, buddy! Here, Max?"

This time, the dog slowly moved his head around, gazed at her for a second or two with mournful eyes, then turned back to stare into the ground again.

And in that moment, Melanie lost her heart to him.

She would bring him home, she vowed, and give him so much love he would eventually forget the horror of losing his first owner in such a hideous way. "Don't worry, Max," she said, "I'll be back for you. We'll get through this."

He didn't respond, and she left him, knowing the next few days were going to be tough to get through until she could come back and claim him.

Liza was alone when she got back to the reception room. She seemed excited about something, but her first words were, "Where's the dog?"

Melanie repeated what the assistant had told her. "I have to call back in a couple of days to see if he's ready to be released. I should have called before we left. I didn't know the dogs went through all those tests before they could be adopted."

"Ah, well, at least you got a good look at him." Liza got up from her chair. "And you'll know if he has any problems before you make the decision to adopt him. Did you like what you saw?"

"He's adorable." Melanie led the way out to the parking lot, feeling brighter than she'd felt in a very long time. "He looks like a sheepdog, sort of, and has the most gorgeous eyes. His name is Max, and I don't care if he does have problems. I'm going to bring him home, and I think he's going to be a great addition to our family."

Liza nodded. "I'm looking forward to meeting Max." She waited until they were in the car and pulling out of the parking lot before announcing, "I had an interesting chat with a woman who's also adopting a dog today."

"I saw you chatting to someone. Did you know her?"

"No, we were just sitting there next to each other and started talking. She lost her dog last winter and missed her so much she's adopting another one."

Melanie felt a stab of pain under her ribs. "It's hard to lose someone you love."

"It is, indeed." Liza sounded worried when she added, "You do realize that dogs don't live for very long, don't you? Especially big dogs. How old is Max?"

"I didn't ask. It doesn't matter. We'll just make the best of the time we have together."

"Okay. I can tell you're really set on having this dog." Liza settled herself more comfortably on her seat. "Anyway, this woman I was talking to happens to know the Sullivans."

Melanie shot her a quick glance. "Really? How well does she know them?"

"I don't think they're bosom buddies or anything, but she told me that Brooke goes to the Golden Days Spa in Sully's Landing every Wednesday morning. Apparently this woman's niece goes there, too, and keeps telling her about the fancy clothes Brooke wears."

Melanie frowned, wondering why Liza was making it all sound so important. "That's nice."

"We need a good excuse to talk to Brooke."

It took a moment or two before Melanie finally understood. "Are you suggesting we pay a visit to the spa? I don't think Brooke will be too happy if we burst in there asking personal and possibly incriminating questions about her husband."

"We won't burst in there. We'll be there getting a facial or pedicure. The best thing about a spa is that it relaxes you, and a relaxed person is far more likely to talk."

Melanie suddenly realized her foot was pressing down on the accelerator. She released the pressure until the car had slowed down to the speed limit. "I've never been to a spa," she said, totally unsure if she ever wanted to go to one.

"Neither have I." Liza's voice rose a notch. "It will be another exciting adventure we can share."

Melanie wasn't sure that adventure was the right word. "Even if we go there, there's no guarantee we'll be able to even get near Brooke. Don't they have private rooms or something?"

"Probably, but she has to come out of the room sometime. We'll have to find out what time she gets there and get there before her, so we can wait for her to come out. She'll be nice and relaxed, and we'll act surprised to see her."

"I sincerely hope you're not going to mention the fact that her husband is responsible for Angela Morelli's pregnancy."

"Of course not. We'll just casually ask her a question or two."

"Like why she or her husband lied about where they were when Angela died? She's not going to admit to that, no matter how relaxed she is."

"Maybe, but she might give us a clue we can work on. It's worth a shot."

Melanie was silent, turning the prospect over in her mind.

"Come on, Mel. It'll be fun. We could both use some relaxation after all the hauling around of stuff we've been doing."

Melanie sighed. "It's probably expensive."

"We're in so deep now, what will a few more bucks matter?"

"You're determined to do this, aren't you?"

"Darn right I am."

Knowing she'd lost the battle, Melanie gave up. "All right. We'll go to the spa. Just be prepared to be thrown out of there if Brooke takes exception to us probing into her private life. Remember Noriko's warning?"

"You worry too much." Liza looked at her watch. "It's almost one thirty. Let's stop in at the hardware store and have lunch."

"So you can flirt with Doug again?"

Liza snorted. "So we can ask him if he's heard anything new from his brother."

Not entirely convinced, Melanie smiled.

Chapter 10

The only vacant table in the hardware store was next to the bar, where a couple of men sat loudly discussing the latest baseball game won by the Hillsboro Hops. Melanie would have preferred a quieter spot to eat lunch, but Liza settled on her chair with such a look of relief, Melanie guessed her hip was giving her trouble again.

Before she could sit down, a loud voice bellowed at them from behind the bar.

"Hey, English! Looking for that glass of wine?"

Liza rolled her eyes as all faces turned her way, but a faint flush in her cheeks told Melanie that despite her protests, her grandmother liked the exuberant owner of the hardware store. "Not unless you're paying," she called out, earning a snicker from the men at the bar.

Seconds later, Doug Griffith appeared at the table, carrying two glasses of white wine. "On the house, as promised," he said as he set the glasses down.

Liza looked up at him. "I thought I told you I don't drink before five o'clock."

"You did." He pulled out a chair and sat down. "I didn't believe you."

Melanie grinned while Liza pretended to be shocked. "I beg your pardon?"

Doug leaned toward her. "Are you telling me you've *never* had a sip of wine before five?"

Liza looked defiant for a moment, then smiled. "I might have had a glass with lunch now and then, but I don't like to make a habit of it."

"Aha. I knew it." Doug pushed a glass toward her. "Go ahead. Live a little."

"If you insist." She reached for the glass and took a cautious sip. "Very nice. Thank you."

Doug nodded. "You can't do much better than Oregon wine." He pushed the other glass closer to Melanie. "Here, try it."

Melanie tasted the wine. It was surprisingly smooth and buttery mellow. "It's real good," she said, putting down the glass.

"We only sell the best in here." Doug beamed as he leaned back. "So what have you two been up to lately? Have you opened the inn yet?"

"We can't until this investigation is over." Liza sighed. "The police keep putting the case on hold. At this rate, it will be next year before we can open." She looked hopefully at Doug. "I don't suppose you've heard anything? Like when they can finish up our case?"

Doug looked uncomfortable. "Did you hear about the murder here two nights ago?"

"Yes, we did." Liza leaned forward. "Did you know her? The woman who was stabbed?"

"No, I didn't." Doug looked sad. "I heard she just moved down here from Seattle a few weeks ago. Got divorced and decided to start a new life." He shook his head. "You never know when it's all going to end for you. You have to grab every moment and make the best of it."

"You do, indeed." Liza took a deep sip of wine and set down the glass.

"Anyway," Doug said, "I guess with this new murder case, the cops won't be worrying about something that happened seven years ago. It's hard to believe something like this could happen in our little town. Two murders in one week. Doesn't seem possible."

"Actually, only one happened recently," Liza pointed out.

"True, but they both made headlines in the newspaper and on TV." Doug pushed back his chair. "Not good publicity for the tourist business. Our town depends on the visitors spending their hard-earned dollars here to keep us going through the winter."

"Well, I just hope the police find whoever stabbed that poor woman and put him in jail. It's not a comfortable feeling to know someone was killed right on your doorstep."

"Good thing we're getting a dog," Melanie said. "At least we'd have some warning if someone tried to break in."

"That woman had that dog with her," Liza reminded her. "She still ended up in the morgue."

"He put up a good fight, so I heard." Doug stood up, nodding at the bar as someone called out his name. "He got a couple of knife wounds trying to save her. Anyway, enjoy your lunch. Good to see you both."

Melanie stared at his back in dismay as he strode off. "Max got cut? Why didn't that woman tell me that? I didn't see any bandages or anything."

"They don't put bandages on cuts anymore." Liza took another sip of wine. "They put glue over them. My neighbor's dog was spayed, and she just had glue on the incision."

"Poor Max." Melanie's heart ached for the dog. "What he must have gone through that night."

"I hope he doesn't have problems because of what happened." Liza frowned. "I wonder if they have dog psychologists."

"I believe they're called behaviorists, and they're really specialist dog trainers."

"Seriously? Well then, we'll take him to one of those if he has problems."

Melanie studied her for a moment. "You're worried about Max coming home with us."

Liza smiled. "I'm worried about you. I know how much this means to you. I just don't want you to have any more big disappointments."

"I won't be disappointed. I'm prepared for anything. I just want to give Max a good home and help him forget what happened."

Liza reached out for her hand. "I hope he can help you forget what happened."

"I'll never forget." Melanie squeezed her grandmother's hand and let it go. "But I'll get past it. And so will Max."

"Good." Seemingly satisfied, Liza picked up the menu. "Now let's order lunch. I'm hungry."

Later that night, as they sat in the kitchen finishing a Cobb salad, Melanie announced, "You were right about the wallpaper in the living room. Since we have some time on our hands, I think we should strip it and paint the walls. I can't stand to look at those prancing peasant women any longer. They look deformed."

Liza raised her eyebrows. "I don't think they're peasants. Those clothes were probably the height of fashion when the paper was pasted on the walls."

"Exactly. More than a hundred years ago. Antique or not, that paper has to go. If we're going to provide a comfortable lounge for our visitors to relax in, they shouldn't have to stare at buxom maidens chasing moths in a swamp."

"Meadow."

Melanie puffed out her breath. "What?"

"It's not a swamp, it's a meadow, and they're chasing butterflies."

"Whatever. In any case, it shouldn't take too long to get that stuff off the walls. What do you think?"

Liza thought about it. "I guess it would give us something to do other than worrying about murders. We can't visit the spa to talk to Brooke until Wednesday, though I would like to talk to Josh Phillips."

"We could call the newspaper office and ask them for his phone number."

"Oh, didn't I tell you? He gave me his card when he came to interview us." Liza frowned. "I put it somewhere. I'll have to look for it."

"So we're agreed on tackling the wallpaper in the living room?" Melanie got up from the table and began stacking the plates.

"Agreed. We'll start first thing in the morning. After I've called Josh."

"Why don't we invite him for lunch? We'll need a break by then, anyway."

"Good idea." Liza pushed herself up from her chair and picked up two glasses. "I'll help you with the dishes, and then I'm going to take a book to bed. It's been a long day."

Melanie took the glasses out of her hands. "You go ahead. It will only take me a moment to do the dishes."

Liza looked relieved. "I'll see you in the morning, then. Sleep well."

"You too." Melanie watched her grandmother leave the room, then carried the plates and glasses to the sink. Her thoughts turned back to earlier that day and the memory of Max sitting slumped in a cage, looking at her with those mournful eyes.

How long, she wondered, would it be before she could bring him home and make him feel safe again? How long would it take for him to heal, both physically and emotionally, and put the past behind him? Would he ever forget his previous owner and learn to love her and Liza? Would he accept his new life and forget the old?

Those were questions she could well be asking herself, she thought as she stacked the dishes in the dishwasher. In many ways, she and Max were sharing the same problems. Starting a new life in the hopes of escaping from the memories.

They needed each other. She couldn't wait to bring him home.

She dreamed about the dog that night. He was running across the beach, and she was chasing after him, her feet sluggish in the sand. Ahead of them a man appeared, waving a knife. She screamed out Max's name as she struggled to reach the dog before the man with the knife got to him.

She woke up in a cold sweat, relieved to see sunshine peeking through the blinds.

This time, she was first in the kitchen and had read most of the newspaper by the time Liza wandered in.

"Any more news about the murder?" she asked as Melanie got up to pour her grandmother a mug of coffee.

"There's a couple of paragraphs about Ellen Croswell— more or less what Doug told us about her. She moved down from Seattle two months ago. She worked at that fancy restaurant on the seafront."

"The Villa?"

"Yes, that's it. The police have no suspects yet, but they're conducting a thorough investigation and trying to reassure everyone that the streets are safe. They're talking to Ellen's ex-husband, but it doesn't say if they suspect him of killing his wife."

Liza looked worried. "That happens so often—women leaving their husbands and getting killed by them. Why is it that some men are so driven by jealousy, they kill the person they love the most just so no one else can have them?"

"I don't know if it's a matter of jealousy or power. Some men are so controlling, they'd rather see their possessions destroyed than fall into the hands of someone else. It's more a matter of pride."

"That's terrifying."

"Yes, it is." Melanie placed the mug of coffee in front of her.

Liza sat looking at it as if she were seeing right through it.

Watching her, Melanie could tell something was disturbing her. "You're worried about Gary, aren't you?"

Liza shrugged. "Not really." She peered up at her. "Are you? You did say he wasn't giving up easily."

Melanie laughed. "Gary is a lot of things, but he's not a killer. Besides, the divorce was fourteen months ago. I would think if he was going to do something drastic, he would have done it by now."

"Well, I just hope you're right." Liza reached for the paper. "Are you done with this?"

"Yes. I'm going to cook breakfast." She went to the fridge and opened the door. "Scrambled eggs?"

"Sounds good."

Taking the carton of eggs out of the fridge, Melanie felt a stab of uneasiness. She could still picture Gary's face when he'd stormed out of the ballroom. Then again, her ex-husband had often lost his temper and slammed a few things around, but he'd never touched her in anger.

Determined to put those memories to rest, she took a bowl out of the cabinet and started cracking eggs into it. "We need to start working on the breakfast menus," she said as she added a dash of cream to the eggs and started whisking them. "I have a couple of cookbooks, but I need to go online and find some good recipes."

"We probably should keep it as simple as possible," Liza said, turning the pages of the newspaper. "We'll have at least fourteen or more breakfasts to make when the inn is full."

Melanie dropped four halves of English muffins into the toaster and added a dab of butter to the frying pan. "We should be able to find enough good recipes that are not too complicated. After all, it's breakfast. Not dinner."

"Right. We can serve cereals and fruit and yogurt."

Melanie sprinkled salt and pepper into the eggs and whisked them again. "We're an inn, not a health bar. It's the only meal we serve, so it should be a good one. Like more of a brunch than just breakfast."

"Okay, then how about an English breakfast?" Liza started counting off on her fingers as she chanted, "Porridge, kippers, eggs, sausage, ham, bacon, fried potatoes, fried tomatoes, fried mushrooms, fried bread—"

"On the other hand," Melanie said, pouring the eggs into the sizzling pan, "we don't want to kill our guests. I was thinking of something like omelets or frittatas. We can add fruit and cereal, muffins and scones."

"Oh, yes. That all sounds good." Liza folded up the paper and laid it on a chair. "What do you think we should do with the tables in the dining room? Push them all together to make one big table, or scatter them around for individual couples?"

"Definitely keep them separate." Melanie flipped the eggs onto two plates just as the muffins popped up in the toaster. "Most people prefer their own personal space. Luckily, the dining room is big enough that we have room to get around seven tables."

"We'll have to get rid of the one that's in there now, then."

"We can sell it. It will help with the expenses."

"I guess it would be better to keep the tables separate. One of us will have to wait on the tables while the other one cooks."

Melanie buttered the muffins and added them to the plates. "We can take turns until we can afford to hire someone to help out."

"That would be nice." Liza smiled as Melanie placed a plate in front of her. "There's so much to think about. So much to do. I hope you're not having second thoughts about all this."

Melanie sat down opposite her. "Of course not. Are you?"

"Not for a second." Liza nodded at the window. "How many people have that view from their kitchen?"

Melanie followed her gaze to where the heaving ocean glittered in the sunlight. Far out in the distance, a smoky-blue smudge revealed a ship creeping across the horizon. A few early risers roamed the beach, looking for sand dollars or agates or chasing a dog into the water. One little boy dragged a kite along the sand, and another sat furiously digging a hole.

As always when she sat looking out at the scene, she could feel the tension draining away. Yes, there was a lot to do and so much to think about. But right then, she wouldn't trade places with anyone in the world. Even with all the problems and delays, she was falling in love with the inn and couldn't wait for the day when they could open the doors to their eager guests.

"I'm going to call Josh," Liza announced as she put the last plate in the dishwasher. "Then we'll tackle that wallpaper. Between the two of us, we should get it done in a couple of days."

Melanie headed for the door. "While you're doing that, I'll take off all the outlet covers and switch plates."

She was in the hallway when Liza called out, "We need to turn off the circuit breakers to the living room. With all the water we'll be using, we don't want to risk frying the electrical system."

"Or us. Good catch." Melanie came back into the kitchen, grabbed the flashlight off the shelf, and unlocked the basement door. "I'll go do that now."

Liza was already at the table, dialing Josh's number on her cell phone.

Leaving her to talk to the reporter, Melanie flipped the light switch for the basement and crept down the steps, trying not to think about the eerie laughter they'd heard down there.

The light from the single bulb barely reached the corners, leaving most of the walls in darkness. Melanie stood for a moment at the bottom of the stairs, listening to the silence with her heartbeat thudding in her ears. All was quiet, and only slightly reassured, she moved over to the wall that held the fuse boxes.

The cold, damp air seemed to seep into her bones, and she shivered as she tugged open the box and stared at the breakers. The rooms were listed alongside, and she focused the flashlight on them, searching for the living room.

At that moment, she heard a slight whisper of sound, as if something moved behind her. She spun around, the flashlight waving about in her hand, sending the beam dancing over the floor. All she could see were piles of boxes and half a dozen chairs.

Slowly, she trained the flashlight around the room. Nothing stirred. Not a single sound. Darn Liza and her stories of a ghost. Melanie was letting it all get to her.

Shaking her head, she turned back to the fuse box and flipped the breakers listed as the living room. As she did so, something brushed past her hair.

She didn't even wait to close the fuse box door. In three long strides, she reached the steps and bolted up them, slamming the door shut behind her.

Still seated at the table, Liza looked up in alarm as Melanie leaned against the door. "Whatever's the matter? You look as if you've seen a ghost."

"Very funny." Melanie pushed herself away from the door, already scolding herself for being such an idiot.

"Wait." Liza's face lit up with excitement. "You heard him again, didn't you? You heard our ghost."

"What I heard was probably a bat down there. It brushed past my head while I was at the fuse box."

Liza looked disappointed. "Bats don't laugh," she murmured. "Or, at least, I don't think they do."

"Well, if it is a bat, we need to get rid of it."

"There aren't any windows, so we can't chase it out."

"I guess we could call an exterminator."

"Let's make sure it is a bat first." Liza got up from the table. "I'll go down and look. Give me the flashlight."

"I'm not letting you go down there alone." Melanie drew a deep breath. "I'm coming with you." Gingerly, she opened the door to the basement. "I'll go first."

"Wait." Liza opened a cupboard door and took down a fly swatter.

Melanie rolled her eyes. "It's a bat, not a fly."

"Then I'll scare the bugger to death." Liza brandished the swatter like a sword. "Into battle, my lord!"

Melanie was having serious doubts about the wisdom of letting Liza tackle whatever was down there, but the thought that there might be a bat flying around the basement was equally disturbing. She started down the steps with Liza breathing down her neck behind her.

Reaching the bottom, she stepped aside to let her grandmother reach the floor, training the beam of the flashlight on each corner. Not even a speck of dust moved anywhere.

After a minute or two, Liza sighed. "Well, if it is a bat, it's gone to ground. We're not going to find it without poking around those boxes or whatever else is lying in the corners of this room."

"Then we'd better start poking." Melanie advanced on the pile of boxes and started carefully moving them around.

Half an hour later, after a thorough search, she had to agree with her grandmother. There didn't seem to be any sign of a bat or anything else that could have caused that sensation of something brushing past her hair.

"I told you it was the ghost," Liza said as they climbed the stairs once more.

"You still have to prove that there is a ghost."

"Maybe you have to prove that there isn't."

Melanie smiled. "Okay. You win."

"By the way, Josh is coming to lunch," Liza announced as Melanie locked the basement door. "He sounded excited by the invitation."

"He probably can't afford a decent lunch and is looking forward to a free one."

"When did you become such a cynic?"

"Ever since I found out that the man I married is a narrow-minded, narcissistic workaholic with controlling tendencies."

"Ouch." Liza pushed back her chair. "Well, I think that Josh is more excited about seeing you again than a free lunch."

"Well, you can forget that. What excuse did you give him for inviting him for lunch? It's not like you're bosom buddies."

"I told him we wanted to try out one of our recipes that we'll be using for the inn and wanted his opinion. Since we don't know that many people here, it sounded feasible, don't you think?"

"I think—" Whatever she was going to say vanished as the doorbell rang out in the hallway.

Liza frowned. "That can't be Josh already. I told him one o'clock."

For some reason Melanie's nerves had tightened. "Mailman?" She jumped as the doorbell rang again.

"A mighty impatient one if it is the mailman." Liza hurried to the door, and Melanie followed her, praying it wasn't more bad news.

Liza pulled the front door open. "Ben! What a lovely surprise." She turned to look at Melanie, who was trying to appear indifferent. "Look! It's Ben!"

Melanie edged forward far enough to see the police officer standing on the doorstep. He had his back to the sun, and she couldn't read the expression on his face. She stepped closer. "Is something wrong?"

"No, ma'am. I just came to tell you—"

"Come inside." Liza grabbed his sleeve and tugged on it. "We don't need the neighbors wondering why a cop is standing on our doorstep."

"Yes, ma'am."

He stepped into the hallway, and Liza closed the door behind him. "Come in here where we can sit," she said, leading the way into the living room.

He seemed hesitant, looking at Melanie as if confirming the invitation.

Melanie smiled. "You'd better do as she asked. She can get very bossy."

"I've noticed."

It was the first time she'd seen him smile. It completely changed his face, and she felt a little tug in her heart. Reminding herself of all the reasons she didn't need any more complications, she hurried into the living room where Liza already sat on the couch.

Ben followed more slowly, looking around with interest as he sat down. "This is a big room."

"Yes, it is." Liza beamed. "It will be plenty big enough for our guests to relax in, maybe read a good book." She nodded at the bookshelves. "Do you read?"

He shook his head. "I barely have time to read the newspaper."

"Ah, that's a shame. Reading can be very therapeutic." She looked at Melanie. "My granddaughter and I read a lot, though we haven't had much time since we bought this house."

"It must keep you busy." He looked at Melanie. "Running a B and B is a lot of work."

"It is," Melanie said as she sat down next to her grandmother, "but it will all be worth it when we can finally open and meet our guests."

"Well, that's what I came to tell you. I had a word with the chief. Since we've had to put this case on hold for now, he's agreed that you can go ahead and open up the inn, as long as you keep that one room closed and locked. Make sure no one can get in."

"Yay!" Liza clapped her hands. "That's great news. Thank you, Ben. That was really nice of you to talk to your chief." She gave Melanie a look and a slight tilt of her head.

Getting the message, Melanie said quickly, "Yes, thank you, Officer Carter. It means a lot to us."

"No problem." The look he gave her was hard to read. For a moment, she thought he was upset about something, but then his face relaxed. "I'm happy for you. I know you were both worried about the delay in the investigation."

"Yes, we were." Melanie leaned forward. "Speaking of that, have you found out who killed that poor woman the other night?"

His face changed again. "I'm sorry, I can't talk about that. It's an ongoing investigation."

"Then you haven't found the killer yet," Liza said, sounding subdued.

"No, ma'am."

"Melanie is going to adopt the dog," Liza said. "We went to see it yesterday."

"The dog?" Ben looked confused.

"Ellen Croswell's dog," Melanie said. "I want to give it a home."

"Oh." Ben's frown cleared. "That's real good of you."

Melanie looked down at her hands. "I felt sorry for him, losing his owner like that. It must have been terrifying for him."

"He was lucky to make it out alive." Ben cleared his throat. "I heard he got cut a couple of times. Someone told me he had a bruised jaw. He thinks the perp kicked him and knocked him out, otherwise either he or the perp wouldn't be breathing right now. Dogs like that don't give up easy."

Melanie felt a sharp stab of anger toward the monster who had so viciously attacked a helpless woman and her dog.

"Anyway," Ben said gruffly, "I shouldn't be talking about this."

"Well," Liza said, "we do have something we need to tell you about our murder case."

Melanie's nerves immediately went on alert. Ben had warned them not to get involved. She didn't think he would be too happy to learn they had questioned the Sullivans.

Liza, however, had no such qualms. Plunging ahead, she told him about their encounter with the couple at the charity dinner and repeated everything they'd learned from them. "They lied about where they were the night Angela disappeared," she said, "and we'd like to know why."

Ben looked thoughtful. "That does bring up an interesting question. Our detective will probably interview everyone connected with the family at that time when he gets back to the investigation. If he interviews them together, one of them at least will have to change his story."

"I never thought of that." Liza frowned. "I guess you still don't know when that will be?"

"Definitely not until we've solved this new murder case. Everything is on hold until then. And I have to get back to work." He unwound himself from the chair. "I'm sure you two have plenty to do."

"We do." Liza got up and waved a hand at the walls. "What do you think of this wallpaper?"

He seemed a little taken aback by the question. Staring at the walls, he murmured, "Well, it's a little . . . um . . . I guess it's okay."

"Go ahead," Liza said. "You can say it. Hideous, right?"

Ben stared some more, then shrugged. "I'd say it's all a matter of taste. Personally, I don't like wallpaper that much, but it does kind of go with the house."

Melanie had to laugh. "It has to go, period. We're taking it down today."

He pursed his lips. "I'd say you've got quite a job ahead of you."

"It keeps us out of mischief," Liza said as she walked over to the door. "Thank you again, Ben."

"My pleasure." He gave her a quick salute as he followed her out into the hallway.

Melanie trailed after them, wondering if they would be making a mistake removing the wallpaper now that they were cleared to open the inn.

She felt a tinge of excitement at the thought. They still had so much to do, but knowing they could finally take bookings again made a world of difference. The Merry Ghost Inn was about to become a reality after all.

Chapter 11

Liza had barely closed the front door when Melanie said, "I'll have to go to the store. If we're going to impress Josh with our recipe, we'll need some groceries."

Liza looked guilty. "Sorry, I didn't think about that. I just said the first thing that came into my head."

"If we'd known we could open the inn, we needn't have invited him at all, now that we don't have to solve the murder."

Liza looked worried. "I'm not so sure about that. Do we really want to open the inn with the case still hanging over us? The police will continue the investigation eventually. Then they'll be in and out, distracting our guests. Wouldn't it be better to get it over with now and put it all behind us?"

"That's assuming we can solve the case and find Angela's killer. So far, we keep hitting dead ends."

"I wouldn't say that. We have two possible suspects—Paul and Brooke Sullivan."

"And no way of knowing how to prove either one did or didn't kill Angela."

"Well, maybe we'll get closer to that once we can talk to Brooke at the spa. Meanwhile, we can talk to Josh and find out if he knows anything that could help us."

Melanie sighed. "So you want to hold off opening the inn until this is solved?"

"I suppose that depends on how long it takes us. Let's give it another week. If we're no further along in solving the murder, then we'll go ahead and plan the opening. That will also give us a little extra time to get the rest of the work done in the house."

"Okay. I'll go to the store. It shouldn't take me long to get what we need." She started down the hallway to her room. "Maybe you could take the switch plates off while I'm gone. We can start on the walls when I get back."

"We don't need anything elaborate for lunch," Liza called out after her. "Just something simple but good."

Melanie answered her with a wave and went into her room to get her purse.

Minutes later, she was on her way into town. The usual flow of visitors filled the sidewalks, some gawking at shop windows while others were content just to stroll down the street, enjoying the fresh breeze from the ocean.

Already the morning clouds were breaking up, promising another beautiful, sunny afternoon. Melanie parked the car behind the grocery store and paused a moment to take a deep, cleansing breath of air before crossing the parking lot.

She was about halfway across when a sudden, violent shove on her shoulder sent her sprawling sideways. The air pumped out of her lungs as she hit the ground hard, and shock froze her body for a moment or two. She lay still, eyes closed, trying to understand what had happened to her.

Vaguely, she realized that someone was shaking her shoulder, and a woman's urgent voice asked her over and over again if she was all right.

No, she wasn't all right. Pain was shooting through her arm, and it hurt to breathe. She opened her eyes and found four faces staring down at her. Somehow, she managed to get enough air back in her lungs to mutter, "What happened?"

"Someone almost ran you down," the woman told her. "If it hadn't been for this guy here, you'd be dead by now. He saved your life."

"It was nothing," one of the men mumbled. "I'm just happy I saw the car coming at you."

"Maybe we should call for an ambulance," the other woman suggested.

"No!"

She'd spoken with such urgency, the group looked startled.

"I'm fine. Really." She struggled to sit up, embarrassed to notice other people in the parking lot staring at her.

"Some people shouldn't be allowed to drive." The woman who had been shaking her grabbed her arm to help her. "Racing out like that in a parking lot. We should call the cops."

"No, really. I'll be fine." Melanie shook her head, blinking as tiny sparkles danced in her eyes. She turned to the two men. "Which one of you saved my life?"

"He did." The shorter of the two men nudged his companion.

"I don't know about that." Her young savior looked down at his sneakers. "I didn't even think about it. I just did what anyone else would do."

Looking at his flushed face, Melanie felt a tremendous rush of gratitude. She was still shaking and afraid she was going to cry. "Thank you," she said, her voice husky with emotion. "I'm truly grateful to you. Are you visiting?"

The guy nodded, glancing at his friend. "We just came down for the day."

"What's your name?"

"Chris." He nudged his head at the young man next to him. "This is Ryan."

"I'm Melanie." She held out her hand. "Thank you again."

The woman who had helped her up asked, "Are you sure you're okay? Do you need a ride somewhere?"

Melanie shook her head, and again the sparkles danced in her eyes. "I'm okay. Just shaken up a bit, that's all. Thank you."

The woman looked anxious. "You could have been killed. I saw that car coming right at you."

"I did, too," the other woman said. "It was almost like he meant to run you down. We should call the cops. It was a gray car, small—one of those foreign cars, I think."

"A Subaru or a Honda," Ryan said, looking smug.

Melanie stared at him. "Are you sure?"

"Pretty sure." He shrugged. "Some of those cars look alike, and I only got a quick look. It was out of here before I could read the license plate."

Her mind reeling with possibilities, Melanie said quietly, "Well, there's no harm done, so there's really no need to call the police. But thank you all for worrying about me." She looked at Chris. "My grandmother and I will be opening a bed-and-breakfast shortly. It's called the Merry Ghost Inn. I'd like to offer you and a friend two nights' free stay at the inn once we are open. Just give us a call, and we'll be happy to book you."

Chris's eyes lit up. "Seriously? Sweet! Thanks!"

"Awesome!" Ryan said, giving his friend a nudge. "Way to go, dude!"

"Wait." Melanie opened her purse. "I have a brochure." She pulled out the leaflets and handed them out to the little group. "Thanks so much, all of you, for being so kind. I hope you enjoy the rest of your visit."

"Oh, I live here," one of the women said, staring at the brochure. "Isn't this the Morellis' house, where they found a skeleton hidden behind a wall?"

Both the men started to speak at once, and Melanie backed away, saying, "I'm really sorry, but I have an appointment, and I have to get back. Thank you again!" She waved at them, then turned and sprinted for the store.

Worried that one of them might follow her into the store to ask her more questions, she hurried up and down the aisles, grabbing things off the shelf and dropping them in the basket without giving too much thought to what she was buying.

To her relief, she was able to pass through the cashier line fairly quickly. It wasn't until she was in the car and driving home that the questions finally began to penetrate the fog.

Had it been an accident, or did someone really try to hit her? *Like he meant to run you down.* The woman's words kept echoing in her head. Yet she couldn't make herself believe that someone had deliberately tried to hurt her.

It was a gray car, small—one of those foreign cars, I think.
A Subaru or a Honda.

Melanie shook her head, trying to get rid of the shocking suspicion forming in her mind. Gary had a temper, but that didn't make him a killer. She just couldn't believe he would actually try to run her down like that. He was much too civilized and controlled. He would never let his emotions get the best of him.

She had pretty much convinced herself of that by the time she parked the car in the driveway of the inn. Carrying the groceries to the front door, she debated whether or not to tell Liza about what had happened.

There was no point in worrying her grandmother if the whole thing had simply been a matter of a careless driver in too much of a hurry. Certainly she'd seen plenty of those.

She opened the front door, flinching as pain shot up her arm. She'd have to be careful to hide that from Liza's sharp eyes.

Her grandmother called out to her as she passed by the living room door. "I'll be there in a minute. I'm just getting the last cover off the outlets."

"No rush!" Melanie carried the groceries into the kitchen and dumped the bags on the counter. She had almost unpacked them when Liza walked into the kitchen.

"I've got all the switch plates and outlet covers off, and I've already—" She broke off as Melanie turned to face her. "What in heaven's name happened to your face?"

"My face?" Confused, Melanie touched her cheek with her fingers and winced. "Ouch."

"How did you get that graze? Did someone hit you?" Liza came forward, her eyes full of concern. "Melanie, what happened?"

Sighing, Melanie walked over to a chair and sat down. "I should have known I couldn't keep anything from you." Reluctantly, she recounted everything that had happened in the parking lot while Liza looked more worried with each sentence.

"I offered the guys a free two-night stay here when we open," Melanie said, rubbing her arm. "I hope that's okay with you."

"Of course it is. That young man saved your life." Liza came over to her and touched her lightly on the shoulder. "You should see a doctor and make sure there's no real damage done."

"I'm fine." Melanie smiled up at her. She'd left out the woman's description of the car. Liza was worried enough, and the last thing she wanted to do was add to it. "My arm's a little sore where I fell on it, that's all. If it's not better in a couple of days, I'll have it checked out, okay?"

Liza looked unconvinced. "All right, but we'd better not tackle the wallpaper today. Why don't we work on the breakfast menus instead? Maybe your arm will feel better tomorrow. Besides, we have to get lunch for Josh. What did you decide on?"

"Caesar salad and stuffed potatoes. I thought that—" She broke off when she saw Liza's eyebrows shoot up. "What? That's not good?"

"I told Josh we were going to try out a breakfast recipe."

"Oh." Melanie thought about it for a moment. "Well, maybe he'll forget you said that when he sits down to eat my delicious stuffed potatoes."

Liza rolled her eyes. "All this subterfuge is getting confusing. Here, I'll help you put this stuff away." She picked up a lettuce and a slab of blue cheese and took them over to the fridge.

"By the way, talking about the breakfast recipes, I remembered something while you were out. I have a book somewhere of recipes the cooks used at Buckingham Palace. They're a bit fancy, but we might find some good ideas for our breakfasts."

"Seriously?" Melanie swung around in her chair to look at her. "That would be fantastic! We could label on the menu that the meals were served at the palace. What a great idea!"

Liza looked smug. "I thought you'd like it. I'll see if I can find the book."

She left the kitchen, and Melanie sat for a moment longer, trying to get control of her quivering nerves. Memories of her narrow escape kept flashing through her mind. She couldn't remember seeing the car at all. The shove had sent her to the ground, and by the time she'd opened her eyes, the car had disappeared.

Gray, like a Subaru or Honda. No. She would not believe that Gary was capable of such a terrible thing. Gray Hondas were common. It had been an accident, pure and simple. Someone had been in a tearing hurry to get out of the parking lot and just hadn't seen her until the last minute.

She had to believe that or she'd go nuts thinking about it. She got up slowly, relieved to find that nothing seemed to be hurting except for her arm. She flexed it and convinced herself the pain was already tapering off.

She had put the rest of the groceries away when Liza walked back into the kitchen, waving a large book at her. "I found it! It was in the chest under my bed." She sat down at the kitchen table and flipped the cover open. "It has some fabulous recipes in here, but we may have to tone them down a bit."

Melanie looked over her shoulder. "Cod with egg sauce? For breakfast? Quail egg tartlets? Can you even buy quail eggs in Sully's Landing?"

Liza shrugged. "Well, like I said, we'd probably have to modify the recipes somewhat." She turned a page. "Look, here's one for scrambled eggs." She started reading out loud. "Separate the eggs, beat the yolks with salt and pepper, whisk in the egg whites, drop a pat of butter in the pan, stir mixture into the melted butter and cook until set, remove from pan and stir in cream."

"Hmm." Melanie stared at the page. "Same ingredients I use, but a different method. I wonder how much difference there would be in the taste if the eggs were separated and the cream was added after the eggs are cooked."

"If Buckingham Palace did it this way, then you can bet it's a better way. Maybe we should try it tomorrow."

"Great idea. We have to sample all our recipes anyway to make sure they're good enough to serve to paying guests."

Liza sighed. "There goes my diet."

"You're not on a diet." Melanie walked over to the counter and pulled open a drawer.

"I might have been if we hadn't decided to surround ourselves with food. Some of these recipes look delicious. How many do you think we'll need?"

"I've thought about that." Melanie came back to the table with a notebook and pen in hand and sat down. "I figure most people will only stay two or three days. So if we have five standard menus that we use regularly, then maybe another half dozen specialties that we can serve whenever we need something different, that should pretty much cover it. Maybe we can find some recipes in your Buckingham Palace book for our specialty menus. We can always add something really different for holidays."

Liza's smile lit up her face. "I knew I made the right choice when I asked you to be my partner. That's brilliant!"

Melanie shrugged. "Hold the praise until we've figured out the menus. There's a lot of work to go into this."

"Then we'd better get started." She glanced up at the clock. "We only have an hour or so before we have to get lunch."

An hour later, they had agreed on the five standard menus. Quiche for day one, frittatas for day two, then omelets, followed by eggs Benedict, and egg casserole for the fifth day.

"The rest will have to wait," Melanie said as she gathered up the sheets of paper strewn across the table. "I have to bake the potatoes now."

"That will take at least an hour." Liza stared at the clock. "Josh will be here before they're cooked."

"Not if I bake them in the microwave." Melanie took three large potatoes out of the cabinet. "They'll be done in about ten minutes."

Liza shook her head. "I'll never get used to using a microwave. I still remember my grandmother cooking over a coal fire."

Melanie gently pricked a potato with a fork. "Really? Do you have any of her recipes?"

"No. I don't remember what we ate when my sister and I stayed with her. It was probably mostly stews and soups." She got up from the table. "I'll make the salad."

Josh arrived shortly after one PM, by which time the potatoes were baked and stuffed and the salad sat in the fridge ready to be served.

"This is a nice surprise," Josh said as he sat down at the dining room table. "I don't get too many home-cooked meals."

"You don't have a wife or a girlfriend to cook for you?" Liza placed the bowl of salad and a plate of biscuits on the table.

Josh laughed. "No, I don't. I'm not much of a cook myself, so I either eat out or zap something in the microwave."

Liza rolled her eyes. "What would people do nowadays without a microwave?"

Melanie sat the dish of stuffed potatoes on the table. "Liza's not a big fan of microwaves."

"I don't trust them. Anything that cooks that fast can't taste the way it should." Liza sat down and picked up the salad. "Here you go, Josh." She handed him the bowl. "So tell us, what have you heard about the woman who was stabbed the other night?"

If he was taken aback by the abrupt change of subject, he gave no sign. "No more than what you read in the papers. The cops are putting all their resources into finding the killer. It looks like a random killing, but you never know."

"I saw in the paper that the police were questioning the woman's ex-husband."

"Oh, he's been cleared. He had an alibi. He was out of town when she was killed."

Liza shook her head. "That must have been a relief for him."

"I'm sure it was." Glancing around, he added, "This is a big room for a dining room."

Melanie sat down on the chair next to her grandmother. "Yes, it's perfect for us. We'll be able to seat all our guests and still have room to move around."

He nodded at the fireplace. "It should be real cozy in the winter with a log fire going."

"You've seen it before, though, haven't you?" Liza said, reaching for the jug of ice water she'd brought in earlier.

Josh stared at her as if she'd accused him of something. "Sorry?"

Liza smiled. "We were talking to Sharon Sutton, the lady who owns Felicity's Fashions. She happened to mention that she met you a couple of times here in the house when she was visiting with Angela."

"Oh." Josh's face mirrored discomfort as he shifted back and forth on his chair. "It was so long ago I'd almost forgotten. I stopped by here a couple of times to interview the Morellis about the ghost."

"So you knew them quite well?"

"I wouldn't say that." He scooped up a potato with the serving spoon and dropped it on his plate. "They weren't very sociable people, but I did get the story on the ghost. It's supposed to have originated back in the 1920s, when one of the Sullivan daughters met an artist who fell madly in love with her. She encouraged him to the point where he proposed and then turned him down. Worse, she laughed at him and made him feel like a fool for thinking she would ever consider marrying into poverty."

"Oh, that's so mean," Melanie said, taking a helping of the salad. "Leading him on like that and then making fun of him? He must have been devastated."

"He was totally shattered." Josh dug into his potato as if he'd been starving. "He went home and hung himself. He left a note saying he would have the last laugh. Right after that, the daughter complained of hearing laughter everywhere she went in the house. No one else admitted hearing it, and in the end it drove her mad. She died in a mental institution, or as it was once called, a lunatic asylum."

"That's such a sad story." Melanie shivered, remembering the noises that sounded so much like laughter. "But is it really true?"

Josh shrugged. "Who knows? I did some research, and I did find a report of an artist committing suicide around that time, and one of the Sullivan women did end up in an asylum, but I could never find any evidence that they knew each other." He shook his head. "It could be true, I guess. It wouldn't be the first time a rich bitch has driven a man to do something drastic. Most of them have wealth handed to them. They think their money makes them better than anyone else, and they put down anyone who makes an honest living. Some of them should spend a year doing hard labor. That would take the sneering smile off their faces in a hurry."

His voice had grown more bitter with each word, and he stabbed viciously at his potato with his fork.

Exchanging a glance with Liza, Melanie cleared her throat. "So what did you think of Angela Morelli? Did you know she was planning on leaving her husband?"

Josh gave her a hard look that made her uncomfortable. "I didn't know her that well. As far as I could tell, she was okay with living with Vincent. She had enough money to have whatever she wanted, and he didn't bother her that much. He spent most of his time in his office or bedroom."

"So you don't know if she was interested in someone else?"

"Like another guy?" He uttered a short laugh. "I wouldn't know. Like I said, I thought she was okay with her life. I was surprised when I heard she'd left town."

"And even more surprised to learn that her bones were discovered behind her bedroom wall, I bet," Liza said quietly.

Again Josh shrugged. "Not really. I had an idea it might be her when I first heard about it. It wasn't like Angela to do a vanishing act in the middle of the night. She always did things on a grand scale. She would have left in a blaze of glory."

"So do you have any ideas about who might have killed her?"

Liza had managed to sound casual, but even so, Josh couldn't hide his surprise. "Me? How should I know? Like I said, I didn't know her all that well."

He looked so uncomfortable, Melanie felt compelled to rescue him. "Don't mind Liza. We've been doing a little detective work on our own, since the police have put the case on hold. We were hoping to solve the puzzle and put an end to their investigation, but so far, the more we learn, the more confusing things become. We were just hoping you could tell us something that might help."

"Ah, I wondered why you'd invited me to lunch. I didn't think it was for my culinary expertise." He shook his head. "I'd like to help. I really would. But like I told you, I didn't know any of them very well. I was here a couple of times to interview them, and that's about it." He took a bite of his potato. "This is really good. What's in it?"

Melanie smiled. "Thanks. It's just bacon, chives, parsley, and parmesan cheese."

"Well, it tastes great. So how long do you have to wait before you can open the inn?"

He'd deliberately changed the subject, Melanie realized. They weren't going to get anything more out of Josh on the subject of Angela Morelli.

Chapter 12

After Josh had left, amid a flurry of thanks and promises to let them know if he heard any more about the murders, Melanie cleared away the dishes and put them in the dishwasher.

"He didn't say anything about it not being a breakfast recipe," Liza said as she dropped the leftover biscuits into a freezer bag.

"He probably thinks we're two nutty ladies who serve Caesar salad for breakfast."

"Well, he's probably got the first part right." Liza popped the bag of biscuits into the freezer. "So what did you think of his rant about wealthy women who make fun of impoverished men?"

Melanie closed the dishwasher door and straightened up. "I think he had a crush on Angela and she shot him down."

"Exactly what I was thinking. He kept saying he didn't know her very well, but then he said all that about her going out in a blaze of glory, which sounded as if he knew her well enough to make a judgment about her. I wonder if he knows that she was having an affair with Paul Sullivan."

"Probably not, or he would have found a way to make it public. I get the impression that Josh Phillips can be vindictive when crossed."

Liza nodded. "He was rather intense, wasn't he?" She looked at the clock. "So do you feel up to tackling that wallpaper, or are you too sore from your accident this morning?"

"I'm fine. If you can manage it with your aches and pains, I can surely handle it with mine."

"That's my girl." Liza opened the tall cabinet and pulled out a bucket. "If you'll get the fabric softener from the laundry room, I'll fill this with hot water."

Melanie took the bucket from her. "This will be heavy. You get the fabric softener. I'll fill the bucket. I'll meet you in the living room."

"Done. Make sure it's good and hot."

She left the kitchen, and Melanie carried the bucket over to the sink. Turning on the faucet, she replayed in her mind their conversation with Josh. Something he'd said had struck a chord at the time. *It wasn't like Angela to do a vanishing act in the middle of the night.*

But she had done just that. Though not the way he meant. According to Noriko, someone had rung the doorbell in the middle of the night. Had it been Paul Sullivan, swearing that if he couldn't have her, no one else would? Or was it Brooke Sullivan, bent on destroying the woman who was trying to steal her husband? One of them was lying about where they were that night. Why would they lie if they had nothing to hide?

Then again, it could have been someone else ringing the doorbell that night. Maybe Angela had gotten pregnant with another man—someone who couldn't give her the lifestyle she enjoyed—and she'd hoped to persuade Paul it was his baby so he would have to provide for the child. After all, if she had planned to leave Vincent, she would need support for her and the baby.

Intrigued by the new possibility, Melanie heaved the bucket of steaming water out of the sink. She was halfway to the door when Liza rushed in, her eyes wide with excitement.

"I heard it again." She waved the bottle of fabric softener at Melanie. "It was on the stairs, as plain as if he was standing there. He was laughing—a real, hollow laugh that sounded . . ." She shivered. "Threatening."

Liza put the bucket on the table. "I thought you said that ghosts can't hurt you."

"They can't." Liza drew a shaky breath. "That doesn't mean they can't scare the hell out of you."

"That does it." Melanie picked up the bucket again. "Tomorrow I'm calling the housing inspector to see if we can find out what's making that noise."

"They won't find anything." Liza looked a little less shaken. "It's the ghost of that artist. I know it is. And right now, he doesn't sound too merry."

"You're reacting to what Josh just told us about the ghost." Melanie carried the heavy bucket to the door. "I think we need to keep our minds off ghosts and murderers for a while. Grab a bowl so we can mix this stuff and get to work."

A couple of hours later, Melanie stood back to check out their efforts. Between them, they had stripped one and a half walls, leaving another one and a half to go, since the built-in bookcases lined the fourth wall.

"I don't remember it being this hard," Liza said, sinking onto a chair. "That paper is stuck on there like cement."

Her pale cheeks and tired eyes warned Melanie that her grandmother's stamina was deserting her. "I think we've done enough for today," she said, putting down her scraper. "We can finish this up tomorrow."

"Good idea." Liza leaned back on the chair. "I think this room will look bigger once we get it painted and get rid of some of the clutter." She stared at the fireplace. "You know, I think we should sell those antiques. It would help to keep us going until we can open up the inn."

"Really?" Melanie felt a stab of guilt. "I wonder if we should contact Tony Morelli first and make sure he doesn't want to keep any of them. After all, they are his family's heirlooms."

"If he'd wanted any of them, he would have taken them before he sold me the house. I got the impression he couldn't care less about what was in it, which is why he included the contents in the sale. He didn't want to be bothered with it all. He was just happy to get it off his hands and have someone else take care of the junk, as he called it."

Melanie looked at the figurines on the mantel. "He might have changed his mind about that if he'd known they could be valuable. I wonder how much they are worth."

"There's one way to find out." Liza got up slowly from the chair. "We can take some of them to a dealer and get them appraised. That clock, for instance, and the peasant couple, and the candlesticks. I believe they're solid silver."

Melanie felt a burst of renewed energy as she gazed around the room. "What about that painting?" She nodded at a landscape hanging on the wall. "Think it's worth anything?"

Liza tilted her head to one side to scrutinize the painting. "Actually, I quite like that one. I'd like to keep it."

"Okay, we'll take a look around and decide what we don't want to keep and take it all to a dealer. We can go tomorrow morning. Do you know any dealers in town?"

"I think we'll need to go into Portland for this project. Can you look for one on the Internet later?"

"Sure! We can have lunch somewhere nice and make a day of it."

"Sounds good to me." Liza headed for the door. "I'm going to wash up and sit on the deck for a while. I could use some fresh air. Then I'll help you pick out what we want to take to the dealer."

"I'll join you in a minute," Melanie said, picking up the scraper again. "I just want to finish this corner."

"You're a glutton for punishment." Shaking her head, Liza left the room.

Melanie smiled as she tackled the wallpaper again. It felt good to be doing something constructive for a change. They had spent so much time chasing after clues and talking to people about the Morellis and the murder, when they should have been working on getting the house ready to open.

Still, she had to admit she was looking forward to going back to Portland for the day. Much as she enjoyed living in Sully's Landing, there were some things she missed about the city. Like the stores, the restaurants, the walks along the waterfront, the view of the snowy peak of Mt. Hood seeming to float in a blue haze above the city.

There was so much that she had taken for granted when she lived there, and only now was she beginning to realize how truly beautiful and unique was the city of Portland, Oregon. Yes, she was looking forward to returning to her hometown. Smiling, she attacked the remaining strip of wallpaper.

The following morning, right after breakfast, Melanie set off down the coast road with Liza beside her, heading for the highway that would take them through the coastal range pass to Portland.

Leafy spruce, hemlock, cedar, and fir lined the road as they swooped up and around the winding highway, soaring over twelve hundred feet before starting the roller coaster ride that would take them down into the valley.

Melanie parked the car near the waterfront, where she planned to take her grandmother to her favorite restaurant for lunch. Melanie had picked a dealer's shop close by, and the weather was perfect for walking—sunny and warm with a light breeze from the river.

She had packed some of the antiques into a couple of tote bags, and they each carried one as they strolled past shops, cafes, and art galleries, stopping every now and then to gaze into windows.

They found the dealer's shop down a side street, tucked between a Thai restaurant and a barber's shop. A tinny bell rang when Melanie opened the door. The shop seemed dark, and the musty smell reminded her of the basement of the inn. Thinking of that made her remember the ghostly laughing, and she quickly focused on the furniture and tables loaded with figurines, candlesticks, lampshades, jewelry, and a vast display of sports memorabilia.

Liza was already heading for the back of the shop, where the dealer was hovering behind the counter. He was a fussy little man, with a black beard and a thick accent that Melanie didn't recognize.

He spread out the antiques they'd brought on the counter in front of him and started examining each one. He kept nodding all the time he was speaking, and she missed most of what he said, but Liza seemed to understand.

"I don't know how old those are," she said at one point when the dealer held up one of the peasant figurines. "Everything came with the house we bought. I do know they are quite old, at least pre–twentieth century, I'd say."

The dealer frowned and picked up the boy peasant. "This not old," he said. "This copy." He shook the girl peasant at her. "This antique." He raised the boy peasant again. "This not."

Melanie stared at him. "Are you saying that one of those is a fake?"

The dealer's dark gaze switched to her. "Yes. That is what I say. One old, the other . . . not antique."

Liza groaned. "What about the other antiques? Are they genuine?"

"I tell you. One moment." He picked up the clock and turned it upside down, stared at it for several seconds, then put it down again. "The rest okay. I take them all." He named a figure and shrugged, as if apologizing.

Liza seemed to be turning the offer over in her mind. "I think we need a second opinion," she said at last. She looked at Melanie. "What do you think?"

Still puzzling over the dealer's evaluation, Melanie said quickly, "I absolutely agree."

Liza turned back to the dealer. "Thank you, but I think we'll take them all back home."

"I give you fair deal," the dealer protested as Melanie started putting the antiques back into the tote bags. "You not get better one anywhere."

"We'll see about that." Liza swept the peasant pair into her bag. "Thank you for your time."

She trotted to the door, leaving Melanie to collect the rest of the antiques.

"You make mistake," the dealer said as Melanie scooped up the clock.

"Maybe." Melanie smiled at him. "But we'll learn from it." Carrying the heavy bag, she followed Liza out into the sunshine.

"That was weird," Liza said as they walked back toward the river. "I can't believe one of those figurines is a fake."

"It doesn't make much sense." Melanie paused to study a bookstore window display. "Why would only one of the pair be a copy? Do you think he was trying to con us?"

"I don't know, but anything's possible." Liza stared at the jacket of a best-selling novel that looked like a scene out of *Star Wars*. "It's hard to tell. I thought by coming into the city, we'd get more money for the antiques, but it's hard to trust someone you don't know."

"We have to trust someone if we're going to sell them."

"Well, I do know a dealer in Seaside. Diane Henning. I don't know her well. I only met her once, but she seems to know her antiques, and she's a lot easier to understand. If we're going to haggle over prices, I'd rather do it with her."

"We're going to haggle?"

"Of course we are. How else will we get a good deal?" Liza peered at the window again. "I'd love to go in there and browse, but it's a little hard when we're carrying so much stuff."

"We'll come back later, if you like. We can put these bags back in the car, go have lunch, then come back here to browse."

Liza grinned. "You have the best ideas." She turned away from the window. "I'm looking forward to lunch."

"I was thinking," Melanie said as she fell into step alongside her, "I wonder if any of those books in the living room are worth anything."

"Oh, I never thought about that. We'll have to take a look when we get back."

"It will take hours to go through them all." Spotting a fast-moving car, she caught hold of her grandmother's arm as she was about to cross the street. "Careful. Wait for the walk sign. We've had enough close encounters lately."

Liza stepped back. "I'm getting used to strolling across the road in Sully's Landing. There are no traffic lights or walk signs to worry about there."

"Well, you'd better worry about them here if you don't want to be flattened by a bus."

Liza frowned. "I can imagine that happening here in the city, but somehow the idea of it happening in a parking lot in Sully's Landing is totally unbelievable."

Melanie ignored the twinge of uneasiness. "I guess it can happen anywhere." She stepped off the curb as the walk sign blinked on. "You just have to watch out for yourself." Leading her grandmother by the arm, she crossed the road and reached the sidewalk on the other side.

"Well, all I can say is there's been a lot of strange things going on down there lately." Liza looked up at her. "You need to do more than watch out. You need to be very careful."

"You worry too much." The uneasiness was growing into a nagging anxiety. Determined not to let it get to her, she started walking briskly down the street. "I made reservations at the restaurant. We'd better hurry or we'll be late."

Trotting to catch up with her, Liza said breathlessly, "You might want to slow down a bit, or you'll end up with a wheezing old hag sitting opposite you."

Melanie laughed and slowed her pace. "Sorry, but you'll never be an old hag."

"I feel like one sometimes." Liza took her arm. "Okay, let's go do my favorite things—eat good food and drink good wine."

"I thought you never drink before five PM."

"I just told Doug that so he wouldn't bug me."

"I got the idea that you liked him bugging you."

Liza snorted. "I'll never admit to that."

The restaurant overlooked the river, and Melanie was happy when the hostess led them to a table by the window. From there, they could watch young couples holding hands as they strolled by, men in business suits walking briskly past the crowded tables and colorful umbrellas, the occasional biker weaving in and out among the pedestrians, and kids licking on ice cream cones as they danced alongside their parents.

Out on the river, a yacht glided serenely across the water while smaller boats darted around in wide circles. Traffic poured across the wide bridges, a direct contrast to the peaceful scene below.

The shrimp salad tasted as good as it sounded on the menu, and Liza seemed to enjoy her fish and chips. After the meal, they headed back to the bookstore and spent an enjoyable hour browsing the shelves before heading home.

Melanie slept well that night and awoke the next morning to hear rain pattering on the window. She showered and dressed before opening the front door to bring in the newspaper. Outside on the porch, the wind whipped her hair into her eyes, and she snatched up the paper and quickly closed the door.

The best place to be when the weather was stormy was right there in the kitchen, with coffee brewing in the pot and a clear view of the angry ocean. Standing at the window, she could see the branches on the spruce trees bowing in the wind while the sea gulls screamed in protest as they swooped low over the sand.

She was still enjoying the view when Liza spoke from behind her. "It always amazes me how fast the weather can change down here. Such a difference from yesterday."

"I know, but it's fun to watch from here." Melanie pointed at the window. "Look, there are people out there on the beach already. They don't seem to mind the rain."

"They're probably looking for agates or sand dollars." Liza poured herself a mug of coffee. "The storms send them in on the tide."

"Sounds like fun."

"It is, but you have to be really careful. See those logs?" She pointed to where a couple of hefty sawn-off tree trunks sat on the sand. "They come in on the tide as well. If you get hit by one of those, it could kill you. This part of the coastline is notorious for its sneaker waves—like miniature tsunamis. One of those can sweep you out to sea before you even have time to yell. So many people have lost their lives because they weren't paying attention. The Oregon coast is beautiful, but it's treacherous as well. You have to treat it with the utmost respect, or it can zap you when you least expect it."

Melanie stared at the white-tipped waves charging to shore. "Wow. That puts a whole new perspective on it."

Liza laughed. "Don't let it scare you. It's just a matter of common sense." She sat down at the table and opened the newspaper. "Have you read this yet?"

"Not yet." Melanie joined her at the table. "I was wondering what you wanted to do about the antiques. You said you knew a dealer in Seaside?"

"Yes." Liza flipped open the front page of the paper. "It can wait a day or two. I guess we should finish stripping the wallpaper in the living room. I know I—" She broke off, staring at the paper, then added, "Oh my goodness. We're in the paper again. Josh wrote another article and mentioned us."

Melanie sat up. "Seriously? What does it say?"

"Well, he's talking about Ellen Croswell's murder. Then he mentions the finding of Angela Morelli's remains. Oh, listen to this." She started reading out loud. "*There have been no new developments in the case since the police are concentrating on finding the person who stabbed Ellen Croswell.*"

"I feel so bad about what happened to her. She must have been miserable in her marriage, and to go through a divorce, and perhaps begin to recover, only to have her life taken away from her before she had time to enjoy it—it just isn't fair."

"Life very often isn't fair."

"Does Josh say if she had children?"

Liza looked up. "It doesn't say. Why do you ask?"

Melanie cradled her coffee mug in her hands. "I was just thinking, if she had kids, they'd not only lost their mother, they'd lost their dog as well. I wouldn't feel right about taking Max away from them."

Liza's face softened in sympathy. "I'm sure if she had kids, they would have been mentioned by now. In any case, even if they did exist, they would probably be somewhere where they couldn't take the dog. There's a reason that dog is in the shelter."

Melanie nodded. "I guess you're right."

"Why don't you call the shelter today and see if Max is ready to come home?"

"I think I will." A rush of excitement took her breath away, and she took a sip of coffee, reminding herself that the dog had been injured and might not be ready to adopt yet. "So where does it mention us in the article?"

"Oh, right." Liza adjusted her glasses and peered at the page again. "*The owners of the soon-to-be-opened Merry Ghost Inn are eager to see the case solved and are doing a little sleuthing on their own. Meanwhile, the facts behind the murder of Angela Morelli remain a mystery.*"

Melanie gulped. "I hope the detective doesn't see that and get mad at us for interfering in his investigation."

"We're not interfering." Liza passed the front section of the paper over to her. "We haven't gone near the crime scene since they taped up the room. All we're doing is asking a few people a question or two. He can't get mad about that."

"I don't know. Ben wasn't too happy when he found out we'd been asking questions."

"At first, perhaps. I think he was just worried we'd get into trouble or something. He didn't say anything when he was here the other day. In fact, he seemed grateful to get the information we gave him." She paused, looking at Melanie over her glasses. "You call him Ben when you talk about him. Why don't you call him that to his face?"

Disturbed by the question, Melanie shrugged. "I don't know. I guess I don't want to sound too personal."

"Why not?"

"Maybe I don't want him to get the wrong idea."

"He seemed disappointed."

"That's your starry-eyed imagination at work again."

Liza sighed. "Why am I the only one around here who senses romance in the air?"

"Because you're a hopeless romantic. Maybe you should stop worrying about me and direct your energy toward Doug Griffith. That's probably the romance you're sensing."

"Trust me, I'm in no way interested in a relationship with that man."

"I'll remind you of that when you're dating him."

Liza rolled her eyes. "My dating days are long gone. I'm much too busy with this house to waste my time dillydallying with a man."

Melanie uttered a shout of laughter. "You sound positively Victorian."

Liza pushed back her chair. "It's my turn to make breakfast. Why don't you call the animal shelter while I'm cooking?"

"I will." Melanie got up, still holding her half-full mug of coffee. "Are you going to try out one of our recipes?"

"I am." Liza walked over to the counter. "Get ready for my awesome sausage and broccoli frittata."

"I can't wait." Still carrying her coffee, Melanie headed for her room, where she'd left her cell phone. Seated on the bed, she dialed the number and waited. Now that the moment was here, she could hardly stand the suspense. Would Max be ready to come home? How badly was he hurt? Was she being totally insane to bring an injured, traumatized dog into the house with so much to do? Would she have time to give him the care and attention he needed?

A sharp voice interrupted her thoughts, and the questions vanished. *Yes*, she assured herself. She was ready to welcome Max into her home. Taking a deep breath, she spoke into the phone. "My name is Melanie West, and I'm inquiring about a dog named Max. I was hoping I could come and get him today."

Hardly daring to breathe, she waited for the answer.

Chapter 13

Liza was standing at the stove when Melanie burst in a few moments later.

"We can pick him up today!" She danced over to her grand mother and flung her arms around her shoulders to give her a mammoth hug. "We can go right after breakfast."

"That's great." Liza hugged her back. "I'm so happy for you. For us both. It's been years since I had a dog in the house. Max will be a great companion for us."

Melanie drew back. "You don't think we're taking on too much, what with all we have left to do in the house?"

"No, I don't. Once he settles down, he'll practically take care of himself. He will give us an incentive for walks on the beach, he'll guard the house, he'll—" She broke off as a sound interrupted her. It was loud, it was close by, and it was unmistakably the sound of deep-throated laughter.

Liza yelped and dropped the oven mitt she was holding onto the floor.

Melanie bent to pick it up, her heart bumping.

"Go away," Liza said sharply.

Only silence answered her.

"That was weird." Melanie went to the basement door and opened it. "We must get someone out here to figure out where it's coming from." She stuck her head through the doorway and listened. "I can't hear anything now."

"He's probably gone." Liza sounded calmer. "His sense of humor needs some work. I wish we'd asked Josh for the name of that artist he said had died. I'd love to give our ghost a name."

"Your ghost." Melanie shut the basement door. "I'm still betting on a technical explanation for that sound."

"He's going to convince you before too long."

"He'll have to do something a lot more spectacular than laughing."

"You'll see." Liza opened the oven door. "My frittata is done. Are you ready to eat?"

The frittata was everything Melanie could have imagined— light, fluffy, and just enough seasoning to add flavor. "This will be perfect on our daily menu," she murmured as she put down her fork. "That was really good."

Liza beamed. "I'll sort through my Buckingham Palace book tonight and see what we can use for our specialties."

"I think we can definitely use their version of scrambled eggs. See if you can find out what they served with it."

"I'll do that." Liza glanced at the clock. "We'd better get moving if you want to pick up that dog."

Melanie jumped up from her chair. "I'm ready. Let's go."

"We have to do the dishes first."

"We'll put them in the sink and do them later." She grabbed Liza by the arm and started dancing around the kitchen. "We're bringing Max home today!"

Liza shook her head. "I haven't seen you this excited since your wedding day." Her face changed, as if she realized she'd said something she shouldn't have, then she headed for the door, adding over her shoulder, "I'll get my sweater and meet you at the car."

Sobering, Melanie stared after her. She had been so excited to get married. She had known Gary only a few short weeks before he'd proposed. He'd insisted that the wedding take place shortly after that. If only she'd taken more time to get to know him, she might have thought twice about rushing into a marriage. If she had, she wouldn't now be facing a future with no hope of giving birth to a child.

Pushing away the memory, she hurried down the hallway to her room. She would not think about that now. Today she was bringing home a new baby who needed her.

Maybe it wasn't the same, but Max would help fill a void that had tortured her for far too long. Liza was right. It was time to put the memories behind her and move on. Not to forget, for that would be impossible, but to live in the present instead of the past. Maybe Max would help her do that.

She had a hard time stopping herself from speeding as they drove north again to Warrenton. Several cars were parked outside the shelter, and once more there was a line at the counter when she walked into the building with Liza hot on her heels.

A young couple with a small child passed them on their way out, leading a frisky Chihuahua on a leash. The little girl danced out the door, hugging herself in her excitement. Melanie knew exactly how she felt.

Reaching the counter after what felt like hours, she greeted the assistant. "I'm here to pick up Max. I called earlier and was told he's ready to come home."

The woman smiled. "Yes, he is, but first you have to fill out an application. Then wait over there until we call your name. You'll be taken to a room where you can visit with Max and make sure you're a good fit."

"I already know I want to take him home," Melanie said, trying not to sound impatient.

"But we don't know if he'll want to go home with you."

Taken aback, Melanie stared at her, wondering if she was joking. The assistant looked perfectly serious, however, and feeling a little offended, Melanie took the form from her and walked over to a couple of empty chairs by the far wall.

"How in the world are they going to know if Max will want to go home with us?" Liza demanded when Melanie repeated what the assistant had said. "They'll have him fill out a form?"

"I guess they can tell if a dog is going to like his new owner. They're probably just making sure he goes to a good home." Trying to convince herself that Max was going to immediately fall in love with her, she began to fill out the application.

Half an hour later, just when she felt the waiting was becoming unbearable, Melanie's name was called. A smiling young assistant led them to a bare room with a concrete floor, a couple of benches, and a glass wall that divided them from the cages on the other side.

Dogs barked, whined, and howled as Liza sat down. The assistant left them alone and returned shortly, leading a shaggy dog on a leash. After firmly closing the door, she unhooked the leash from the dog's collar. He sat down, his jaw drooping on his chest.

Feeling that same tug in her heart she'd felt the first time she'd seen him, Melanie held out her hand and called softly, "Max. Here, buddy."

The dog's head lifted slightly, then drooped again.

"He's a little unhappy right now," the young assistant said. She bent down and tugged on his collar. "Come on, Max. Let's be sociable."

As if he understood, Max slowly got up and allowed himself to be led over to Melanie.

She held out her hand, and he sniffed at it, then looked around as if seeing the room for the first time. On the other side of the glass, a dog yelped, and Max's ears pricked up. He stared for a moment, then limped over to the wall to stare at the cages. His soft whine almost broke Melanie's heart.

She got up and walked over to him, knelt down on the hard floor, and laid her hand on his neck. Noticing the shaved hair and the scar on his chest, she felt a deep flash of anger. How could someone do that to such a beautiful creature?

The cut on his front leg looked even more painful, and she vowed right there and then that she would shower this dog with love and make him forget the terrible thing that happened to him and his beloved owner.

"We'd like you to come home with us, Max. Liza and I will take really good care of you. I promise."

She felt him tense up under her fingers, but after a second or two, he turned his head. For a long moment, he stared deep into her eyes, then slowly reached out and licked her face.

Melanie swallowed hard. Getting to her feet, she said firmly, "We're taking this dog home with us." She looked at Liza for confirmation and received a nod and a smile of agreement from her grandmother.

The assistant seemed happy. "You'll need to fill out some additional forms." She clicked the leash back onto Max's collar. "I'll show you where to go."

She led them back to the reception area and pointed to a door. "Over there." Before Melanie could answer, she'd led Max away and disappeared around the corner.

"So what do you think?" Melanie asked as they walked over to the office. "Do you think I'm doing the right thing?"

"Do you think you're doing the right thing?"

"Yes, I do."

Liza smiled. "Then that's all that matters. He seems like a good dog. He risked his life to save his mistress."

"He must have been heartbroken that he failed." They reached the door of the office, where a young man beckoned to them from behind a desk.

It took another twenty minutes to fill out the paperwork, and to assure the serious-looking assistant that she and Liza were capable of taking care of Max, and no, there were no children in the house.

"He's been through a lot," the man said, "so don't be surprised if he has behavioral problems until he settles down. He needs to be handled with a kind but firm hand and given a safe place to sleep at night so that he feels secure. I assume you intend to keep him in the house?"

"Oh, absolutely," Melanie assured him.

"Good. We don't release dogs to anyone who keeps a dog outside." He pushed another form over to Melanie. "Here's the medical report. The cut in his chest wasn't that deep and is healing nicely. The one on his leg might need some attention. You have a certificate for a free initial exam with a veterinarian, and that should be taken within a week from now. The name of his previous vet is on the form. You can either use that one or choose your own. You will need a leash. If you don't have one with you, you can buy one in the shop. Wait at the counter and someone will bring Max out for you."

Thanking him, Melanie left the office with Liza trotting along beside her.

"I never realized that so much went into adopting a dog," Liza said as they headed for the corner, where a counter displayed leashes, collars, toys, and pet food. "It's wonderful that they care so much about their animals."

"It's impressive." Melanie watched a woman carry a cat in her arms to the door. "It's surprising how many people are here adopting pets. Good to know they are finding homes."

"And sad to know that so many of them don't."

After buying a leash, some pet food, and a couple of toys, they went back to sit in the reception area again. It seemed an eternity until a woman appeared in the hallway with Max at her side.

He limped toward them, his head swinging from side to side as he stared at all the activity going on.

"I'll take him out to your car," the woman said as she clicked Melanie's leash to his collar. Feeling like dancing, Melanie followed her out into the sunshine, with Liza following behind.

They reached the car, and Melanie opened the back door. At first, Max refused to get in and sat down on the ground. It took all three of them to get him onto the back seat and close the door on him.

"He'll settle down," the woman assured Melanie. "If you have any questions, feel free to call us. We're here to help in any way we can."

Thanking her, Melanie climbed into the car, fastened her seat belt, and waited for Liza to join her.

She seemed to take an exceptionally long time to get in. Looking out the window, Melanie could see her grandmother standing near the rear of the car, gazing hard at something in the distance.

Melanie turned her head and found Max staring at her with anxious eyes. "It's all right, Max. You're going home. You'll love it there. It's right on the ocean. You'll be able to run on the beach and play in the water. You'll have a nice bed to sleep in—" She uttered a soft gasp. "We don't have a bed for you. How could I forget that? We'll have to stop at a pet store on the way home. We'll get some treats for you, too." She shook her head. "There's so much to remember." She reached out to pat his head. "Don't worry, Max. We'll work it out together."

Max feebly thumped his tail on the seat.

Melanie was still smiling when Liza finally crawled into the car next to her.

"What were you looking at?" Melanie turned the key in the ignition. "I was just about to come and get you."

Liza stared straight ahead as she clicked on her seat belt. "Oh, nothing."

Disturbed by her expression, Melanie said sharply, "You were looking at something. What was it?"

Liza shrugged. "I thought I saw Gary's car, that's all. I'm sure it wasn't. After all, there are plenty of those little cars running around. I've seen so many of them lately. They must be really popular."

Melanie tried to ignore her stab of apprehension. "I'm sure my ex-husband is far too busy taking care of his clients to be chasing around after us." She put the gear into reverse and backed out of the spot.

"Of course he is." Liza settled herself more comfortably on the seat. "I'm letting my imagination run away with me. That's what happens when you read too many mystery novels."

Feeling only a little better, Melanie managed a laugh. "You haven't had time to read too many lately."

"I read at night. When you're as old as I am, you don't need as much sleep." Liza yawned. "Though I must admit, I've been sleeping a lot recently."

"I'm not surprised, with all the work we've been doing." Melanie was about to suggest Liza take it easy for a couple of days when a movement in her rearview mirror caught her eye. Max's head was in the way, but she could see enough to notice the small gray car coming up fast behind her.

Instinctively, she slowed down, pulling over to the right to let it pass. There was nothing coming in the opposite direction, so the car had plenty of room to get by. To her dismay, however, as the driver drew level, he swerved over toward her.

Melanie slammed on the brakes and felt a heavy thump on the back of her seat. Liza cried out and smacked her hands on the dashboard.

The car narrowly missed them as it sped past and disappeared around a curve.

Thoroughly shaken, Melanie brought the car to a halt and immediately turned around. Max whined as he jumped back onto the seat. "Are you all right, buddy?" She reached out and patted his neck. "I'm so sorry. That was not a good way to start our relationship."

"Did you see the driver?" Liza asked, her voice shaking.

"No, I was too busy trying to keep us on the road." Memories surfaced of another car narrowly mowing her down in a parking lot. She hesitated to ask the question, afraid of the answer. "Did you see him?" she asked at last.

"No." Liza sounded stronger. "He went by too fast. It could have been anyone."

"Like you said, there are an awful lot of those cars on the road."

"Yes. They're very popular."

"They are."

"It was just another road hog in a hurry, that's all."

"I'm sure."

"You don't think—?"

"No, I don't." Having cut her grandmother off before she could say what was on both their minds, Melanie deliberately changed the subject. "We have to stop at the pet store and buy Max a bed."

"Oh. I thought he would sleep on your bed."

"Well, both you and Max can get that idea out of your heads." Having settled that matter, she forced herself to put her suspicions about her ex on hold and pulled out onto the road again.

She found the perfect bed for Max at the pet store. It had a lovely soft pillow to lie on and padded walls to keep out the drafts. She also bought him a bag of rawhide sticks and some meaty chews. She gave him one of the chews when she got back into the car, and he gulped it down as if he hadn't eaten in weeks.

She could hardly wait to get back to the inn and see how he reacted to his new home. Liza seemed just as excited as they parked in the driveway. "You take him in," she told Melanie as she started to climb out of the car. "I'll bring the shopping bags."

"Leave the bed," Melanie said, scrambling out her side. "I'll come back for it." She leaned in to grab Max's collar and fastened the leash to it. "Come on, buddy. You're home!"

To her surprise, the dog pulled back from her and braced his front legs. No amount of coaxing would make him budge, and she finally had to ask Liza to push him from behind while she dragged on his collar.

The second he was out of the car, he lunged for the street. Taken by surprise, Melanie was dragged past the house before she managed to dig in and haul Max to a stop. This, she warned herself, was not going to be as easy as she'd imagined.

It didn't help matters to see Liza leaning against the car, helpless with laughter.

Taking a firm hand, Melanie leaned down to Max's ear. "This is your home now. Let's go!"

Something in her voice must have penetrated, as he surged forward and dragged her up to the driveway again.

Liza pushed herself away from the car, wiping her eyes. "That dog will be taking *you* for walks," she said as she pulled the shopping bags out from the trunk. "You might want to buy a pair of good running shoes."

"Very funny," Melanie said, feeling slightly out of breath. Max was no lightweight to be hauling around.

Somehow, she got him into the house and closed the front door. The second she unhooked his leash, he took off, in and out of rooms, stopping to sniff here and there. Before she could stop him, he bounded lopsidedly up the stairs, and she could hear him thumping down the hallway.

"Good thing the door to the skeleton room is closed," Liza said as she emptied the things they'd bought onto the kitchen table. "The cops would probably arrest him for disturbing a crime scene."

"He can't disturb it any more than it already is," Melanie said, picking up the bag of rawhide sticks. After several minutes of tempting the dog with one of the sticks, he finally ventured down the stairs again.

Liza had brought his bed in and laid it in the corner of the kitchen. "We spend most of our time in here, anyway," she said when Melanie questioned her with a look.

Max apparently decided it was a good place to sleep, and before long was quietly snoring in his bed.

"I think we should take those antiques into Seaside this afternoon," Liza said as they sat at the table with sandwiches and iced tea for lunch. "I'm anxious to find out if that dealer in Portland was telling the truth about the peasant boy."

Melanie swallowed the last of her sandwich before answering. "I can't understand why only one would be a fake. It just doesn't make sense."

"Nothing makes sense." Liza picked up her tea. "Like that car this morning. That driver barely missed us—almost like he was swerving at us on purpose."

"He was probably distracted by a cell phone or something."

The bitterness must have sounded in her voice, as Liza looked mortified. "I'm sorry, Mel. I didn't mean to bring back bad memories. It's just that you seem to be having problems with cars lately."

Small gray cars in particular, Melanie thought. Could it have been the same car that had barely missed her in the parking lot? *Was it Gary's car?*

"What's the matter?" Liza asked sharply. "You look as if you're going to be sick."

Melanie shook off the disturbing questions in her mind. "I was just thinking about that car," she said, making an effort to sound casual about it. "I'm sure it was just carelessness. If someone had really wanted to run us off the road, he could easily have waited until we were just ahead on that curve above the cliffs. We wouldn't have had a chance up there."

Liza shuddered. "Well, from now on, you need to be extra careful when you're out on the road. I think I'm going to call Noriko Chen." She got up from her chair. "I'll talk to her while you're doing the dishes."

Melanie stared at her. "Why are you calling Noriko?"

"I want to ask her about Josh Phillips, to find out what she knows about him and his crush on Angela."

"I don't understand. What has Josh Phillips got to do with anything?"

Liza reached the door and looked back at her. "Maybe nothing. But he drives a gray car." She disappeared before Melanie could reply.

Staring after her, Melanie pictured herself standing on the ladder, paintbrush in hand, while Josh came up the steps with a newspaper in his hand. He'd parked his car in the driveway, but she couldn't remember what it looked like.

Had Liza really remembered it, or was her imagination putting pictures into her mind? Josh? No, she couldn't imagine that friendly, cheerful man deliberately aiming his car at her. Why on earth would he do that, anyway? She could more easily picture Gary behind the wheel.

She shot up from her chair, horrified with where her thoughts were leading her. Was someone really trying to kill her? Liza had pointed out that her granddaughter bore a resemblance to Ellen Croswell. In the dark, she could have been mistaken for her. Then there was the car in the parking lot and now the car that morning. The more she thought about it, the less it seemed like accidents and more like attempts on her life.

Her first instinct was to grab her phone and dial 9-1-1. She actually had her phone in her hand when common sense prevailed. It was all in her head. The police would probably laugh at her. Ben would laugh at her, thinking she was a pathetic, psychotic moron with delusions of persecution.

The kitchen door opened, making her jump. Liza walked in, shaking her head. "Noriko wasn't there. She's on sick leave. They wouldn't tell me what was wrong with her. I hope it isn't anything serious."

It was hard to think of that dynamic little woman being laid low with an illness. "She's a really strong lady," Melanie assured her grandmother. "I'm sure whatever it is, she'll handle it."

"I hope so. I really like her." Liza walked over to the sink. "I'll help with the dishes, and then we can take the antiques into Seaside." She glanced at Max, who was awake and watching them, his head on his paws. "What do we do about him?"

"We can either take him with us or shut him up somewhere where he can't do any damage."

"Well, that answers my question. I can't see you locking him up, so I guess he's coming along with us." She nodded at him. "You'd better take him outside first and show him where his preferred bathroom is going to be. I'll finish up here."

"Good idea." Melanie picked up the leash and walked over to Max's bed. He sat up as she approached, his ears pricking with expectation.

"We're going for a walk," Melanie told him as she fastened his leash to his collar. "You're going to love your new bathroom." She paused at the door, with Max tugging on the leash to get outside. "You don't really think that Josh would try to hurt us, do you? Why would he?"

Liza turned around, her face a mask of worry. "Right now I don't trust anyone connected to the Morellis. Someone killed Angela Morelli and could still be in town. If he found out we were trying our best to find out who he is, he might do anything to stop us."

Melanie stared at her. "You think Josh Phillips killed Angela?"

"I think he has to be on our list of suspects. He was supposedly fond of her, and he sounded awfully bitter about women who look down on the working class. It's possible he made a move on Angela and she cruelly rejected him."

Melanie had to smile. "You sound like a Victorian novel."

"Rejection and revenge never go out of style."

Her smile fading, Melanie tried to picture Josh killing a defenseless woman. "I just can't see him doing something like that."

"Everyone is capable of murder when driven far enough." Lisa turned back to the sink. "That's what makes it all so complicated—and so very interesting."

Not so much if you're the target, Melanie thought. She still couldn't imagine Josh Phillips as a vicious killer, but Liza's words unsettled her. The thought that Josh, or someone else, could be stalking them with the sole purpose of preventing them from investigating the murder was not a comfortable thought.

Deciding she really needed some fresh air, she gave in to Max's tugging and let him lunge out the door.

Chapter 14

The smell of sand and seaweed greeted Melanie as she led Max out onto the grass. With the salty breeze in her hair and the sound of sea gulls crying overhead, all her fears and suspicions seemed to melt away. The cloudless sky was mirrored in a calm sea, and below her, people strolled along the sand, enjoying a perfect day at the beach.

Several dogs leapt and raced along the water's edge, and, straining at the leash, Max whined as he stared down at the scene.

"I know you'd love to be down there with all your pals," Melanie said as she led him across the lawn, "but it will have to wait a while. Now do your thing so we can go into town and sell our antiques."

Max soon obliged, and a few minutes later, they were on their way to Seaside.

The dealer's shop was at the far end of town, nestled on the corner of a small tree-lined side street. The familiar musty smell of aged artifacts greeted her as Melanie stepped inside.

She would have liked to examine a beautiful little bureau that had to be well over a hundred years old, but Liza, as usual, was in a hurry to get to the counter.

Diane Henning, a pleasant, matronly woman, examined each piece that they'd brought, murmuring now and again as she peered through her magnifying glasses. Finally, she put the last vase down and smiled at them. "I can offer you a round figure for the whole collection, or I can price each one, in which case I wouldn't be taking them all."

Liza raised her chin. "Are you saying that some of them are not antiques?"

Diane shook her head. "No, they are all at least fifty to a hundred years old, with the exception of this one." She held up the peasant boy. "This is an excellent piece, very well crafted, but it's not antique. It's not as heavy as the original, and if you compare the hands to the female"—she picked up the other peasant—"you can see the difference. Hands are difficult to create."

Melanie leaned closer to look at the hands. "They do look a little different, but unless you actually studied them, it wouldn't be noticeable."

"Yes, it's a shame." The dealer laid both pieces down carefully on the counter. "Had they been a genuine pair, I could have offered you much more. If you want to sell all these in a bundle, I'll take them, but if you want a separate price on everything, I won't be taking this pair. Or these." She held up a pair of candlesticks. "These are old, but they are silver-plated and not very good quality."

Liza looked at Melanie as she answered. "We might as well let them all go?"

Melanie nodded in agreement.

The figure Diane gave them was slightly more than the offer from the Portland dealer, and Liza beamed when she accepted the check.

"I saw you mentioned in the local paper," Diane said as Liza tucked the check into her purse. "I read that you and your granddaughter are opening the Morelli house as a B and B." She looked at Melanie for confirmation.

"We are," Melanie said, wondering if the whole world knew who they were. "It's called the Merry Ghost Inn."

"Right!" The woman's face lit up. "A real-life ghost! Have you seen it yet?"

"No, I don't—" Melanie began, but Liza interrupted her.

"We hear him a lot," she said, giving her granddaughter a forbidding look. "He likes to laugh at us."

"What does he sound like? Doesn't it scare you?" Diane was practically foaming at the mouth in her excitement.

"We should go," Melanie said firmly, then grabbed her grandmother's arm. "I don't want to leave Max too long in the car. It's warm out there."

"Oh, right." Liza smiled at the dealer. "Thank you for everything, and I hope the antiques go to a good home."

Max seemed happy to see them when they returned to the car and soon settled down again.

"We should have gone to Diane in the first place," Liza said as they drove back to Sully's Landing. "I liked her better, and we got a better price."

"Well, at least we know the Portland dealer was telling the truth about the peasant boy."

"I know. That's really weird, though." She laughed. "Diane seemed thrilled to know we'd heard the ghost."

Melanie sighed. "I guess I just have to get used to acting as if I believe in the thing."

"You won't have to act before long. He'll find a way to convince you."

"You truly believe he's real?"

"Yes, I do. Ghosts do exist, whether we want to admit it or not. There have been plenty of eyewitnesses who are convinced of that. Just because scientists don't have hard evidence yet doesn't mean they're not there. It simply means we haven't yet found the technology to prove it. Strange things happen that can't be explained any other way than the presence of ghostly spirits. We may not be able to prove that ghosts exist, but so far no one has proven that they don't."

Melanie took a moment to absorb all that. "Well, at least he's a friendly ghost."

"A good thing, too. We don't want to scare our visitors away."

"You don't think that the presence of even a friendly ghost will scare people away?"

"I think that most people, when faced with what seems impossible, want to see for themselves whether it's real or not. The doubters will come to prove us wrong, the enthusiasts will come to enjoy the spectacle, and the curious will come just to find out what all the fuss is about."

Melanie laughed. "In that case, we should have a full house for the entire year."

"Wouldn't that be a blessing?" Liza patted her purse. "At least we have some funds to pay the bills for a while longer."

It was later that night when Liza brought up the subject of the fake figurine again. Sitting in front of the TV in the living room, she was watching a news story about a sea turtle being rescued in Seaside when she announced, "I can't get that peasant boy out of my head. I just don't understand why only one of the pair is a fake."

Leaning back in her chair, Melanie murmured, "Maybe the real one got broken and the Sullivans replaced it."

"That's possible, I suppose. Though why would they replace it with a fake? You would think they'd buy another genuine pair."

"It probably had sentimental value to someone." Half asleep after the long day, Melanie glanced at Max. He was already asleep on the rug, his head on his paws. Much to her satisfaction, he'd eaten a full bowl of his dog food and looked utterly content.

She thought back to earlier that day, when he'd whined at the scene on the beach below. A swift pang of sympathy accompanied the thought that he might have been whining for his former mistress. She wanted so badly to get down on the rug with him and give him a warm hug.

Just then, however, Liza startled her with an explosive, "Oh my good heavens!"

Sitting up, Melanie frowned at her grandmother. "What's wrong? Do you have a pain?"

Max lifted his head, stared at Liza for a second or two, and went back to snoozing.

Liza had both hands at her throat, and Melanie was about to grab her phone when her grandmother said, "What if it was the murder weapon?"

"What? What murder weapon?"

"The peasant boy." Liza's voice rose with excitement. "What if the killer used it to hit Angela Morelli? He would have to get rid of the evidence, but then someone would notice it was missing. So he would have to find a copy to replace it."

The more Melanie thought about it, the more logical it sounded. "I guess it's possible, but how would anyone prove it?"

"I don't know, but I think we should buy back that pair of peasants and take them to Ben. He might be able to track down the missing one."

"If it is the murder weapon. Besides, with the case on hold, there's not much he or anyone else can do right now."

"Maybe not." Liza got up from her chair. "But it will give us a good excuse to see him again. First thing in the morning, I'm going to call Diane and ask her to hold onto the figurines until we can go and fetch them."

"Why don't we just go out there and get them tomorrow?"

"Because tomorrow is Wednesday. We have an appointment at the spa, remember?"

Melanie inwardly groaned. The prospect of bombarding the haughty Brooke Sullivan with questions about her private life was not exactly appealing.

Liza patted her shoulder. "You can take that ghastly look off your face. You must be the only woman I know who doesn't salivate at the idea of a spa session. Just remember this is all for a good cause. Now I'm going to bed. Have a good night's sleep, and you'll feel better in the morning."

Melanie seriously doubted that, but she managed a smile as Liza left the room. "Come on, Max." She got up and held out her hand. "Come on, buddy. Time to go out outside."

Max rolled his eyes up to look at her but didn't even twitch a muscle.

She finally had to clip the leash to his collar and tug on it before he'd consent to get up and follow her outside.

The moon was so bright, for an instant she was tempted to take him down to the beach. The memory of what had happened to Ellen Croswell banished that idea. Despite the moonlight, the deserted sands looked dark and forbidding, and the image of a man with a knife was too vivid in her mind.

"You'll have to be content with the yard for now," she told him. "We'll only take you for walks in broad daylight until that demon is caught."

Max looked up at her as if he understood, and she bent down to give him a hug. Just then, however, his ears pricked up, and he uttered a low growl deep in his throat.

Chills chased down Melanie's back as she spun around, staring into the shadows. She could see nothing, and she laid her hand on Max's neck to reassure him. He growled again, and she could feel the dog's hairs bristling under her fingers.

"What's wrong, Max?" she whispered.

Her heartbeat thudded in her ears as she strained to hear whatever had alerted the dog. Max started forward, tugging on the leash with his nose in the air.

Holding him back, Melanie peered at the side of the house, where Max seemed to be focusing his attention. She could still neither see nor hear anything, and after a moment, she pulled the dog back into the house and locked the door.

After making sure all doors were locked, she secured every window, peering through each one to make sure no one was skulking around out there. She had just fastened the last one in the kitchen when a soft chuckle brought Max to a fighting stance again.

He growled and then barked, standing with all four legs braced as he glared at the basement door.

"I'm not going down there," Melanie told him. "There are no windows in the basement, and that door is the only way out. If someone is down there, they will have to stay there." With that, she walked over to the basement door, turned the key in the lock, and slipped it into her pocket. "There. Now let's go to bed."

"What in the world is all the noise about?" Liza demanded from the kitchen door. She looked half-asleep, wrapped in her robe with her hair standing in clumps all over her head.

Max whined and sat down while Melanie told her grandmother what had happened. "I don't know if he saw something or heard something or what it was that disturbed him, but he was definitely upset."

"He probably heard our ghost," Liza said, walking forward to pat the dog on the head. "Did you hear him laughing, Max?"

Melanie decided not to mention the fact she'd heard the noise again. "I'm taking his bed into my room. That way, I'll know where he is, and I won't have to worry about him wandering around the house in the dark."

"Plus, he'll be protection for you," Liza said. "Good idea."

"Not that I need protection." Melanie picked up Max's bed.

"I'm not so sure about that." Liza pulled her robe closer around her throat. "I'm glad you brought Max home. He makes me feel a little more secure, knowing he's in the house."

Melanie agreed with her, though she wasn't about to admit it. "We have to take him to the vet before the end of the week."

"Make the appointment then, and we'll take him." She patted the dog's head again. "'Night, Max. Sleep tight." She nodded at Melanie. "You too."

As if in answer, Max uttered a soft growl.

"He's just trying to adjust," Melanie said as she tugged on his collar. "Come on, buddy. It's time for bed."

After settling the dog in her room, she climbed into bed and soon fell asleep, only to wake up a short time later when a heavy thump landed by her side. A warm body snuggled into her back, and, sighing, she gave in to the idea that from now on, she would have to share her bed with a big, hairy animal that snored.

In spite of the unfamiliar intrusion, she slept well and woke up to find the dog asleep at the foot of the bed. The moment she moved, he lifted his head and stared at her, as if trying to remember who she was.

"It's okay, Max." She held out her hand. "You're home now and safe."

He gazed at her for a long moment, then yawned, stretched, and jumped off the bed.

This time, she let him out into the yard without his leash, though keeping a stern eye on him until he came limping back to the door.

Liza called Diane Henning right after breakfast while Melanie stacked the dishes in the dishwasher.

Listening to her grandmother as she talked to the dealer, Melanie could tell something was wrong. Liza's voice had risen a notch or two, and she sounded agitated. "What? When?" She listened to the voice on the phone, then said more quietly, "I see. Okay, well, thank you. No, that's okay. 'Bye."

She hung up the phone and turned to look at Melanie. "Diane's assistant sold the figurines last night, after Diane had left."

"Already? That was fast."

Liza sat down at the table again. "Yes, it was. She told me who bought them."

The odd expression on her grandmother's face quickened Melanie's pulse. "Who was it?"

"It was Brooke Sullivan."

Melanie felt her jaw drop. "Brooke? But how—? Why would—?"

Liza smiled. "It seems we'll have a lot to talk about when we see dear Brooke this morning."

Still confused, Melanie stacked the last dish in the dishwasher and closed the door. "What makes you think she'll be willing to talk to us?"

"We'll invite her to lunch. I noticed at the charity dinner that she really enjoyed her wine. There's nothing that loosens the tongue like a spot of alcohol."

Melanie shook her head. "You're devious."

Liza grinned. "I know. This is fun." Her expression changed. "Or it would be, if we didn't have a possible stalker to worry about. I think we should talk to Ben. At least tell him what's been going on and let him decide if it's something we should worry about."

"I hate to keep bugging him. After all, we don't know for sure that it's not all just a matter of coincidence. No one has been hurt, just shaken up, that's all."

"For now." Liza got up from the table. "I really don't want to wait until someone does get hurt. Better to be safe than sorry."

"All right." Melanie glanced at the clock. "I guess we'd better get going if we're going to make our appointment at the spa." She looked at Max. "You'll have to stay here, buddy, and guard the house."

The dog looked disappointed as they walked out the door without him. Melanie felt guilty for some reason, as if she were abandoning him when he needed her the most.

Reaching the driveway, Liza stopped so suddenly, Melanie almost ran into her. Seeing her grandmother staring at the ground, she followed her gaze. To her dismay, red chalk marks had been drawn across the white concrete.

"Who in the world would do that?" Melanie looked out into the street. "It must be kids. Why would they think it's okay to play in our driveway? That's going to take some scrubbing to get rid of, unless we get some heavy rain." She looked up at the bright-blue sky, where just a few fluffy white clouds floated overhead. "Doesn't look like much chance of—"

"Look at it," Liza said, sharply interrupting her.

Something in her voice jerked Melanie to attention. She stared at the chalk marks trying to make sense of them. "I can't make out what it is."

"Look at it the other way up."

Frowning, Melanie walked around the scribble and stared at it again. "It looks like . . ." Her voice trailed off as she realized what she was staring at.

"A skull and crossbones," Liza said quietly. "It's another warning. Now we have to talk to Ben."

Much as she disliked the idea, Melanie had to agree. "Well, if you want to keep our appointments at the spa, we'll have to go see him later this afternoon." She fished her phone out of her pocket and took a picture of the drawing. "There. He can see it for himself."

Liza looked for a moment as if she would argue but then shrugged. "I guess it won't hurt to wait a few hours. We don't want to be late for our massages."

Melanie paused with her hand on the door of the Suburban. "Massage?"

"Yes. I booked us Swedish massages." Liza hurried around the back of the car and disappeared inside.

Climbing into the driver's seat, Melanie said firmly, "No massage."

"But—"

"I'm not getting naked for a strange man."

"They have women masseuses."

"Or a strange woman."

"You can keep your underwear on."

Melanie sighed. "Look, why don't I cancel my appointment and wait for you in the reception area? That way we can be sure to connect with Brooke when she's finished with her appointment."

Liza looked disappointed. "I guess that makes sense, but you don't know what you're missing. A good massage can make you feel incredible."

"I'll take your word for it."

Melanie drove into Seaside with one eye on the rearview mirror but saw no sign of a small gray car behind her. She did see a couple of gray cars coming from the opposite direction, but they soon disappeared, and she reached the spa without encountering any problems.

The vision of the crude skull and crossbones drawn in the driveway stayed with her while she tried to concentrate on an article in a travel magazine. Liza's massage took over an hour, and although several people came and went through the door, Brooke wasn't one of them.

Melanie hoped that the woman had arrived early, in which case she expected to see her walk into the reception area any minute, but when Liza emerged, looking thoroughly relaxed and happy, Brooke still hadn't put in an appearance.

"She's here," Liza said when Melanie told her she hadn't seen Brooke. "She was in the next cubicle to mine. I heard her talking, but I couldn't hear what she said. She must be having a longer session than mine."

She walked over to the counter to pay her bill, and just as she dropped the receipt in her purse, Brooke sailed out of the massage room, heading for the counter.

Liza waited for her to pay her bill, then confronted her with a cheery, "Good morning, Brooke! Fancy seeing you here! I was just telling my granddaughter . . ." She nudged her head at Melanie. "You do remember Melanie, right? I was just telling her I thought I recognized that voice next to me in there."

Brooke looked puzzled. "I'm sorry, I don't—"

"The charity dinner. We sat and had a wonderful conversation while Melanie danced with your husband."

Brooke's frown cleared. "Oh, now I remember. It's Lila, isn't it?"

"Liza. We were wondering if you'd like to have lunch with us. I know this wonderful little restaurant in Gearhart that you'll simply adore. They have the best wine list in the Northwest."

Brooke looked about to refuse when Liza took her arm. "We simply won't take no for an answer, will we, Melanie?"

Melanie smiled. "Absolutely not."

"But—"

"You can ride with us," Liza said, leading a reluctant Brooke to the door. "We'll drop you off back here afterward to get your car."

Following behind them, Melanie grinned, knowing how impossible it was to oppose her grandmother once she'd made up her mind about something. Brooke Sullivan was going to have lunch with them whether she wanted to or not.

The drive to Gearhart took only a few minutes, and following her grandmother's directions, Melanie found the corner restaurant and parked outside. Inside the cafe, she felt as if she'd stepped into a Victorian parlor.

Lace curtains adorned the windows, and yellow daises, blue asters, and pink carnations thrived in window boxes. Huge photographs of people in Victorian clothes hung on the walls, and shelves of antiques decorated every room. The entrance led off into several small rooms, all barely big enough to hold two or three tables. White, lace-edged tablecloths covered the tables, and on each one, candles flickered in silver candlesticks.

Melanie was pleased to see no one else in the room when they sat down. It would certainly help to have a private conversation.

"Charming," Brooke murmured as she took a seat. "I'm not really dressed for this."

Looking at the woman's designer jeans and purple silk shirt, Melanie tried to envision what Brooke might have worn instead—something a lot more glamorous that her own jeans and cotton sweater, no doubt.

Liza waited until they had all given their order before turning to Brooke. "I heard that you bought a pair of figurines from Diane Henning yesterday."

Brooke looked a bit startled by this blunt statement. "Yes," she said cautiously. "Diane called me and told me that you had brought in some of the antiques that were left at the house when we sold it. The Morellis had bought a few of them from us, and Paul always regretted that he'd let go of the peasant pair."

"They are beautiful," Melanie said, hoping Liza's forthright manner wouldn't upset the woman.

Brooke looked at her as if seeing her for the first time. "Yes, they are. They belonged to Paul's grandmother. I don't think he meant them to be sold with the rest of the antiques. So when Diane described what you'd brought in, I decided to buy them for his birthday."

The server arrived with the wine just then and assured them their lunch would follow shortly.

"I imagine he was really surprised and happy to see them again," Liza said when the server left the room.

Brooke frowned. "I haven't given them to him yet. His birthday is next week."

Liza leaned forward and lowered her voice. "Were you aware that one of them is a fake?"

Brooke had raised her wine glass halfway to her mouth. Her hand jerked, and some of the wine spilled over the edge of the glass as she stared at Liza. "A fake? What are you talking about?"

"The peasant girl is genuine; the boy is a copy." Liza lifted her own glass. "I'm surprised Diane didn't tell you."

Brooke looked stunned. She took a gulp of her wine and set the glass down heavily on the table. "Diane wasn't there when I picked them up. Her assistant sold them to me." She shook her head. "I wondered why they were so reasonably priced. Now I know."

"I'm sorry." Liza actually looked apologetic. "I thought you might have known. I'm sure your husband must."

"I think he would have told me. This will probably be a huge shock for him."

She looked so dejected, Melanie felt sorry for her. "You don't have to tell him."

Brooke looked her straight in the eye. "He'll know. He doesn't miss anything. What I don't understand is what happened to the original and when the copy was made."

"Good questions." Liza looked around to make sure they were alone. "We think the peasant boy was the murder weapon used to kill Angela Morelli."

If Brooke had looked stunned before, she looked positively flabbergasted now. She drained her wine glass, then gazed at Liza, then Melanie, then back again to Liza. "You know who killed Angela?" she said, her voice faint with shock.

"No," Liza said, "but we think whoever did kill her used the peasant boy as a weapon and had to get rid of the evidence. We think he covered his tracks by buying a copy to replace it."

Brooke shook her head. "Unbelievable. Who would do something like that?"

Liza exchanged a glance with Melanie, then said quietly, "Brooke, I know how this is going to sound, but there's something we have to ask you. You told me that Paul was with you in Hawaii when Angela was killed, but he told Melanie that he was in New York. He couldn't have been in two places at once."

A pink flush spread over Brooke's cheeks. Before she could answer, the server arrived with the food, and the women had to wait to continue the conversation.

Melanie kept glancing at the door, praying that no one else would be seated in the same room. In those close quarters, there was no way they would be able to have a private conversation.

"Look," Brooke said the second they were alone, "I don't know why I'm telling you this, but Paul was right. He was in New York when Angela was killed. And I was in Hawaii. Alone. I told everyone that Paul was with me that week because I didn't want everyone to know we were having problems with our marriage. We—"

She broke off as the server returned with a bottle of wine and refilled Brooke's glass. After being assured there was nothing more she could get for them, she left them alone again.

Brooke looked close to tears, and Melanie felt a deep urge to go over and hug her. She managed to restrain herself but felt a stab of guilt as Liza said, "I'm sorry. This is none of our business, and we shouldn't—"

Brooke held up her hand and groped for her purse under her seat. Taking out a tissue, she blew her nose and tucked the tissue in her pocket. "It's all right. It's a relief to talk to someone. I can't talk to any of my so-called friends. They'd blab everything all over town." She managed a weak smile. "I get the feeling I can trust you to keep what I say to yourselves."

"Of course," Liza said brightly. "We wouldn't dream of tattling about your private business to anyone."

Melanie wanted to kick her. If Brooke said anything incriminating about her husband, they would have to report it to the police. She couldn't possibly make a promise like that. Holding her breath, she waited for Brooke to speak.

Chapter 15

Brooke took another sip of wine before continuing in a voice so soft, it was hard to catch her words. "We were going through a really bad patch in our marriage at the time. I knew Paul was having an affair with Angela. I could see it in their faces when they were together, and there were too many unexplained times he was absent. He kept saying he was working late, but I knew that wasn't true."

Liza must have shared Melanie's discomfort, as she covered Brooke's hand with hers. "You don't have to tell us anything else."

"Yes, I do. I need to get it off my mind, and the best way to do that is to talk to someone about it—preferably someone who isn't close to us." She took another sip of wine. "When I found out Angela was pregnant with Paul's baby, I was devastated. I thought about leaving him, but I would have given up so much, and I had worked so hard to get there, I couldn't do it. I couldn't confront him with it, because he wouldn't have believed me. I know he didn't believe Angela when she told him. He thought he was infertile."

Liza raised her eyebrows. "He *thought* he was?"

"Yes." Brooke stared down at her glass. "He wanted children. I didn't. He threatened to divorce me if I didn't agree. We had a prenup, and I would have ended up with nothing. So I took birth control pills without telling him."

Melanie had a hard time reconciling with that. "And he never found out?"

Brooke shook her head. "When I didn't get pregnant, he insisted we get checked out to find out why. Luckily for me, I answered the phone when the doctor called back with the results. I told Paul he was infertile. When the papers came, I got rid of them. He took my word for it and to this day doesn't know the truth. If he ever found out, he would never forgive me. I know that. So please, I beg you, don't ever breathe a word of this to anyone else. I can't lose him. I can't lose my home and my life here. It would destroy me."

Melanie was fast losing her sympathy for the woman. Brooke Sullivan and Angela Morelli had both deceived their husbands. Both had stayed in a bad marriage for the wrong reasons. Seeing Brooke looking so desperately unhappy, she had to wonder how all that money and privilege could possibly compensate for losing the love and respect for a cheating husband.

"I have to ask you this," Liza said, "but I'll understand if you don't want to answer. Are you quite sure your husband was in New York the night Angela Morelli was killed?"

Brooke's face seemed to turn to stone. "I have never asked him to prove it. And that's all I have to say."

Liza started to say something else, but just then, the hostess arrived with a couple of customers in tow and seated them at the next table. "Let's eat," Liza said. "The food is getting cold."

After that, the conversation turned to more mundane topics. Brooke seemed to recover from her depression and actually looked animated as she described her visits to Hawaii, Paris, and Hong Kong. "My favorite vacation is to hire a yacht in the Bahamas," she said as they were all enjoying a chocolate mousse for dessert. "I'd love to take our yacht, but it takes far too long to get there by sea. Paul wanted to do that one year. He wanted to see the Panama Canal, but the thought of being cooped up with him for that long was too dismal to even think about."

Her laugh had sounded forced, and Melanie was glad when they were finished with the meal and could leave. She'd had just about enough of Brooke Sullivan and her overprivileged lifestyle.

On the way back to the spa, Brooke once more lapsed into a quiet mood and barely spoke while Liza chattered on about their plans for the inn. When they reached her car, Brooke climbed out of the Suburban and, before closing the door, thanked them for lunch. "I had a nice time," she said, "but I think I talked too much. I hope you will remember your promise to keep my secrets."

"Of course," Liza assured. "I hope we have an opportunity to do this again."

Brooke's expression suggested that was unlikely, but she smiled and waved as she took off in her Porsche.

"Well, that was interesting," Liza said as Melanie drove back onto the coast road. "Can you imagine making your husband believe he was infertile? That should be one of the seven deadly sins."

Melanie slowed down for the curve, her gaze automatically going to her rearview mirror. The road was clear behind her, and she relaxed her tense shoulders. "If he was so certain Angela's baby wasn't his, he'd have no motive to kill her."

"I thought about that. But then Angela was convinced it was his, especially if he was the only one she'd been intimate with. She could have threatened to tell Brooke about the affair."

"I don't think he would have worried about that enough to kill her. It doesn't seem that their marriage was all that great. I'm surprised they're still together."

"So you're saying he didn't have a motive to kill Angela?"

Liza sounded disappointed, and Melanie smiled. "I didn't say that. Remember Noriko told us that Paul had business dealings with Vincent Morelli? I think Paul had much more to lose if Vincent found out his wife was sleeping with him. From what I've heard about the Morellis, they're connected to some very powerful and evil people on the East Coast."

"Oh!" Liza was silent for a moment. "How do you know all that?"

"I looked them up on the Internet. I was curious about them."

"Goodness. I had no idea."

"Do you think Brooke suspects her husband of killing Angela?"

"I think she's afraid to know the truth and is ignoring the whole thing."

"It can't be too comfortable living with a possible murderer."

"Apparently, she feels that her lifestyle makes it worth the risk."

"That's sad."

"It is." Liza tapped on the window. "Here's the turn. We're going to talk to Ben, remember?"

"I'm just going to call him. I can show him the picture of the drawing later. I'm eager to get home and see if Max survived being left alone for so long."

"I'm sure he'll survive—though I'm not so sure about the contents of the house." Liza leaned back on her seat. "Anyway, Orville will take care of him."

Melanie flung her a quick glance. "Orville?"

"Yes. I've decided to call our merry ghost Orville. We have to give him a name. We can't keep calling him 'the ghost.' It sounds so Hollywood."

Melanie wasn't sure she was comfortable with that. It made whatever was making those odd noises seem more tangible somehow, and that was really disturbing. "Why Orville?"

"I don't know. It just seems a good name for an artist. I'll have to ask Josh if he knows the name of that artist who hung himself. Until then, we'll call him Orville. It's a good name. One of the Wright brothers was named Orville."

"Then your ghost should be happy with it."

"Our ghost."

Melanie let that go. There was no point in arguing with her grandmother. Liza was convinced the ghost was real, and nothing was going to shake her from that.

Max seemed happy to see them, though his exuberance amounted to a slight wagging of his tail and a swift lick on Melanie's hand when she petted him. Reminding herself to make an appointment with a veterinarian, she took him outside to the lawn.

He stood for some time staring down at the ocean, then uttered a soft whine and turned his head to look at her.

Her heart ached for him as she asked softly, "Do you want to go for a run on the beach?"

His tail waved slowly from side to side.

Taking that for a yes, she smiled. "First, I have to make a call." She took her phone out of her pocket and checked the speed dial list for the number of the police station. The woman who answered her informed her that Ben was out on patrol and assured her she would give him a message when he returned.

"Okay, buddy, now it's your turn," she said as she led him back inside to get his leash. "I'm taking Max for a walk on the beach," she told Liza, who was dozing on an armchair in the living room. "It's time he went back down there. I think he misses it."

"He probably misses Ellen," Liza said, reaching out to pat Max's head. She gave Melanie an anxious look. "I thought you were going to call Ben."

"I called him while I was outside. He wasn't there. The assistant is going to give him a message."

Still looking worried, Liza nodded. "Be careful down there."

"It's broad daylight, and there are a ton of people out," Melanie assured her, though she had to hide a twinge of apprehension. "We'll be just fine." She looked down at the dog. "Won't we, Max?"

From somewhere out in the hallway came the sound of husky laughter.

Max barked while Melanie's nerves jumped. "First thing tomorrow, I'm calling the housing inspector."

"It costs hundreds of dollars to have an inspection."

"It will be worth it to find out what is making that noise."

"Orville won't be happy about that."

"Orville," Melanie said grimly as she led Max to the door, "can go to purgatory."

Liza's eyebrows rose in alarm. "I hope he didn't hear that." She looked up at the ceiling. "She didn't mean that, Orville. Really."

Shaking her head, Melanie led Max outside into the warm, breezy air.

The lane sloping down to the beach was a couple of blocks away. Cars were parked on either side of the road beneath the bent and twisted shore pines, and Max strained at the leash as they neared the low wall that guarded the sand.

The familiar smell of seaweed and driftwood seemed to clear Melanie's mind as she followed Max down the gritty steps to the beach. She felt nervous about letting him off the leash, but he kept tugging at it, and in the end she unclipped the hook and set him free.

At first, he just stood there and looked into the distance, and she wondered if he was looking for Ellen, but then another dog barked. Max turned his head and lurched toward the ocean.

She followed him, hoping fervently that he wouldn't plunge into the water. A couple of other dogs were frolicking along the water's edge, and Max joined in the fun. Although his movements were hampered by his injured leg, he seemed to enjoy the party and eventually limped toward her, tongue hanging out of his mouth.

It was the liveliest she'd seen him since she'd brought him home, and she patted his wet head, happy that he seemed to be recovering from his ordeal. "I know you miss her," she said softly, "but I hope one day soon you'll put the past behind you and look forward to the future in your new home. You and I together, buddy. That's how we'll get through this."

Max licked her hand, and she clipped the leash to his collar again. "Time to go home and rest that leg," she told him as she led him back toward the steps.

Trudging through the soft sand, she passed several people sunbathing on short deck chairs. One woman kneeled on a blanket, helping a little girl hunt for treasures in the sand. They were laughing together, striking a chord deep in Melanie's heart.

She wondered if her own mother had ever played with her on a sun-washed beach like this one. There was so little she remembered about her mother—just a vague, shadowy figure who vanished whenever she tried to see her more clearly.

Thinking of her mother reminded her that she hadn't heard anything more from her research with the nursing homes. She needed to work on that some more, she told herself. With the help of the Internet, one day she'd find out what had happened to her mother.

Reaching the steps, she began to climb, her mind still dwelling on the fascinating possibilities of the Internet. There were so many avenues open to her on there that would never have been possible without a computer. She could find just about anything she wanted if she knew where to look. There was so much knowledge to be found right at her fingertips.

Pausing for breath at the top of the steps, she took a last look back at the beach. Max tugged at the leash, and she turned back to the lane.

An idea hit her, and she halted, dragging Max to a surprised stop. Was it possible? Her excitement began to build as she considered the prospect. If she could track down where the figurine copy was made, she might learn the identity of Angela Morelli's killer.

Eager now to get home, she started forward, urging Max on. "Let's go, buddy. We have work to do."

Reaching the house, she found Liza still snoozing in the living room. After settling Max in his bed, Melanie hurried to her room and turned on the computer. It took only a few minutes to find several companies that crafted custom-made copies of antiques. An hour later, she still hadn't found anything that resembled the peasant figurine close enough to fool anyone.

Disappointed with yet another dead end, she wandered into the living room to find Liza awake and reading a book.

Her grandmother looked up when Melanie dropped onto a chair. "How did Max like his romp on the beach? Where is he, by the way?"

"He loved it, and he's asleep in the kitchen right now." Melanie sighed. "I've been trying to find out where the figurine copy was made, but I've had no luck so far. I was hoping it would help us find Angela's killer."

Liza closed her book and laid it beside her on the couch. "Even if you did find out who had it copied, that wouldn't necessarily mean that person was the killer. Someone could have been helping him or maybe was asked by the killer to have a copy made without being told why. We don't even know for certain that it is the murder weapon."

Leaning back on her chair, Melanie groaned. "None of this makes sense."

"Well, we can tell Ben everything we've found out so far. Has he called yet?"

Melanie shook her head. "He's probably busy, or maybe the assistant forgot to give him the message."

"He'll probably call tomorrow. Maybe his detective can make sense of everything."

"If they ever finish investigating the case." Melanie got up. "I'm beginning to think that room will be sealed off forever."

"I sincerely hope not." Liza's frown made her look tired. "We can't hold out much longer."

Feeling depressed now, Melanie headed for the door. "I'm going to hose off the driveway and get rid of that skull and crossbones."

"Don't you want Ben to see it first?"

"I have a picture of it. That should be enough. I'll cook dinner when I get back. Maybe a glass of wine will help us feel better."

"I think the only thing that will make us feel better is if we open up the inn now, even with that room sealed off."

Feeling utterly miserable, Melanie nodded. "I guess that's what we'll have to do."

They were both quiet during dinner, and even the glass of wine failed to lift Melanie's spirits. Soon after Liza stacked the dishes in the dishwasher, she announced she was going to bed.

Hoping to get her mind off their problems, Melanie decided to watch some TV before following her. She was engrossed in an episode of her favorite cop show with Max at her feet when Liza wandered into the living room wearing her bathrobe.

"Have you seen my nightgown?" she asked when Melanie looked up at her. "I always put it under my pillow, but it's not there."

Melanie studied her for a moment. "Did you put it in the wash?"

"No, of course not. It was clean yesterday. I've only worn it one night."

"You had a lot on your mind this morning, thinking about our meeting with Brooke. You might have dropped it in the wash without thinking."

Liza lifted her chin. "I might be getting on in years, but I'm not senile. Not yet, anyway."

Melanie smiled. "I'm thirty-two, and I do absent-minded things when I'm stressed out about something. Let's go look in the hamper, just to satisfy my inquiring mind."

Without a word, Liza turned around and headed for the bathroom. Lifting the lid of the hamper, she said stiffly, "See? It's not there. I told you I hadn't put it in there."

Melanie reached out and hugged her. "I just wanted to make sure. It has to be somewhere. I'll get you a clean one, and we'll look for it tomorrow."

"I can get a clean one. I just don't understand what happened to the other one."

As if in answer to her, a hollow laugh made them both jump. Max barked and loped out into the hallway. The laughter seemed to linger, echoing in the rooms upstairs. Max lunged for the stairs, but Melanie caught hold of his collar, holding him back.

Peering up the steps, Liza murmured, "I think it's coming from up there."

"It's all over the house." Melanie struggled to hold Max still while he kept growling deep in his throat. "I thought it was in the basement, but you're right, that is definitely coming from upstairs."

Before she finished her sentence, the laughter stopped as suddenly as it had begun. Max, however, was still straining to get upstairs.

"I'd better get him into my room." Melanie tugged on his collar. "Come on, buddy. Time for you to go to bed."

"It's time for me, as well." Liza gave a last glance up the stairs. "Though I'm not sure I can get to sleep now."

"I'll bring you a mug of warm milk. That always does it for me." Melanie started down the hallway, tugging a protesting Max along with her. "Just as soon as I get this animal settled."

She heard Liza close her bedroom door as she opened her own. Stepping inside the room, she let go of Max's collar. "Stay here. I'll be back soon."

Max looked up at her with mournful eyes.

Feeling guilty, she patted his head. "It's okay, buddy. I know you were just trying to protect us. You're a good boy."

Max answered with a wag of his tail.

She was about to turn around when she caught sight of something lying on the floor by her bed. Frowning, she picked it up and uttered a gasp of surprise when she recognized Liza's blue nightgown.

"Wait there," she told Max, then hurried from the room.

Tapping on Liza's door, she called out, "Are you in bed yet?"

Liza's muffled voice answered her. "No, come on in. That was quick."

Melanie opened the door and walked in, holding up the nightgown. "I haven't got the milk yet. I think this is yours."

Liza eyes widened as she gazed at her nightgown. "Where did you find it?"

"Lying on my bedroom floor." She laid the nightgown on the bed.

"What on earth?" Liza picked up the gown and examined it. "How in the world did it get there?"

From down the hallway, the ghostly laughter echoed once more.

Melanie felt a cold chill down her back as Liza stared at her. "Orville," she whispered. "He must have put it there."

Melanie shivered. "Ghosts can't move things."

"Oh, yes they can. There have been all kinds of reports from people who have had things moved around in their house with no other explanation." Liza stared at the door. "I just didn't think Orville was capable of that."

Melanie struggled to bring things back to normal. "It must have been Max. He could have taken your nightgown and dragged it into my room. He thinks it's his room, so that would make sense."

"There's just one problem with that. How did he open the door? I always keep it closed."

"You could have left it open without realizing it. With everything on our minds lately . . ."

"It was closed when I came to bed. Do you think Max would stop to close the door after he took my nightgown?"

Melanie felt an urge to sit down and sank onto the side of the bed. "Why? Why would a ghost take your nightgown out of your room and leave it in mine?" Even as she asked the question, she was aware of how ridiculous it sounded.

Liza shook her head. "I don't know. Maybe he was trying to prove to you that he does exist. He must know you don't believe in him."

"Well, there are better ways to convince me." Melanie got up from the bed. "I'm going to get your milk now, then I'm going to do some research online."

"About ghosts?"

"About a missing mother." She left the room and walked down to the kitchen, every nerve twitching. The house seemed unusually cold, and she checked the thermostat. It showed a comfortable seventy-two degrees.

Trying to shake off the creepy feeling that she wasn't alone, she hurriedly poured milk into a mug and set it in the microwave. Seconds later, she carried the mug down to Liza's bedroom and once more tapped on the door.

Hearing no answer, she carefully opened the door and peeked in. Liza lay in bed with her eyes closed, and Melanie crept over and set the mug down on the bedside table. After assuring herself that her grandmother was still breathing, she crept out again and gently closed the door.

Max greeted her with a furious wagging of his tail and several licks on her hand when she returned to the room. After playing tug-of-war with him with one of his toys for a while, she settled him on the bed and sat down at the computer.

As she expected, there were still no replies to her queries from nursing homes. She had to think of another angle. She tried to remember things Liza had told her about her mother. She had met Melanie's father in high school. They had gone to the same college, and after graduating, Janice had taught at a grade school until she became pregnant with Melanie. She'd given up her job, intending to be a full-time mother. She was thinking of going back to teaching when Melanie's father was diagnosed with terminal cancer. Janice stayed home to take care of him, and in a few short weeks he died, leaving her to raise their little daughter alone.

Melanie's heart ached for her mother. She could only imagine the agony she must have gone through. Even so, a question surfaced—one that had tortured her for years. Had something happened to Janice to prevent her from coming home to her little girl, or had she stayed away by choice?

Staring at her computer, Melanie finally had to accept the truth. Until now, she'd managed to convince herself that she was conducting the search for her mother for Liza's sake. She'd assured herself over and over again that it was simply curiosity that had kept her focused on the project—that and the desire to reunite her grandmother with her daughter.

But it went deeper than that, and it was time she acknowledged it. It was the doubt, the heartbreaking possibility that kept her at her computer in such a frustrating search. She needed to know. Had her mother abandoned her?

If so, someone somewhere must know where she was. Tapping her fingers on the keys, Melanie frowned.

Her mother had been a grade school teacher. If she was still alive, it was possible she was still teaching somewhere. Without much hope, Melanie started the mammoth task of researching grade schools in England.

Her concentration kept wavering, and she found herself straining to hear the sound of laughter. The mystery of Liza's nightgown kept taunting her. Part of her wanted to convince herself that Max had taken the nightgown, while another part kept telling her that Max couldn't have opened or shut the bedroom door. It just didn't make sense.

Giving up on her research, she crawled into bed, comforted by Max's warm body lying next to her. Visions of Liza's nightgown kept drifting into her mind. Another thought started nagging at her. Another nightgown. Something her mind was trying to tell her.

She snapped her eyes open as the thought clarified. Sitting up in bed, she tried to concentrate. Max stirred and uttered a soft groan of protest.

She had to make sure. Quietly, she slipped out of bed. "Wait there," she whispered to Max as she slipped into her robe and left the room, closing the door behind her.

It only took a moment to reach the kitchen and open the bottom drawer beneath the counter. Finding the newspaper cuttings she'd saved, she read again the articles about finding the skeleton. With mounting excitement, she carried the clippings back to her room and turned on her computer. Moments later, she found what she was looking for—the TV news reports of the murder.

After viewing them, she leaned back in her chair and raised a triumphant fist in the air. "Gotcha!" she said out loud.

Max whined.

"I did it!" she told him, forgetting in her excitement to keep her voice down. "I solved the murder!"

Chapter 16

Max whined again, and wary of waking Liza, Melanie hushed him with a warning finger. She badly wanted to tell her grandmother what she'd discovered, but it could wait until morning. Liza needed her rest.

She lay in bed, staring at the shadowed ceiling, going over and over in her mind everything that had happened in the past few days—her and Liza's conversations with Noriko, Sharon, Josh, Paul, and Brooke. The "accidents" that had come close to harming her. The skull and crossbones drawn in the driveway. It all made sense now. First thing tomorrow, she would call Ben and tell him everything.

She finally dozed off, only to dream of being chased in the dark by a shadowy creature down a long alleyway. The smell of smoke made her cough. Something was making a horrible whining noise, and there was a dog barking somewhere close by. Really close.

She woke up with a start. An alarm was beeping in the hallway, and Max was at the door, his urgent barking warning her that something was wrong. She scrambled out of bed, grabbed her robe, and flew across the room to open the door.

Max dashed out into the hallway, still barking. Liza's door opened down the hallway, and her sleepy voice demanded, "What the blazes is going on?" The question ended in a cough as she clutched her throat. "Is that smoke?"

"We have to get out of here. Now!" Melanie grabbed her grandmother's arm and gave her a little push. "Get out. I'll be right there." Without waiting for an answer, she rushed back into her room and grabbed her cell phone. Racing back out into the hallway, she almost fell over Max, who was running frantically back and forth between her and the open front door.

Together they flew outside, where Liza stood shivering on the porch. "It's in the garage," she said, pointing at the doors from which smoke poured into the night. "The rest of our inventory is going up in flames."

Melanie thumbed 9-1-1 and gasped out her address to the dispatcher. Moments later, the distant sound of a siren assured them the fire department was on the way. Flames were already licking through the roof of the garage, and Melanie pulled her grandmother off the porch and down the driveway.

Neighbors were beginning to gather in the street outside, and by the time the fire engine arrived, there was a small crowd in front of the inn.

"We're going to lose everything," Liza said, her voice cracking. "After everything we've gone through, we're going to lose it all."

Melanie fought back tears as she hugged her grandmother. "We're insured. We'll rebuild."

"I'm not sure I want to now," Liza said as she wiped away her own tears. "Maybe someone is trying to tell us something."

"Are you two okay?"

At the sound of the deep voice behind her, Melanie swung around. Officer Ben Carter stood gazing down at her, his face creased with worry.

"We're fine." She gave him a wobbly smile. "At least physically. We're not doing so good emotionally."

"I'm sorry." He looked over her shoulder. "Is that your dog?"

Melanie followed his gaze, sick with guilt that she'd forgotten Max. The dog sat by a tree, and she could see him trembling in the glare of the fire engine's headlights. She called out to him, but he just sat looking at her, as if afraid to move.

"I'll be right back," she told Ben, then hurried over to Max. Putting her arms around him, she spoke soothingly in his ear. "It's all right, buddy. You were a good boy. You woke us up. Good dog."

He licked her cheek, and she hugged his furry body. "You've been through so much," she whispered, "and now this. It looks like we'll all have to find a new home now."

"I just talked to the fire chief," Ben said, appearing from behind her again. "He thinks he can save the house, though there will probably be some smoke damage. It looks like they're getting it under control."

She nodded, afraid to trust herself to speak.

"Come and sit in my car." Ben took hold of her arm. "Your grandmother's waiting in there for you."

Max growled, and Melanie laid a hand on his head. "It's okay, buddy. He's a friend."

Ben led them both back to the car and graciously allowed Max to jump into the front seat. Liza sat in the back, looking frail and a little scared.

Melanie climbed in beside her and smiled up at Ben, who stood holding the door. "Thank you."

He nodded. "I'll be back in a while. Hang in there." He closed the door and disappeared behind the crowd of onlookers.

"It's amazing how many people enjoy watching someone else's disaster," Liza said, gazing out the window.

"I'm sure they're all concerned for us." Melanie followed her gaze. "They are our neighbors, after all."

Just then, a woman broke away from the group and hurried over to the car. She tapped on the window, and Melanie opened her door.

"I'm Paula Richards," she said, holding out her hand. "We're all so sorry about this."

Melanie took her hand and shook it. "Thank you. I'm Melanie West, and this is my grandmother, Elizabeth Harris."

"Yes, of course I know who you are. You two are quite the celebrities in town." She leaned in and offered her hand to Liza. "I just want you to know that several of us are offering a place for you both to stay . . ." She paused and glanced warily at Max. "And your dog, of course, until you get settled again."

Melanie had to swallow past the lump in her throat. "That's incredibly kind of you. We both appreciate that very much, but I think we'll be all right. Officer Carter said they could probably save the house, so I think we can manage."

"Ah, you've met Ben." The woman smiled. "He's a good man. Well, let us know if you need somewhere. I live down the street at 742 Cedar Lane. If you need anything at all, just let us know." She smiled, nodded, and sped off back to the crowd.

"That was so nice of her," Melanie murmured.

Liza answered her, but Melanie's attention was caught by a face in the crowd. The petite woman detached herself from the rest of the onlookers and started walking quickly down the street. "I need to talk to Ben," Melanie said, her hand on the door handle.

"He must have been worried about us," Liza said as Melanie opened the door. "He told me he heard about the fire and recognized the address. He came right over here to see if we were okay."

"That's nice, but right now I have to speak to him about something else."

She started to close the door, but Liza called out, "Wait! Aren't you going to tell me?"

"When I get back." The roar of an engine lifted Melanie's head just as a small gray car shot past them. She shut the car door and hurried over to where a couple of firemen stood talking to the police officer.

Ben looked surprised to see her, but his expression changed when she said urgently, "I need to talk to you. Now."

He moved away from the curious firefighters and started leading her back to the car. "What's up?"

"I think I know who did this." She waved a hand at the smoldering garage. "She killed Angela Morelli. It was Noriko Chen, and right now she's getting away."

Even in the dim light, she could see the shock and doubt on Ben's face. "The nurse? What makes you think she killed

Vincent's wife?" He looked back at the house. "Or set fire to your garage?"

"I'll tell you later. Right now, you have to arrest her and stop her getting away." She could hear the desperation in her voice and made an effort to calm down. "She went that way." Her hand shook as she pointed in the direction the car had gone.

Ben put a warm hand on her shoulder. "Okay, let's slow down a little. I can't just go and arrest someone without good cause."

"You have good cause. She tried to burn down our house. She killed Angela Morelli. She tried to kill me—"

"Whoa, wait a minute. We need to talk about this." He opened the door. "Get in."

"But Noriko! She—"

"If there's anything in your story that holds up, we can question her later. Now get in."

There was no ignoring the order, and Melanie obediently scrambled in and sat down.

"Are you going to tell me what's going on," Liza demanded, "or do I have to drag it out of you?"

Before Melanie could answer, the front door opened, and Ben climbed into the driver's seat. Max growled, sniffed at the hand Ben offered him, and licked it.

"Good boy," Ben said, then twisted around in his seat to look at Melanie. "Okay, let's hear it."

For some reason, Melanie felt tongue-tied. Sitting in the close confines of a car with Ben Carter gazing into her eyes was an unsettling experience. Although her robe covered her sleep shorts and tank top, she felt underdressed and vulnerable. Thanks heavens for the presence of her impatient grandmother.

"Go on, tell us," Liza said, giving her a hefty nudge in the arm.

Brought back to earth with a jolt, Melanie cleared her throat. "Uh . . . well, it was the nightgown."

Ben raised his eyebrows.

"My nightgown?" Liza's voice rose in disbelief. "Whatever are you talking about?"

Melanie decided it was easier to talk to Liza than keep looking at Ben. "Yes, your nightgown. After we found it in my room, I kept thinking about it, and it triggered a memory. Do you remember talking to Noriko about the murder, when she said she thought at first a cab driver rang the doorbell that night?"

Liza frowned. "Yes, I remember that, but what does that tell us?"

"It's what she said after that." Excited now, Melanie turned back to Ben. "Noriko said that Angela was wearing her nightgown when she died, so whoever rang the doorbell must have killed her after she'd gone to bed."

Ben looked skeptical. "Okay," he said, drawing out the word as if struggling to understand.

"There was never any mention of Angela's nightgown in the newspaper reports."

Liza stirred impatiently at her side. "I still don't see what . . . oh!"

"When I read the reports," Melanie said, "I wondered at the time why Josh hadn't mentioned the nightgown. It seemed like such an interesting detail about the discovery of the skeleton."

Liza nodded. "I didn't even notice that. I wonder why he didn't mention it."

"It wasn't in the police report," Ben said. "We don't release every piece of information."

"Anyway," Melanie went on, "just to make sure, this evening I watched the news report again online and checked every report written about the murder. Nowhere does anyone mention the nightgown."

"So you're saying," Liza said slowly, "that the only way Noriko could have known about the nightgown was if she'd killed Angela."

"How else would she know Angela was wearing it when she died? She said Angela was wearing a coat when she saw her packing a suitcase. She said she went to bed after that, and in the morning Angela was gone."

"But what about the visitor who rang the doorbell?"

"I don't think there was a doorbell ringing that night. I believe Noriko made it up to make it look like someone came into the house and killed Angela." Melanie turned back to Ben. "Someone has been stalking me for the past few days. Twice I nearly got hit by a gray car, and a gray car almost ran us off the road. I just saw Noriko driving away in a gray car. I remember now seeing one in the parking lot outside the nursing home where she works. We parked right next to it."

"How in the world did you remember that?" Liza shook her head. "I barely remember going there."

"I came close to hitting it when we parked," Melanie said, leaning back on her seat. "I took a good look at it when we got out, just to be sure I hadn't bumped it. I remember thinking at the time that it looked like Gary's car."

Ben lifted his head. "Gary?"

"Her ex," Liza said. "A real jerk."

"Granny!"

"I keep telling you not to call me Granny."

"Okay, ladies. Simmer down." Ben rubbed his chin. "Tell me more about this car running you down."

"Well, the first time it was Gary's car when I was crossing the street, but after that I think it was Noriko's car. They look alike. It was in the parking lot of Martin's grocery store, and if it hadn't been for a very nice young guy, I wouldn't be here talking to you now. He said it came right at me, and he shoved me out of the way." She paused, shuddering as she visualized the scene again. "He saved my life."

"Did you see the driver?"

"No, I didn't even see the car that clearly. The people who helped me up afterward told me about it."

"Did anyone see the driver?"

"I don't think so. No one mentioned her."

"So you don't really know if it was your ex, Noriko Chen, or someone else."

Melanie frowned. "No, but—"

"Did you see the driver of the car tonight?"

"No, but I saw Noriko walking away from the house just now, then the car went by and . . ."

"Are you positive it was Noriko Chen you saw? It's hard to see clearly in the dark."

"I'm sure it was her." Even she could hear the uncertainty in her voice.

"What kind of car does your ex-husband drive?" Ben pulled a cell phone from his pocket.

Melanie was beginning to feel as if she were on trial. "A gray Honda Civic."

"You said someone tried to run you off the road."

"Yes, on the way back from Warrenton. It came really close to us as it passed us."

"And it was a small gray car?"

"Yes."

"Those Hondas are pretty common, and there are several look-alikes. Could you tell the make of the car that passed you that day?"

Melanie slumped back on her seat. "No, I couldn't."

"And you didn't see the driver."

"It went by too fast."

Ben looked at Liza. "How about you? Did you see the driver?"

Liza sounded defensive. "The car had tinted windows. I couldn't see that clearly."

Ben thumbed something into his phone.

"Look," Melanie said, trying not to sound too irritated, "I know we can't prove anything, but how did Noriko know about the nightgown? Why was she standing outside our house, watching it burn down, when she lives in Tillamook?"

"And what about the skull and crossbones drawn on the driveway?" Liza chimed in.

Ben frowned. "The what?"

"Skull and crossbones," Melanie repeated. She clicked on her cell phone and found the picture. Holding it out to him, she added, "Someone drew a skull and crossbones on our driveway. We believe it was a warning."

Ben peered at the picture. "That could have been kids. They love to chalk all over the sidewalks."

Melanie felt like screaming at him.

"I guess I could talk to Detective Dutton and see if he wants to bring in Ms. Chen for questioning," Ben added, saving Melanie from exploding with frustration. "Meanwhile, I'll take you two to a hotel." He glanced at Max. "I know one that takes dogs. The fire chief doesn't want anyone in the house until they've determined the cause of the fire."

"How long will that take?" Liza asked, sounding disgusted.

"It shouldn't be too long. You wouldn't want to stay in there anyway. It doesn't smell too fresh right now."

"I don't have my purse," Melanie said, glancing at the house. "We just dashed out of there without stopping to pick anything up."

"And we need clothes and my meds," Liza added.

"I'll check with the fire chief and see if it's safe for you to go in and get what you need." Ben opened the car door. "Wait here until I get back."

Melanie waited until he was striding away from the car before muttering, "He didn't believe one word I told him."

"He's a police officer," Liza said, patting her arm. "He has to be careful about jumping to conclusions. Besides, technically this case is on hold until they find the person who stabbed Ellen Croswell."

Melanie gestured at the house. "I'd say that this is good cause to reopen our case, wouldn't you?"

Ben returned a short while later and opened the door on Melanie's side. "They have the fire under control. You can go in and get what you need. The guys will lock up when they leave.

The garage and its contents are pretty much gone. There's been some damage to the living room and dining room and a couple of bedrooms upstairs, but the kitchen seems okay. We won't know the full extent of the damage until the smoke clears."

"You're sure we can't sleep in there?" Liza asked.

"Positive." Ben glanced across the street to where the group of neighbors had begun to disperse. "You'll be safer in a hotel."

Melanie wasn't sure if he meant safer from the fire or if he believed she might not be entirely paranoid about being stalked. Right then, all she wanted to do was get some sleep. Liza looked shaky as she walked around the back of the car, and Melanie took her arm. "Why don't you stay here, and I'll get what you need?"

"No, I want to get dressed and pick up my meds." She squeezed Melanie's hand. "I'm fine. Just tired."

Max barked just then, making Melanie jump. She looked up at Ben. "I'll take my car to the hotel. Just tell me where it is."

Ben looked as if he would argue, but after a moment's pause, he shrugged. "Okay. You can follow me out there. I just want to be sure you get there okay." He opened the door and took hold of Max's collar. "Come on, big guy. You can get in your own car."

Max jumped out, wagging his tail.

"My keys are in my purse," Melanie said, giving Max a pat on the head. "I'll be right back."

Inside the house, the smell of smoke and chemicals was overpowering. "I guess Ben was right," Liza said, holding her nose. "We couldn't have slept here tonight. It smells like scorched cow dung."

"Let's just get dressed, grab a few things, and get out of here." Melanie headed to her room, leaving her grandmother to collect her own belongings. It took only a few minutes for her to pull on jeans and a sweater and grab a change of clothes and her laptop.

Liza was coming out of the bathroom when Melanie got there. "I've got my meds, makeup, and hair spray." She held up a toiletry bag. "I guess I don't need anything else. It's not like I'm going to bump into the president or Engelbert."

"The hotel will probably have whatever else we need." Worried to see her grandmother looking so tired, she hugged her. "Are you okay?"

"I will be if we can get some sleep tonight." Liza gestured down the hall, where a couple of burly firefighters in heavy gear were checking out the walls. "Do you want to see the damage?"

Melanie shivered. "Not tonight. At least the house is still standing. The insurance should cover the repairs. I'll call them first thing in the morning."

Liza gave her a weary smile. "I guess we'll get the renovations done after all."

Melanie grinned. "I can think of better ways to do it, but whatever works is good enough for me."

"Me too." Liza looked over her shoulder. "Now let's get go get some sleep."

Ben led them to the hotel, then left, promising to get back to them as soon as he had any news. They opted to share a room with two queen-sized beds, one of which Max immediately claimed by leaping onto the middle of it and sprawling out with a contented sigh.

They wasted no time in getting to bed, and Melanie was on the point of dozing off when she heard Liza murmur something.

Turning over to face her grandmother's bed, Melanie asked sharply, "Are you okay?"

"Yes, I was just thinking about Orville."

Melanie had to think for a moment. "Oh, the ghost. What about him?"

"I think he was leaving us clues."

"Clues?"

"Yes. Remember you said you saw lips drawn in lipstick on the mirror?"

Melanie struggled to clear her mind. "Yes, but you put it there."

"No, I didn't. It was Orville, and I think he was trying to tell us that the killer was a woman."

Melanie shook her head. "Are you serious?"

"Absolutely. And what about my glasses that we found on the mantelpiece? That must have been Orville, too. Trying to tell us about the figurines. What's more, I think he put my nightgown in your room so that you'd connect it to Noriko. That was probably her room when she lived there."

Melanie didn't want to think about that. Right then, she desperately needed to go to sleep. "Okay, if you say so," she said, then turned over again.

Despite all the trauma of the night, she slept well and woke up to hear loud snoring and see sunshine streaming through the slits in the blinds. It took her a moment to remember where she was, and then the memories came pouring back.

Glancing at the clock on the bedside table, she sat up. It was almost nine. The snoring was coming from Max at the foot of her bed, and she nudged him with her toe. He woke up with a grunt, then stretched, yawned, and slowly sat up.

Liza was facing the other way in her bed, and Melanie squinted at her. She couldn't tell if her grandmother was breathing, and, concerned now, she slid out of bed and poked Liza's shoulder.

To her immense relief, Liza mumbled something and rolled over onto her back. "What are you doing in here?"

Melanie smiled. "I slept here, remember? We're in a hotel."

Liza blinked. "Oh, right." She struggled to sit up. "I'm starving. Does this place have room service?"

An hour later, they had showered and dressed and were enjoying a breakfast of cereal, fruit, and eggs Benedict. Their waiter had also obliged with a small bowl of pet food for Max, who gobbled it up and then sat waiting for them to drop something on the floor while they ate.

As soon as Melanie had stacked the dishes on the trolley and wheeled it outside, she called the insurance company. "They want us to take pics of the damage," she said when she clicked off her phone. "We should go back there this morning and get them."

"You might want to call Ben and let him know," Liza said. "I wonder if they've found out what caused the fire."

"I'll ask him." Melanie dialed the police station. The woman who answered told her that Ben was not at the station but was expected to return shortly. She promised to give him a message, and Melanie hung up.

"He's not there," she told Liza. "I just hope he gets the message this time. We'll go ahead and take the pictures, and we'll talk to him later. Max has an appointment with a vet this afternoon. We can take him after lunch."

Minutes later, they arrived back at the inn. In the daylight, the damage looked formidable. The blackened walls next to the garage were a stark contrast to the rest of the house. The fire had burned a hole in the roof, and tiles were scattered all over the lawn. Parked in the driveway, Melanie felt sick, wondering what it would take to restore the place to its former glory.

"It looks so sad," Liza said as she climbed out of the car. "I'm almost afraid to go inside and look at it. Poor Orville must be desolate."

Melanie rolled her eyes. Only her grandmother would be worrying about a ghost while looking at the ruins of her livelihood. "Look at the porch. It's covered in soot. After all the work we did painting it. How depressing. Let's just get the pics and get it over with."

Leaving Max in the car, she walked up the steps and unlocked the front door, wrinkling her nose at the acrid smell of smoke.

"We need some air fresheners," Liza said as she followed Melanie down the hallway. "Preferably something exotic, like Hawaiian orchids."

Walking into the living room, Melanie groaned. Smoke and water stains covered the walls, and a lump of plaster hung down from the ceiling. Dark stains dotted the carpet as well as the couch and armchairs.

"This will all have to be replaced." Liza loudly cleared her throat. "Thank goodness we hadn't finished stripping the wallpaper and hadn't painted yet. That would have been a colossal waste of time." She walked over to the bookshelves. "Some of these books are ruined. What a shame."

Melanie followed her and put an arm around her shoulders. "The insurance agent assured me they would take care of everything. We'll have to make a list of everything that was lost and then get estimates for the repairs. They'll be sending an adjustor out to look at all this," she waved a hand at the room, "and hopefully it will be settled and the repairs done before the end of summer."

Liza looked mournful. "Meanwhile, we have to survive somehow."

"I thought about that." Melanie took out her cell phone and started snapping pictures. "I can get a job while we're waiting. The insurance will pay for the hotel for now, but we should be able to stay here while the repairs are being done. Our rooms and the kitchen are okay, though it might be a bit noisy. We can handle that. Right?"

Liza nodded, though she didn't look too happy.

The dining room didn't look quite as bad when Melanie walked in there moments later, and she took the pictures she needed, while Liza headed for her room to pick up more clothes.

After taking photos in the kitchen, Melanie tapped on Liza's door. "I'm just going upstairs to take pics up there," she called out. "I'll be back in a minute." Without waiting for an answer, she headed for the stairs.

As she reached the upstairs hallway, she could hear Max barking. She'd left the car parked in the shade with the windows halfway down, but now she wondered if it might be getting too warm for him.

It should only take her a couple of minutes to take the pictures, she assured herself as she hurried into the bedroom at the end of the hall.

What she saw when she opened the door horrified her. A gaping hole in the sloping ceiling was open to the sky, and wallpaper hung off the walls in strips. The carpet squelched as she walked across it, and a broken lamp and ornaments were scattered all over.

Mentally promising herself she would have a tarpaulin put over the roof, she took the pictures, shuddering at the sight of so much chaos. The insurance company would have a hefty bill by the time it was all restored.

The second bedroom was only slightly better. Melanie worked quickly, as Max was still barking, and she was beginning to worry about him.

The yellow tape was still across the door to the bedroom where Angela's remains had been found. Melanie hesitated for a moment, then opened the door and ducked underneath. The insurance agent was adamant that she take pictures of the whole house. Detective Dutton would just have to deal with it.

Standing in the middle of the room, she aimed her phone at the walls. There didn't appear to be any damage anywhere, and she clicked off the camera and turned to leave.

Catching a glimpse of a shadow in the doorway, she thought she was imagining things, but then the figure moved and walked into the room.

"I warned you, but you wouldn't listen," Noriko Chen said. "Now I have to do something I hoped wouldn't be necessary."

Chapter 17

Shock held Melanie rooted to the spot as she stared at Noriko's face. The nurse's eyes glittered with spite, and dark-red splotches stained her cheeks. "You couldn't keep your nose out of my business," she muttered, "and now you'll pay the price."

Staring at the wicked-looking knife in Noriko's hands, Melanie's knees buckled as she slowly backed away. Outside in the car, Max's barking sounded frantic. Was he just wanting out, or did he know she was in danger?

Another thought struck her, filling her with dread. "My grandmother. Did you . . . ?"

"She's lying comfortably on her bed." Noriko's smile was even more terrifying than her scowl. "She's tied up for now." She laughed—an evil sound that chilled Melanie's bones.

Noticing the plastic hose in Noriko's other hand, Melanie edged another step backward. She had to play for time. With any luck, Max's barking would raise concern from someone. She sent up a silent prayer. "I don't know why you are doing this, Noriko. We have no reason to hurt you."

"You sent the police to my house. They are looking for me and it's all your fault. They would never have opened up the case again if it hadn't been for you and your interfering grandmother."

"I don't know why they are looking for you—"

"Yes, you do!" Noriko took a step forward, sending a stab of fear through Melanie. "Somehow you found out I killed Angela Morelli and you told the police. No one was ever supposed to find her. I closed that door in the wall and left her there to rot." She waved the knife at the wall. "Then you had to go digging around in here until you found her."

"We found her by accident," Melanie said, backing up another step. "We were going to strip the wallpaper—"

"I don't care how you found her!" Noriko yelled. "You told the police. And now they are looking for me."

Melanie took a deep breath and calmed her voice. "I'm sorry Angela gave you so much trouble. It must have been hard working for her."

"I didn't work for her. I worked for Vincent. He was a good man, and she was . . ." Noriko's voice broke, and she took a moment to control it. "She had everything a woman could want, and she was throwing it all away. She was going to leave him—to abandon him when he needed her the most. He didn't deserve that. I begged her to stay. She said terrible things to me. She accused me of—" Once more, she broke off, struggling for control.

Melanie backed up again and felt the hard edge of the dresser behind her. She could go no farther.

"I lost my temper," Noriko said. "I took one of the figurines from the fireplace and hit her with it. I didn't mean to kill her."

Her voice got really quiet. "I didn't mean to kill anyone. That lady with the dog. I thought it was you. I was just trying to frighten her, but then the dog attacked me, and I had to use the knife, and somehow she got in the way."

Stunned, Melanie grabbed the dresser behind her for support. "You killed Ellen Croswell?"

Noriko's voice rose again as she took a step forward. "I didn't mean to. It was all your fault. You wouldn't give up. I kept trying to frighten you so you'd let go of it, but you took no notice. And now the police are looking for me. So I have to burn down the house. Then all the evidence will be gone, and you and your grandmother will be gone, too." She held up the knife and took another step forward.

There was no more time for thought. Springing toward Noriko with her arms outstretched and locked, Melanie hit her hard, one hand on the shoulder and the other deflecting the arm holding the knife. Noriko stumbled backward, and Melanie leapt past the nurse, heading for the door just as a burly figure filled the doorway.

Her momentum took her into his arms, and, looking up into Ben's face, she thought she'd never seen anything so beautiful in all her life.

He held her for a second, then let her go and walked into the center of the room where Noriko sat slumped on the floor, all the fight taken out of her. "I heard everything from the hallway. Noriko Chen, you are under arrest for the murders of Angela Morelli and Ellen Croswell. You have the right to remain silent . . ."

Melanie didn't wait to hear any more. She sped down the stairs and down the hall to Liza's room. Flinging open the door, she rushed inside and caught her breath at the sight of her grandmother lying helpless on her bed, her hands and feet bound with masking tape.

"Thank God you're okay," Liza said as Melanie tugged at the tape. "I thought that witch was going to burn us down with the house. That's not the way I want to go out."

"Me neither." Melanie's hands shook as she pulled off the tape from Liza's hands. "Did she hurt you?"

"Nothing I can't deal with." Liza sat up and rubbed her wrists. "Is Ben up there with her? Did she attack you?"

Melanie pulled the last of the tape from Liza's ankles. "She didn't get the chance. Ben's arresting her right now."

"I can't tell you how happy I was to see him poke his head around the door." Liza worked her legs around to the edge of the bed. "When he pulled the tape off my mouth, I told him you were upstairs and that Noriko had gone after you. He didn't wait to hear any more. He took off like a bullet out of a gun."

"His timing was perfect." Remembering those brief moments in his arms, Melanie smiled.

A loud clattering on the stairs told her that Ben was escorting his prisoner to his car. Max was still barking, and she hurried to the door. "I'm going to get Max out of the car. I'll be right back."

"No rush. I'm going to make a cup of tea." Liza stood up, steadying herself with one hand on the bedside table. "A Brit's cure for everything."

"I'll join you as soon as I get Max." Melanie ran down the hallway and out of the front door.

Ben's car was parked out on the street. He was closing the door as Melanie ran out into the driveway.

She pulled open the back door of the Suburban, and Max leapt at her, tail wagging, trying to lick her face. "I'm okay, buddy," she said, giving him a hug and receiving a wet tongue on her cheek in return.

She held him with one hand on his collar as Ben walked toward her. "Looks like you were right," he said when he reached her. "You solved two murders. You might want to reconsider your occupation."

She laughed, warmed by the approval in his eyes. "Only one, actually. I didn't know Noriko had killed Ellen Croswell until she told me."

"Neither did we. Thanks to you, we can close both cases."

"You heard what she said?"

"The last part of it. We'll get the rest out of her."

"I'm glad to be of help. How did you know Noriko was here?"

"I didn't." He glanced back at his car. "I got your message that you were here taking photos, so I drove by to make sure that everything was okay. Parts of the house are not safe to be around, so you need to be careful."

"I've got all the evidence I need of the damage."

"Good. Anyway, Max was barking up a storm in the car, and I just got the feeling that something was wrong, so I went in to take a look. I couldn't see you anywhere, so I opened the doors to the rooms down the hallway, and that's when I found your grandmother tied up on the bed." He frowned. "Is she okay? She was pretty frantic about you being in danger upstairs. I didn't wait to see if she was hurt."

"She's fine. So am I, thanks to you." She smiled up at him, unsettled when he continued looking at her as if seeing her for the first time.

He seemed to collect his thoughts, and he stepped back. "I'd better get my prisoner to the station."

She nodded, feeling tongue-tied. He seemed to have that effect on her. He started to walk away, and she blurted out, "You will let me know what happens to Noriko?"

He paused and looked back at her. "She'll go to trial and probably prison." He turned away, then paused again.

Heart thumping, she waited as he slowly turned back to her. "I'll tell you the whole story later. How about dinner?"

Somehow, she'd known he was going to ask her out. Maybe she'd been waiting for it. She hesitated for a moment longer, then said quietly, "I'd like that."

His smile warmed her heart. "Good. I'll get back to you." He lifted his hand in farewell, then turned and strode to his car.

Max was straining at his leash, and Melanie rushed back into the house with him bounding along beside her.

Liza was waiting for her in the kitchen, seated at the table with a mug of tea in front of her. "So what's happening with our killer nurse?"

"Ben's taking her to the station. He says she'll go to jail." Melanie poured herself a mug of tea. "He's going to tell me what happens later. Over dinner."

Liza's eyes lit up. "Good for you! I told you he was interested in you."

"It's just dinner."

"Ah, but it's what it could lead to that matters."

"It's not going to lead to anything. I told you, I'm not interested in getting involved with anyone right now."

Liza leaned forward. "Something tells me you're already involved."

Realizing she was protesting too much, Melanie changed the subject. "I think Max must have seen Noriko and recognized her. That's why he was barking so frantically. Ben said that she'll go to trial. I wonder if Josh will be covering it in the paper."

"Probably. I hope she gets what she deserves." Liza visibly shuddered. "When I think what could have happened . . ."

Melanie laid a hand on her grandmother's arm. "Don't think about it. It's over. The insurance will pay for the repairs and renovations, all our problems will be solved, and we'll be able to open in time for the fall festivities."

"I didn't know there were festivities here in the fall."

"We'll make sure there are some."

Liza sighed. "I haven't heard Orville since the fire. I wonder if he's okay."

Melanie took a sip of her tea. "If he really is a ghost, I don't think he has to worry about being killed again—do you?"

As if in answer to her, a hollow laugh echoed down the hallway.

* * *

Almost a month later, the insurance adjustor had examined the house, the estimates for the repairs had been approved, the roof and electrical wiring had been repaired, and Melanie and her grandmother were finally able to move back into the inn.

"The first thing I want to do," Melanie said as she parked in the driveway that morning, "is pull that police tape off the bedroom door."

"If someone hasn't done it already." Liza climbed out of the car and stood for a moment, gazing up at the roof.

Max whined, and Melanie scrambled out and opened the back door. The dog leapt from the car, bounded toward the lawn, and joyfully christened it.

Smiling, Melanie joined her grandmother. "He's so happy to be home. Now that his leg has healed, he needs room to run. He's been so confined in that hotel."

"Haven't we all." Liza was still gazing at the roof, a pensive look on her face.

"Are you okay?" Melanie put an arm around her grand-mother and hugged her.

Liza sighed. "We came so close to losing it all."

"But we didn't." Melanie followed her gaze. "The roof looks a lot better without all that tarpaulin covering it."

"Yes, it does." Liza's eyes glistened with tears. "It's good to be home. Let's go make some tea."

The house still smelled of smoke, and while Liza put the kettle on for tea, Melanie ran around opening up all the windows, allowing the fresh sea air to sweep throughout the inn. The yellow tape had been removed from the bedroom door, but she still felt a cold shiver as she walked down the hallway.

Seated in the nook later, a mug of tea in front of her, she finally felt herself begin to relax. "I think we should have the secret room sealed up before the decorators start work in there," she said as Liza sat down at the table.

"Good idea." Liza cradled her mug in her hands. "There's still so much work to be done. The porch and upstairs balcony will have to be renovated. Those two bedrooms windows that are cracked will have to be replaced. Four of the ceilings will have to be repaired."

"And the entire house needs repainting," Melanie finished for her.

"We will be into fall before it's all done. Thank goodness Sharon offered you that job helping out in her shop for the summer." She looked anxious. "How do you feel about working in a dress shop?"

Melanie laughed. "It will be a change from a stuffy stockbroker's office. I'm looking forward to it." Her smile faded as she studied her grandmother. "What about you? You'll be alone here all day."

"I'll have Max for company, and there will be plenty to keep me busy. We should be able to take reservations soon."

"I'm so looking forward to that." Melanie glanced at Max, who was still sniffing around the kitchen, exploring every nook and cranny. "It's all turning out all right, after all. Angela's killer will pay for her crimes, my ex-husband is back in Portland and out of my hair, the inn will soon be as good as new, and Max is all healed up." Watching the dog, she felt a pang of guilt. "I just wish that Ellen Croswell hadn't gotten killed."

Liza leaned forward. "You have to stop blaming yourself. What happened to Ellen wasn't your fault."

"If she hadn't looked like me, and if we hadn't investigated Angela's murder, Ellen would still be alive."

"And you wouldn't have Max. I bet she's looking down on you right now, happy that you're taking such good care of him."

Only partly reassured, Melanie shook her head. "I guess I'll always feel a little responsible for what happened. I just hope she forgives me."

"I'm sure she does."

Melanie took a sip of her tea. "I can't wait to get back on my computer. I'm tired of peering at my phone."

Liza reached out and patted Max's head. "No luck on the research on your mother yet?"

"Nothing. I was hoping that I'd hear from one of the schools I contacted, but it looks like it's another dead end."

"I'm sorry, Mel. I know how frustrated you are. Maybe you should give it a rest for a while. Something will turn up eventually. I'm sure of it."

Right on cue, the sound of ghostly laughter answered her.

Max barked, and Liza smiled. "See? Orville agrees with me. All is well at the Merry Ghost Inn."

Liza's Awesome Sausage and Broccoli Frittata

8 eggs, lightly beaten
¼ teaspoon salt
¼ teaspoon black pepper
1 tablespoon snipped fresh basil or 1 teaspoon crushed dried basil
2 tablespoons olive oil
1½ cups chopped broccoli
¼ cup thinly sliced green onions
½ cup crumbled cooked pork sausage
½ cup shredded cheddar cheese

Combine eggs, salt, pepper, and basil, then set aside. Heat oil in a large skillet and add broccoli and onions. Cook, uncovered, over medium heat for about 5 minutes or until vegetables are tender, stirring occasionally. Stir in sausage.

Pour the egg mixture over the vegetables and sausage in the skillet. Cook over medium heat. Run a spatula around edge of skillet as mixture sets, lifting edges so the uncooked portion flows underneath. Continue cooking and lifting edges until egg mixture is almost set. Sprinkle with cheese.

Bake in a preheated oven at 400 degrees for 5 minutes or until cheese is melted and top is set.